Dragon HUNT

WATER DRAGONS BOOK 1

CHARLENE HARTNADY

Copyright August © 2018 by Charlene Hartnady
Cover art by Melody Simmons
Edited by KR
Website Simplicity

Proofread by Brigitte Billings (brigittebillings@gmail.com)
Formatting by Integrity Formatting
Produced in South Africa
charlene.hartnady@gmail.com

Dragon Hunt is a work of fiction and characters, events and dialogue found within are of the author's imagination and are not to be construed as real. Any resemblance to actual events or persons, either living or deceased, is purely coincidental.

No part of this book may be reproduced in any form or by any electronic or mechanical means, including information storage and retrieval systems, without written permission from the author, except for the use of brief quotations in a book review.

First Paperback Edition 2018

"Because thirty-five is the cut-off for taking part in the program." She had to undergo a whole lot of testing – including ones of the medical variety – and she'd been selected anyway. "I'm so done with guys running away as soon as they realize I'm serious."

"How is being a part of this program going to change anything? I love you long freaking time, but you do tend to scare men away. You're a little … pushy."

"I'm not pushy! I know what I want and I go after it. After everything I've been through, I'm not interested in anything less, and shifters actually want to settle down. They want kids. They want what I want. For once, I'm going to meet someone who doesn't run scared at the prospect of commitment and family." She sucked in a deep breath.

"Human guys also want commitment." Ruth raised her brows, taking another sip of her coffee. "They want kids."

"Just not with me they don't. None of them wanted anything other than sex or casual dating. Sure, they're more than willing to take the plunge as soon as they move on to the next one, but not with me."

"Have you ever stopped to consider that you're maybe coming on just a little too strong? You can't start out a relationship talking about marriage. Guys can't handle that."

"I'm not coming on too strong. I'm done wasting my time… that's all." Jolene took a sip of her own coffee, feeling the warm liquid slide down her throat. "I know what I want. Casual sex, endless dating…" She shook her head. "That's not it. Even living together. Have you ever heard the saying, 'why buy the cow if you can get the milk for free'? No…not for me. Never again!"

CHAPTER 1

She should be happy.

What was she thinking? She *was* happy.

Happy, excited and nervous all rolled into one. Nervous? Hah! She was quaking in her heels. This was a huge risk. Especially now. Her stomach clenched and for a second she wanted to turn around and head back into her boss's office. Tell him she'd changed her mind.

No.

She would regret it if she didn't take this opportunity. Why now though? Why had this fallen into her lap now? What if it didn't work out? She squeezed her eyes closed as her stomach lurched again.

"You okay?" Rob's PA asked, eyebrows raised.

Jolene realized she was standing outside her boss's office, practically mid-step. Hovering.

"Fine." She pushed out the word together with a pent-up breath. She *was* fine, she realized. More than fine, and she had this. The decision was already made. Her leave approved. She was doing this, dammit. Jolene smiled. "I'm great."

"Good." Amy smiled back. "Just so you know," she said under her breath, looking around them to check that no-one was in hearing distance, "I'm rooting for you." She winked.

"Thank you. I appreciate that," Jolene said as she headed back to her office, trying not to think about it. Not right now. It would make her doubt her decision all over again. She'd made the right one. The only thing holding her back was fear of failure. It was justifiable and yet stupid. She wasn't going to live with regrets because fear held her back. She was going to embrace this. Give it her all and then some. Her step suddenly felt lighter as she walked into her office. *Do not look left.* Whoever designed this building had been a fruitcake. This floor was large and open-plan. Fifty-three cubicles. There were only two offices. One was hers, and one was—*Not looking or thinking about her right now.* Both offices had glass instead of walls. Why bother? Why even give her an office in the first place if everyone could see into it?

It had something to do with bringing management closer to their staff, or the other way round – she couldn't remember. The Execs were on the next floor. *Not going there and definitely not looking left.* She could feel a prickling sensation on that side of her body. Like she was being watched. Jolene sat down at her desk and opened her laptop. Her accepted leave form was already in her inbox. She had to work hard not to smile. It was better to stay impassive. Especially when anyone could look in on her. This was going to work out. It would. All of it.

No more blind dates.

No more Tinder.

No more friends setting her up.

She was done! Not only was she done with trying to find a partner, she was done with human men in general.

Jolene bit down on her bottom lip, thinking of the letter inside her purse. She'd been accepted.

Yes!

Whooo hooo!

It was all sinking in. She couldn't quite comprehend that this was actually happening.

The sound of her door opening snapped her attention back to the present. She lifted her head from her computer screen in time to see Carla saunter in. No knock. No apologies for interrupting. Not that Jolene had been doing anything much right then, but still. She could have been.

A smug smile greeted her. "I believe I'm filling in for you starting Friday for three weeks." Her colleague and biggest adversary sat down without waiting for an invitation. "Rob just called to fill me in."

"Yes," she cleared her throat, "that's right." Jolene nodded. *Don't let her get to you.* "I have too many leave days outstanding and decided to take them."

Carla folded her arms and leaned back. She seemed to be scrutinizing Jolene. It made her uncomfortable. "Yeah, but right now? You're either really sure of yourself or …" She let the sentence drop. "I believe you're going on a singles' cruise?" The smirk was back. Carla's beady eyes—not really, they were wide and blue and beautiful—were glinting with humor and very much at Jolene's expense.

It was her own fault. She should never have told Rob about why she was taking this trip. Why the hell had he told Carla? It was none of her damned business. *Stay cool!* She smiled, folding her arms. "I thought it would be fun."

"You do know that I'm about to close the Steiner deal, right? Work on the Worth's Candy campaign is coming along nicely as well."

"Why are you telling me this?" Her voice had a definite edge which couldn't be helped. Carla irritated the crap out of her.

The other woman shrugged. "It might not be the best time for you to go on vacation. Not that I'm complaining. It works for me." Another shrug, one-shouldered this time.

Jolene pulled in a breath. "I need a break. That's the long and short of it."

"Yeah, but right now and on a singles' cruise…do you really think you'll meet someone?" She scrunched up her nose.

"Why not? It's perfectly plausible that I would meet someone. Someone really great!" she blurted, wanting to kick herself for the emotional outburst.

"It's not like you have the greatest track record." Carla widened her eyes. Unfortunately, working in such close proximity for years meant that Carla knew a lot about her. In the early days, they had even been friends.

"But you should definitely go," Carla went on. "You shouldn't let that stop you," she quickly added. Her comments biting.

"I'm not going to let anything stop me. Not in any aspect of my life," Jolene replied, thrilled to hear her voice remained steady.

Carla stood up, smoothing her pencil skirt. "I'll take care of things back here. The reason I popped in was to request a handover meeting, although I'm very much up to speed with everything that goes on around here." She gestured behind her. "I'll email a formal request anyway." She winked at Jolene.

Jolene had to stop herself from rolling her eyes.

"Perfect." She refolded her arms, looking up at Carla who was still smiling angelically.

"I need you to know that I plan on taking full advantage of your absence."

"I know." Jolene smiled back. "I'm not worried."

The smile faltered for a half a second before coming back in full force. "You enjoy your trip. Good luck meeting someone." She laughed as she left. It was soft and sweet and yet grating all at once. Like the idea of Jolene actually meeting someone was absurd.

That woman.

That bitch!

Stay impassive. Do not show weakness. Do not show any kind of emotion. She forced herself to look down at her screen, to scroll through her emails.

Two minutes later, there was a knock at her door. Jolene looked up, releasing a breath when she saw who it was. Ruth smiled holding up two cups of steaming coffee.

Jolene smiled back and gestured for her to come in.

"I was in here Xeroxing—our printer is down yet again – and thought you could use a cup of joe." Ruth ran the admin department on the lower level. Her friend moved her eyeballs to the office next door to hers. The one where Carla sat, separated by just a glass panel.

"You were right," Jolene exclaimed.

Ruth sat down. "Are you okay? That whole exchange looked a little rough."

"I thought I kept my cool. Are you saying you could see how badly she got to me?" Carla was all about pushing buttons. She only won if Jolene retaliated and she'd learned a long time ago it wasn't worth doing so.

"You looked fine. What gave it away and – only

because I know you so well – was the way you tapped your fingers against the side of your arm every so often. I take it when 'you know who' said something mean." Ruth handed her the coffee and took a seat.

"Mean doesn't begin to cut it. Thanks for this." She held up the mug before taking a sip.

"What's going on?"

"Things have happened so quickly, I didn't get a chance to tell you. I'm going on vacation." Jolene briefly told her friend all about her real upcoming plans, as well as about what had transpired between Carla and her.

Ruth smiled. "I can't believe you're this excited." She looked at her like she had lost all her faculties. "It's not that big of a deal. Quite frankly, I'm inclined to partly agree with Carla, for once." She made a face. "Maybe you shouldn't be going on a trip right now."

"It's a huge deal, and you're right, I'm excited," Jolene gushed. "One in five hundred applicants are accepted, and I'm one of them. The shifter program is just the place for a woman like me. I'm ready to settle down, to get married and to have kids. Lots of kids. Four or five … okay, maybe five's too many, but four has a ring to it. Two boys and two girls."

"Two of each." Ruth chuckled under her breath.

She smiled as well and shook her head. "Actually, I'm not too phased about that. I just can't believe they actually selected me."

"You're nuts!" Ruth laughed some more. "Why's it so hard to believe? Just because you've had a bad run doesn't mean you're not…worthy."

"I'm thirty-four. I turn thirty-five in two months' time."

"And that's a big deal why?"

"You seem to think it's going to be different with a shifter. Can't say I know too much about shifters." Ruth shrugged. "Except that they're ultimately guys too."

"For starters they're hot. Muscular, tall and really, really good-looking."

"Okay, that's a good start." Ruth leaned forward, eyes on Jolene.

"They have a shortage of their own women, just like with the vampires. It's actually the vampires who are helping them set up this whole dating program."

"Oh!" Ruth looked really interested at this point. "No women of their own you say, now that's interesting."

"I didn't say no women, just not many women. Their kind stopped having female children, so there's a shortage. They have a natural drive to mate and procreate, which is exactly what I'm looking for." Jolene put her coffee down and rubbed her hands together. "I can't wait to get my hands on one."

"You might just be onto something here. Where do I sign up?" her friend whisper-yelled while smiling broadly. "I can't believe you told Rob you're going on a cruise. Where did you come up with that?"

"I shouldn't have said anything at all." She shook her head. "I don't know why I disclosed as much as I did."

"Yeah!" Ruth raised her brows. "I can't believe he told," she looked to the side while keeping her head facing forwards, "her."

"I know. Thing is, I've made up my mind. I'm going."

"That cow is going to move in while you're gone. She might just get the edge in your absence and take the promotion out from under you."

"I realize that, and yet I can't miss out on this

opportunity. I'm willing to risk my career over this. It's a no-brainer for me." She sighed. "Don't get me wrong, I'm freaking out about it, but as much as I love my job, having a family would trump everything. I have a good feeling about this."

"Those shifters sound so amazing." Ruth bobbed her brows.

"I'll show you the website online. They only take three groups a year and then only six women are chosen each time. Just a handful from thousands of applications." Jolene's heartbeat all the faster for getting accepted. She was so lucky! Things had to work out for her. They just had to.

"You say these shifters are hot and pretty desperate?" Ruth smiled, her eyes glinting. "Why didn't you tell me about this sooner? We should have entered together."

"Not exactly desperate, but certainly looking for love. Ninety-six percent of the women who sign up end up mated…that's what the shifters call it, mated. It's not actually the same as marriage, it's more binding. Ninety-six percent," she shook her head, "I rate those odds big time."

"I can't believe you didn't tell me sooner." Even though she was still smiling, Ruth narrowed her eyes. "I thought we were friends."

Jolene made a face. "I didn't tell you anything because I didn't want to jinx it."

Ruth rolled her eyes. "I wouldn't get too excited until you get there. Until you actually meet them." Ruth snickered. "With your luck, you'll get one of the bad apples."

"You shut your mouth. Don't be putting such things

out in the universe."

Ruth looked at her with concern. "I don't want you getting your hopes up, that's all."

"Well too late, my hopes are already up." Jolene was going to win herself a shifter. Someone sweet and kind and loving. A man she could spend forever with. "I just wish it wasn't right now. This isn't a good time to be leaving."

"Not with that big promotion on the horizon." Ruth shook her head. "Not when *she* could take it."

"We're both on the same level. We both started at the same time. I hate how evenly matched we are."

"You're the better candidate though. I've never known anyone to work as hard as you."

"Carla works hard too. She's also brought in several big clients in the last couple of months, and she's not going on vacation. She'll be here day in and day out, whispering sweet nothings into Rob's ear."

Ruth made a face. "It's not like that, is it?"

"No, no." She waved a hand. "Sweet nothings of the business kind. It's still a threat just the same to me, and honestly, that's the only downside to this. I stand a good chance of losing to Carla if I go."

"But you are still going anyway." Ruth took a sip of her coffee, frown lines appearing on her forehead.

"I have to." She pushed out a breath. Hopefully, Ruth was wrong about the whole 'bad apple' thing.

CHAPTER 2

Storm was just about to take a bite of his burger when he spotted his brother walking towards him. Tide grinned as they locked eyes. He weaved between tables. "Did I read that right?" he asked as he took a seat.

"Read what right?" Storm took that big bite, tasting ground venison, fresh tomato, and pure goodness. Tide looked at him like his hair had just turned purple or something. "What?" Storm asked around his food.

"You signed up for the hunt? You?" His brother didn't give him a chance to talk. "Mister *I love to fuck around*. Mister *I'm never settling down*. You of all dragons."

Storm shrugged. "I'm bored, so I thought I'd try it."

"Bored?" Tide shook his head. "You do realize that you'll be expected to try to win a female if you actually capture one..."

"What do you mean 'if'?" Storm snorted. "Of course, I'll catch one. I quite like the idea of a hunt. Of capturing a sweet human." He licked his lips and it had nothing to do with the barbeque sauce clinging there.

"Of mating one?" Tide cocked his head, looking skeptical.

"Fuck no!" Storm put down his burger. "I see how

pussy-whipped the three of you are. You!" he snorted. "You're the worst of my brothers and I never expected it. Not from you. Torrent, okay fine, but you…" He shook his head. Tide had always been with him on this until he'd met Doctor Meghan. "Look," Storm had to smile, "your female is mighty fine. She—"

Tide growled, his eyes narrowing.

Storm had to laugh. "See what I mean? I can't even say something about Meghan without you getting all bristly. She's my sister-in-law, I would never go there."

Tide looked at him hesitantly. "Let's leave my mate out of this. If you take part in the hunt and capture a female, you will be expected to win and mate her. If you're not ready for that, then you shouldn't take part."

Storm leaned back in his chair. "I'll win her and have a little fun with her. Then I'll send her packing."

"That would be a dick thing to do." Tide shook his head. "Even you should know that."

"I would be completely honest with her. I always am. I'd give her a chance to try to convince me to settle down." Not that she would be able to…ever. "I'd let her use whatever techniques she saw fit to try." He bobbed his brows.

Tide tossed out a laugh. "You're full of shit. You really are."

"No." He shook his head. "It is what it is. What harm can it do?"

"No female is going to agree to that. You can forget it. They join this program in order to meet and mate with us. Not to fool around. You're within your rights as an eligible male to take part, but I wouldn't recommend taking this stance. Whomever you end up winning is going to be pissed off."

"Don't be too sure, you haven't seen me through the eyes of a female." Females loved him. They loved the way his dark hair contrasted with his amethyst eyes. They loved his muscles. Loved his cock even more. He only needed to click his fingers on a stag run, and the females would come running. Two females had even fought over him once. There'd been scratching and hair pulling, the whole nine yards. "No female would turn down some fun with me. I guarantee it. Plus, I did say she could try to change my mind."

"Isn't that a two-way street though?"

"I'll try as well, I'll try plenty…and I'll make the stay worth her while." He'd use his tongue, his hands and most certainly his cock. Storm planned to try really, really hard to please the female before sending her on her away.

Tide sat back in his chair. "To think I was just like you once. Your good looks will only get you so far. Trust me, I know. After that…you can forget it. No human female is going to fall for your shit for very long. You might even end up being the one who falls on their face."

It was Storm's turn to look at his brother like he had lost his mind. *Not happening!* "Let's wait and see." Storm picked his food back up and took another big bite.

"It would be so funny if you ended up mated." Tide grinned, looking smug.

Storm couldn't help but laugh. It was hard to do with a mouth full of food, but he managed anyway. "Not happening, bro."

Not a chance.

CHAPTER 3

Oh, good lord!
 Jolene had not signed up for this. No way in hell! Her thighs burned. Her feet hurt. She was sweaty. Her t-shirt was sticking to her back, and underboob sweat was a thing. It existed. It was very real and happening to her right at that moment.

She stopped for a second, breathing heavily. The girl she was with glanced back. "You okay?" Not a drop of sweat on her young, perky, twenty-something body. Christina was sweet though. Sweet but tough as nails, which could be irritating.

Just a bit longer.
Just one more hill.
Just one more mile.
We're nearly there. All thrown at her in a sing-song voice. A voice that didn't hold a shred of fatigue. *Arghhhh!* "I'm just reminding myself why I'm here. Why I didn't wait at the drop off point like the other women. They were clever."

Christina smiled. "You know why."

"Because the best guys don't want easy pickings." She

panted between every word and then made a snorting noise. "I can't believe that dragon lady actually used the term 'easy pickings.'"

"Used the term." Christina laughed. "More like spat the words out like a curse. I want a prince. I'm only sorry that there aren't any kings left." She sighed. "I'm willing to keep on going to make sure I get one."

Jolene didn't have to think why she put one foot in front of the other right then. "I want to make the guy work for it a bit, I guess. Easy come, easy go as the saying goes." She might really want to settle down, but she wasn't willing to settle. Two very different things. "I ultimately want a sweet guy…" She shrugged. Someone who would love her passionately and completely. "I guess royalty isn't important to me."

"It's a golden chest all the way for me." Christina opened a bottle of water and took a sip. "The way the gold glints off their chests in the sun is amazing."

"The silver tattoos are also pretty spectacular." What was she saying? Everything about these shifters was superb. Gold, silver…it didn't matter.

"Dragons," Christina sighed. "Here I was expecting wolves or bears. I certainly never imagined being a princess and with a dragon shifter."

"Me neither…the dragon shifter part that is."

"We should get going." Christina recapped her water.

"You are a machine," Jolene mumbled, meaning it.

Christina smiled. "Rubbish. You should meet my personal trainer, then you'll know all about working out. See that ridge over there?"

Jolene sighed. "The one that's at least two, if not more, miles away? The one I'm having a hard time seeing because it's so far?"

Christina shook her head, still smiling. "It's barely a mile. One more mile. What's one more little mile?"

One more stinking mile.

One more.

They started to walk, within half a minute, Christina picked up the pace, taking them almost to a steady jog. This girl would be the death of her. A roar sounded behind them. It had her almost falling over her own feet. It had her heart skipping several beats. It had gooseflesh rising on her arms. Her man was here. He was here.

She turned. The shifter moved with startling speed. His muscles had muscles. She was shocked by the sight of him. Her mouth actually fell open.

"My prince has arrived." Christina moved in next to her, the other woman's eyes were just as wide. "They're all pretty hot, but that's next level." She sighed.

He did, indeed, have a golden chest tattoo. "Yes, he most certainly is next level." She still sounded breathless, but at this point, it had nothing to do with the exertion. Those eyes, those lips. She realized with a start that he was close enough for her to see his lips. And such an arrogant smile. It was sexy though.

"Afternoon, ladies. I'm so glad there were two of you with a little bit of fire in your veins." His smile turned into a grin. "I'm happy to announce I think you're both gorgeous." It was like he was trying to decide which one of them he wanted. Looking from one to the other.

Jolene frowned. This wasn't how it was supposed to go down. Her Prince Charming was supposed to fall instantly in love with her at first sight. They were supposed to look into each other's eyes and realize in that same moment that they were meant to be together forever. Done. Sorted.

Instead, his gaze finally settled on Christina, sizing her up. It seemed to take forever before those brilliant purple eyes — with lashes that long did not belong on a man — landed back on her, doing the same. Appraising. Searching. Maybe he was looking for child-bearing hips. She had those. Or boobs capable of feeding a small village. She had those too — and the boob sweat to prove it. If so, she was winning this hands-down.

But no, that didn't seem to be it since he turned those gorgeous eyes back to Christina. "Good afternoon to you too," her competition purred, managing to sound sexy and sophisticated.

"Afternoon…hi…" Jolene panted, still a tad out of breath. They had just crossed the countryside after all. Up and down enormous hills. Around boulders and over fallen trees. It had been exhausting.

The shifter folded his arms across an enormous chest, which was bare. His abs…good lord his abs! She struggled to focus on anything else in the face of those honeys.

"I'm going to have to excuse myself in a moment. I can see by the way you're both looking at me, that you're very interested. I'm going to let the two of you decide who gets me." He widened his arms. Great arms! His biceps were thick and—

Wait a minute! Wait! "Um…" Jolene thought back to their brief training. To everything those shifter women had told them the evening before. "I don't think that's how this was meant to go down. You're supposed to hunt us…go after us…It's not supposed to be the other way around."

The shifter cocked a half-smile as a roar sounded

behind him. He didn't even flinch. That roar was followed by two more. *Oh, good lord!* Three guys were running towards them. The shifter in front of them smirked. "That would be my cue." He winked, looking gorgeous as he did it. "Forget what you were told. I don't know…talk it through…fight it out…" He winked again. "Let me know who the lucky winner is when I get back."

"Wait…what?" *Forget it!* "I'm not fighting." Jolene folded her arms, glancing at Christina. She was bigger than the younger woman, she could just sit on her until she gave up.

"Why not?" Christina didn't sound too impressed. "I think we should at least argue some."

The shifter chuckled. It was throaty and really sexy. "That's more like it. I'll see you ladies shortly." He turned and sprinted away, moving with such power. He also had a good supply of grace for someone that big. His back was sculpted to utter—

Nope…wait up. All that smirking and winking. He was hot, but he came across as a player. That's not what she'd signed up for. It didn't matter that he was sex on legs. It wasn't what she wanted. She'd learned a thing or two over the years. Right now, she trusted her gut.

"Just because I'm smaller than you, doesn't mean I can't take you. I'm stronger than I look," Christina went on.

"That's not it!" Well sort of. Jolene was convinced she could win even though Christina was fitter, the other woman was just too tiny. "It's just that, bottom line, I'm not fighting over a man. I had this conversation with my friend just the other day. I won't do it. Call it a principle." She shook her head.

"So, that means I win by default." Christina smirked. "I get my prince after all, and he's a hottie. Those other three all have silver tattoos." She made a face, pointing over Jolene's shoulder.

Irritation burned inside Jolene. It wasn't because she actually wanted Golden Boy – who was indeed a hottie. It was because she didn't like losing. For just a second, that's what this felt like – like she'd flat-out lost – and she was almost tempted to take on the other woman just to prove she could. Thing was, it would be a fight for all the wrong reasons. Not fighting wouldn't be losing, it was conceding, which was something different. Conceding was a choice. One she decided to make.

There was a yell as the sounds of flesh thudding against flesh filled the air, drawing their attention. Jolene turned. Both their mouths fell open as a bloody battle ensued. One of the three silver dragon shifters was already down. That must have been him yelling as he fell. He rolled on his back, on the ground, cradling a broken arm to his chest, moaning loudly. Even from this distance, Jolene could see that his face was pale and taut with pain.

Golden Boy punched a second guy in the face, taking a punch to the jaw himself. His head snapped back for a split second. Other than that, the hit didn't deter him. In a surprising move, he leaped into the air, elbowing the one guy in the face while kicking the other shifter square on the chest.

There was a cracking noise that made Jolene flinch, and the guy went flying. He tried to get up, but Golden Boy kicked him solidly on the underside of his chin with a crack. There was another thudding noise as the back of his head hit the ground.

"Oh shit!" Christina said.

"He has to be dead!" Jolene yelled, unable to believe what she was seeing.

The last remaining shifter jumped onto Golden Boy's back, but he countered, elbowing him hard in the solar plexus. The shifter made an '*oof*' noise and fell back, managing to keep his footing. Golden Boy turned so quickly it was hard to register the move. One second his back was to them and the next he was facing forwards. It was freaky. The other shifter dropped down, narrowly avoiding a punch, which was also delivered startlingly quickly. He landed on his haunches, dropping back onto his hands and sweeping with his legs.

Golden Boy not only jumped up to avoid the kick but landed on top of the poor shifter, knocking him to the ground. With one…two quick, downward punches, the shifter was out cold, his head lolling to the side.

Moving in a care-free, relaxed manner, Golden Boy stepped off the downed shifter and rose to his full height. His chest heaved a few times, that was the sum total of any sign of exertion. It seemed like he and Christina had a couple of things in common so they would get along great after all.

Jolene felt a pang. Golden Boy was something to behold. She'd made her decision though and was only feeling this way because…conceding still felt like losing to some degree.

The guy with the broken arm was sitting, still cradling the limb. He looked up, fear on his face. At least, it looked like fear. Hard to tell from over there. Golden Boy said something and the guy on the ground responded, his shoulders relaxing.

"What are they saying?" Christina asked, sounding breathless.

"I can't make it out." Jolene shook her head.

"Good lord but that was hot!" Christina held her chest with one hand.

"Violence is not hot," Jolene said with a little too much venom but only because it had indeed been hot. It was wrong of her...of them to think it. One against three and only one blow to the jaw. The guy was skilled. That much was for sure. Golden Boy turned to them, saying something else to the shifter with the broken arm.

"I'm in love," Christina gushed.

"You don't even know his name."

"I don't have to," Christina sighed.

Conceding, not losing! Conceding, dammit! "I wish you many happy years together," Jolene pushed out.

"Thanks," Christina whispered.

※

The male's arm was cleanly broken. No bones protruded from the skin. He would heal quickly. "You have made a wise choice by standing down, Bayou." Storm had no wish to knock a fellow water dragon out, like he had the others.

Bayou nodded. "Thank you for sparing me, my lord." He looked up, looking Storm in the eyes. "I had to try." He looked back down, showing submission.

Storm nodded. "I understand." He laughed. "It was a bad decision."

"I realize that now." Bayou smiled, looking back up.

"I will make my choice quickly." Storm glanced at the females. "You move in straight after. The others will not be far behind." He checked the horizon before turning his gaze back to the females.

This had indeed been fun. So far, so good. There was more in store for him. In store for the lucky female. Storm began to jog back, a frown quickly settling on his forehead. Why weren't they arguing or trying to scratch each other's eyes out? Had they decided so quickly which one would get to go with him? After the display he had just put on, he knew neither of them would possibly be able to resist him.

Yet, they just stood there. His frown deepened. Both females had been acutely interested in him when he'd first arrived. He scented outright arousal on the smaller one. The taller, lush as fuck female had checked him out big time, but she had also seemed a little more reserved.

"And," he rubbed his hands together, "who is the lucky winner?"

"I am! I am!" The pretty little thing jumped up and down.

For a second it looked like she was going to jump into his arms. Storm put up a hand, his frown back. "You already discussed it?" He narrowed his eyes. That was too quick. Too easy.

The small female nodded, smiling broadly.

"There was nothing to discuss." Lush As Fuck folded her arms across a chest a male could lose himself in.

Then he realized what she had just said. "Nothing to discuss? Why is that?"

"Because Jolene over here," the small one said, "wasn't interested in fighting for you. I would've fought." She nodded, her blond ponytail bobbed up and down. "So, I win." More jumping and giggling. "I get you. A prince.

You're mine."

Storm turned to the lush female. Banging body but her features were far more plain. Dark eyes, brown hair. "Jolene," Storm said, liking how her name rolled off his tongue. Liking her name, period. Loving how her cheeks turned a touch pink as he said it. Maybe not as plain as his initial assessment. Also, not so unaffected by him after all. He folded his own arms, sure to flex his pecs.

Jolene shifted, looking uncomfortable as her eyes darted down to his chest and straight back up. More pink bled into her cheeks. Her lips were just as lush as the rest of her. "I don't believe in running after men. If that's what you're looking for, then you can forget it." She shook her head once. "I wish you both a very happy life together." She gave a tight smile to the other female, her gaze moved past him. She was waiting for the next male to come and claim her. She had turned him aside. Dismissed him.

Him.
Prince of Water
Handsome as fuck.
Great conversationalist.
Fucking amazing in bed.
Him.

It took him a moment to realize that the tiny female was at his side, that she'd wrapped her arms around him.

Jolene had just picked up her backpack and was hoisting it onto her back. She was stepping away from him, heading towards Bayou, towards where more males would soon appear.

"Wait," Storm rasped.

She acted like she hadn't heard him. Jolene continued to walk away. From him. Him. *What the fuck!?*

"My name is Christina and we're going to—" Storm pulled away, extricating himself from her arms.

"This is my hunt. My choice. I'm sorry, female." He looked down at the human. "Bayou will take you," he added

Her eyes widened. "What? Why? No…"

He didn't stick around to hear what she had to say. With a low growl, he picked up all that lushness, hoisting Jolene over his shoulder. The female screamed, but he ignored her. Storm sprinted away, just as several males came into sight behind them.

CHAPTER 4

The ground was a blur below her. "Put me down!" Jolene yelled for what felt like the hundredth time.

Her throat felt raspy. Her head felt like it might explode since all of her blood had congregated in her skull.

"Put. Me—" She gasped as he did as she asked.

Thankfully, Golden Boy held onto her arms, or she would've flopped onto the ground. The earth spun. Dizziness hit, she put out a hand, planting it on him to keep from tilting to the side and crumbling to the ground. More spinning and dizziness. Her hair was plastered to her face, which felt hot. Her head felt swollen. She didn't think it was actually swollen, but it sure as hell felt that way.

Golden Boy had run with her like that over his shoulder, like a sack of potatoes, for what felt like forever, but in reality was probably thirty or forty minutes.

The shifter chuckled. He wasn't in the least bit out of breath. "You okay?" he asked, in that smooth, easy baritone of his. At least he had the good grace to sound concerned.

Jolene's mouth felt dry. She licked her lips, hair catching her tongue and mouth. Her breathing was hard. "That was horrible," she mumbled between pants.

"Do you want to sit down for a couple of minutes?" He held onto her arms, still holding her up.

Her hand was still planted on...on steel. Ripped steel. She cracked open one eye. Yup, her hair was covering her face, but she could see through a gap in the strands. Her hand was splayed across the top part of his abs. His skin was very warm, almost hot even.

Jolene removed said hand and used it to swipe the hair from her face and mouth. Where was the band that had held it in place? Somewhere in the wilderness behind them. "Yes, sitting sounds like a good idea. Wait a minute though," she quickly added. "You weren't supposed to take me." She shook her head. "It was decided. Christina was the lucky winner. You should take me back. More slowly this time."

"You were right." Good lord but his eyes were a beautiful color. A vivid light amethyst. Humans didn't have eyes that color. The color of gemstones and fanned by thick, dark lashes. "It was ultimately up to me to decide who I was going to choose. I chose you!" Like it was a done deal.

"No." She shook her head.

Golden Boy frowned. "What do you mean *no?*"

"It's not going to work out. This is all a game to you...I can tell. I've been around enough players in my time to know one when I see one. You are one alright." She could almost see a neon sign on his forehead.

"Player?" He shook his head. "I'm unfamiliar with the term."

"You like to mess around. It's all about sex and a good time. I'm here to find myself a man."

One side of that mouth...*oh, that mouth*...quirked up.

He looked down at himself. At his chest, his guns, lower. "I'm pretty sure I qualify, only I'm a shifter which means I'm much, much better than a mere man."

Jolene tracked his gaze, following along the contours of all that muscle and brawn. Those cotton pants these shifters wore did little to hide their package. Yes…he was distinctly manly. A very manly man…a shifter. "You know what I mean." She snapped her gaze back up to his when she realized she was gawking.

"Not really." He shook his head.

"I want friendship and respect."

"Noted." He folded his arms. "Those I can do."

Jolene was trying hard not to come on too strong but hell, she was here on serious business. These shifters weren't supposed to mess around. "I'm going to just say it."

When she didn't continue he nodded. "Go ahead. I like females who are upfront about what they want."

"I want commitment. I want children…in the not too distant future. If these things scare you, then move on. Go find someone else to track down and to throw over your shoulder. I'll sit right there." She pointed to a fallen tree. "I'll wait for someone who wants what I want. I don't need a prince, thank you," she mumbled.

His jaw tightened, and his eyes narrowed just a smidgen. They seemed to darken. "Those things don't scare me in the least."

That came as a shocker. Golden Boy was a player…he had to be. Everything about him screamed it. His royal heritage, the fact that he was gorgeous and strong and…just plain yum. More than anything, his whole attitude screamed it. He ran a hand through that thick mop of tousled hair. It looked silky soft. "I also want a female and young."

"Oh...okay." She wasn't sure she was buying it. Why was she sensing a 'but' here?

"Only...I don't want all of that just yet."

Hah! She knew it! "Why did you take part in this whole hunt then? It is called a bride hunt, isn't it?" Jolene felt herself frown. "Bride as in partner, wife...mate? Do I need to explain to you how a bride hunt works? I thought a dragon shifter would know."

Golden Boy removed her backpack from his shoulders, setting it down at his feet. Somewhere along the line it had fallen off of her own back. Being jostled upside down would have that effect. She was just lucky she hadn't lost her lunch as well.

He nodded, seeming to think his answer through. "You were straight with me, and I will be straight with you as well."

"I should hope so."

He smiled. It was the first genuine smile she had seen from him. "I think I might like you, Jolene."

She felt this warm fuzzy feeling inside. She was such a girl. Did he really like her? Players played games, so she still couldn't be sure. The warm fuzzy feeling stayed, even if she was a little confused and a whole lot irritated.

"I'm not ready to settle down." He went on, looking sincere, "If I was, you'd be just the female for me."

That made her want to snort and roll her eyes. Such a charming thing to say. Too charming, like he was buttering her up. He didn't even know her. He went on. "I took part in the hunt to have fun. I wanted to see what it was all about. I wanted to spend some time with a human. I would love to spend some time with you." He reached out and squeezed her hand, holding onto it.

That warm fuzzy feeling only magnified. This, despite Golden Boy being a player of note by his own admission. Jolene pulled her hand away. "Well then, head on up the creek, bucko. I'm not interested in you."

"Not interested." He snorted. "You do find me attractive and you would like me to fuck you." He said it like it was a fact. No question marks in sight. "That spells interest right there."

Her mouth fell open. The need to choke on nothing also hit but she managed to suppress that urge. Only just. "I find you both attractive and an asshole," she finally spluttered. "The one counters the other, so I ultimately feel nothing for you. As to the other part of that equation," she shrugged, "I'm not really into sex." All true.

"What? Not into...?" Golden Boy looked completely out of sorts, which was out of character for what she knew of him so far. "How can you *not* be into sex? You're young and attractive and single and...fuck me!" He continued to shake his head, looking lost. "No, I don't get that. You need to explain please."

"There isn't much to explain."

"Please try."

"Fine! I don't mind sex, it's okay. If I'm in a relationship, then we do it, and if I'm not, I don't miss it. There's nothing wrong with it *per se*. I don't need it though. It's not important to me."

She watched as his jaw slowly dropped as she spoke. It was comical to watch.

"So there." She shrugged. "That's it! Not much to explain and no, I don't particularly want to fuck you."

Okay, that wasn't entirely true. Call it curiosity. She'd never been with someone this gorgeous. That in itself would be worth the whole sticky business of having sex. Only, it wasn't enough. Not anymore. She wanted burning love. Two bodies coming together out of passion, pure and unrelenting passion.

"You don't want to fuck me?" He quirked a brow, managing to look both comical and sexy. Then he straightened up, his broad shoulders pulling back. Two deep grooves appeared between his eyes. "You have no idea, do you?"

"No idea about what?"

"How good fucking can be. How amazing we would be together. How—"

"Good lord!" she muttered, her eyes on his cock. "You're getting a hard-on."

"You'd better believe it. Just thinking about fucking does this to me." He pointed at his...well, there, not in the least bit embarrassed at how hard he was getting. "Thinking about being inside you...making you cry out...making you come." His voice was impossibly deep. "It's turning me on in a big way."

She should feel weird about this conversation. She should find him creepy. It didn't happen. Her nipples tightened...*They tightened.* Her girl part did something as well. Gave a clench. That's it...her vagina clenched tight. Her clit did this throb, throb thing. It made her feel...needy. It made her feel like sex. Pity Golden Boy was so arrogant and full of himself. Guys like him made the worst lovers. Not that she was thinking about having actual sex with him, mind you. He was a player, so that was out!

Golden Boy grinned. His nostrils flared a couple of times. "You're aroused." He grinned some more.

What? Good lord, but he had good senses. She had a three-second freak-out, and then Jolene took in a deep breath. "A momentary loss of my faculties. I'm over it."

His eyes turned stormy. "No, you're not." He sniffed again, making this groaning noise. "You have an amazing scent...like candied apples. I wouldn't mind diving right in." He licked his lips. The bastard licked his lips using languid strokes, his eyes burning holes in her.

More throbbing. More clenching. More tightening. *What the hell?*

Golden Boy's nostrils flared, and he grinned. "I can tell you'd like that, Jolene."

"I'd hate it."

"Your body says different."

"My body isn't in charge here, I am. Now, please leave so that whoever heads this way knows I'm available."

"You're not available." He seemed to tower over her. Gone was any trace of humor. His jaw was tight, his eyes filled with intensity. Sex on legs and yet emotionally unavailable What a waste! Golden Boy was the bad apple. All these perfectly lovely apples. All buff and attractive and she had to get saddled with the bad apple of the bunch. The asshole.

"You're right, I'm not available," she countered. "At least, to you I'm not, I—"

Golden Boy wrapped his arms around her and pulled her against him. Against all of his hot, hard muscle. He covered her mouth with his. Good lord but his lips were soft. Then his tongue was pushing between her lips, delving into her mouth. Her feet were being lifted off the ground. Right off. Her. Jolene had always felt attractive but at the same time, she wasn't tiny. She was average height and she had curves. Hips and ass, with maybe a side of thighs. Right then, in his arms, she felt like a feather. The way he kissed her, made her feel like she was the sexiest creature alive. Her chest pushed up against the hard planes of his chest. Her hands dug into his shoulders. She knew that she should pull away. She really did. Instead though, she moaned. All out moaned.

Golden Boy pulled back, his cocky grin back on his face. "See, this could work." He winked at her.

The human made a throaty noise. Her eyes were wide. There were both golden and green flecks within their dark depths. Very pretty. Her cheeks were flushed. Her mouth swollen. Fucking beautiful. Any second now, she was going to beg him to fuck her. Humans were like that. They enjoyed ripping his shirt off of him. Pulling their own clothes off, frantic to have him touch them. Begging him. It was—

She leaned back and cracked him a shot across the cheek. A decent slap for a human. Especially one of the fairer sex. It stung for half a second but was nothing to a dragon shifter. The impact wouldn't leave even the tiniest of marks.

Her face crumpled, and she cried out in what sounded like pain. Storm put her down. Jolene grabbed her palm in her other hand, her face definitely showed pain. "What are you made of? Granite?" Her voice was shrill.

"Oh shit!" He eased his own hand over the two of hers. "Are you okay? I'm sorry you are hurt. You shouldn't have struck me. I mean," he shrugged, "you are welcome to do so but you will need to be more careful, so you don't hurt yourself."

"You mean that didn't hurt you at all?" Her face was still pinched, and she still held onto her hand.

"No, not even close." He could have stopped her twice over, but that would have meant dropping her, which could have hurt her even more. "I take it that you weren't happy with the kiss?" This confused the fuck out of him. Their kiss had been amazing. This female was so soft, so lush and yet so damned fiery.

"Don't do that again." She pointed a finger at him, still holding the hurt one to her chest.

"Why not? I aroused you and you enjoyed it. I could tell by the sounds you were making. The scent coming off you and how your heart was beating."

"I did not get aroused!" She grit her teeth for a moment, looking up. "Okay, it wasn't bad…it's just not what I wanted. Definitely not something I would want again."

"That doesn't make sense because your body is saying different." He glanced down at her chest. Her nipples were all over the place. Hard little nubs, trying to rip free from her shirt.

Jolene gasped, her eyes widening like saucers. She cupped her breasts, her small hands doing a terrible job of it. "Don't look at me like that, it's rude."

"Your breasts are pretty much trying to poke out one of my eyes – make that both my eyes. You could say *they* are looking at *me*."

"That's bullshit! Look," she sounded flustered, "let's cut the crap here. We want different things…very different things. I don't want fun. I want serious. I don't want to have any kind of sex with you, despite what my body keeps telling you. Go away. I'm waiting for my happy ever after, for my handsome prince and you are not him." She shook her head, putting her hands on her hips.

Storm couldn't help the laugh that was pulled from him.

"What's so darned funny?" She scowled at him.

"Handsome prince?" He quirked a brow and touched a hand to his golden mark.

Her eyes widened when she realized what she had just said. "Fine," she practically growled. "You're a prince and you're…okay looking, but—"

"Okay?" He lifted both brows. He'd seen how she looked at him not so long ago. How her gaze kept dipping to his cock. She could deny it all she wanted but that kiss hadn't lied. Their lip-lock had been scorching. She'd loved the hell out of that kiss, hence her adverse reaction.

"Back to the part about you being an asshole and a player and that makes my attraction to you null and void."

He should just leave. Turn around right then and head back into the fray. He could easily steal another male's female. He could do it in a heartbeat. They would come willingly. No work, no fuss. He'd have his cock wet within the hour.

Thing was, he was there for fun. He was there for a little excitement. He was there because he was sick of being bored. Even the stag run was getting tired these days. This female was interesting. She was different. He liked Jolene. Liked everything about her.

A challenge.

That was it. This female was a challenge. He'd never

experienced this before, and he fucking loved it. Storm had never been one to back down from a contest of wills, and he wasn't about to start now. "No, Jolene, I'm afraid I'm not leaving you behind for some other male to snap up. You are *my* prize. I won you fair and square, and that kiss sealed the deal. I plan on having you back in my chamber and under me before the sun comes up tomorrow morning. Back before any of the other three tribes catch wind of you."

Her mouth fell open, but she quickly recovered. "Oh, and this is because you just fell madly in love with me and want me to bear your children? That had better be the reason. Anything else is unacceptable!"

"What?" He frowned. "Have my young? Not a fucking chance. You get me for the next three weeks. I'm going to show you what you've been missing out on."

"I've been missing out on love!" she yelled. "That's all! Love, okay."

Storm knew he really shouldn't laugh at her right then, but he couldn't help himself. "Love? No, love and all that other stuff can wait. You don't need it right now."

"How dare you tell me what I do and don't need." Her face was turning a dark red, and her eyes were narrowed. "I know what I need and three weeks of you isn't it."

"If you mated and had children now, you would miss out. Everyone needs to live a little before settling down. It has nothing to do with me *per se* except that I'm the lucky male who gets to help you out." He rubbed a hand over the stubble on his jaw.

"I'm not sure what you're on, but it looks like it's some good shit." She sucked in a deep breath. "Now...are you paying attention?" Before he could answer, she went on.

"I. Know." She paused. "Exactly. What. I want." She spoke slowly and carefully. Like he was a whelp.

"You have no clue, Jolene. These males from your past could not even class themselves as males." His voice dropped a few octaves, but that couldn't be helped. He moved in closer. "You can't settle down until you've had a decent fuck. One that blows your mind several times over. Until you—"

Crack!

He had to give it to her, her reflexes were fantastic for a human. Her pain threshold, on the other hand, was terrible. Jolene yelped, cradling her hand all over again.

"I told you not to do that." Storm shook his head.

"Oh good, it hurt this time." She smiled, even though her face was still contorted in pain.

"It hurt *you*."

She tried flicking the hand. "I reckon you must be made from granite for real. I think I broke something." She bounced from one foot to the other. "Oh god, it hurts."

"Let me help you." Storm picked her up.

"No, you don't!" she yelled.

"Stop fighting me for a second." He held her to his chest and sprinted. Within minutes they were at the bank of the river.

"Oh, wow!" Jolene sighed as he put her down, noticing that he still held her hand. "How beautiful." She looked around them, her pain temporarily forgotten.

"Come to the river bank, the water is icy, it will soothe you."

Jolene nodded, she followed him to the river's edge and placed her hand in the current.

"You shouldn't keep hitting me." No-one had ever

struck him before, outside of battle. It was fascinating that she stood up to him in that way.

"You were rude. I've never struck anyone in my life."

"I spoke my mind," he countered.

"Exactly. You have a seriously dirty mind."

Storm shrugged. "Females normally like dirty talk."

"Not me."

"If you say so. And?" he asked. "Feeling any better?" He glanced down at her hand. It was still in the water.

"Much." She nodded. Her shoulder slumped. "Just let me go, please. I'm asking you really nicely."

"I take it that even though you are attracted to me, I'm not your type."

"I don't even know your name and no…" She clamped down on her lower lip for a moment. "We want different things, so that means you're not my type at all."

"Well then, you have nothing to lose."

"I have a whole lot to lose. I came here to find myself a future. My clock is ticking. I need to get married and to have children, one of these days it won't be possible anymore. I love cats. I don't have any, but I love them."

He wasn't sure what felines had to do with any of this. Storm frowned.

"I don't want a whole house of them though, and I don't want to be alone." She looked around them. "I love it out here. I want to stay. I want to fall in love. I want more than you can give me."

"I'm not saying you can't have those things but waiting three weeks longer for them to happen won't make too much of a difference, will it?"

"Yes, it will make a big difference!" she practically yelled. "If you're suggesting I stick it out with you for the prescribed three weeks then yes, it will absolutely make a huge difference because I'll have to go home and this will have been for nothing. I left everything to come here."

"You won't have to go home. You can move on to someone else after three weeks. The males would clamber for a chance. You'd pretty much have your pick."

"I can move on to someone else if things don't work out between us?" She looked like she was mulling it over. "I didn't know that." She frowned, shaking her head.

"It's not something we advertise but yes, you could move on. Jolene…" Her heart-rate picked up when he said her name and her pupils dilated. This female was far more interested in this than she realized. "I'm keeping you for the next couple of weeks. You'll share a chamber with me, a bed with me—" She tried to talk. "Let me finish. It's going to happen whether you like it or not. No male will dare try to touch you during that time because I would kill him."

"That's a bit harsh." Her breathing became a little more elevated, and the scent of apples surrounded them. Aroused at his talk of violence. *Interesting!*

"No, it's not in the least bit harsh. I will kill anyone who touches what is mine, even if it is a short-term arrangement."

"Can I talk yet?"

"No." He shook his head. "We're going to fuck and often."

She shook her head, gritting her teeth. Her eyes filled with venom.

"You'll love it!" he growled.

She rolled her eyes. "You're so damned full of it."

"No, I'm not. I'll make a deal with you, you let me fuck

you just once, if you don't like it, you can leave."

"I'm not agreeing to anything." More candied apples hit his nose. She wanted to wrap her legs around him. She wouldn't admit it though. Not yet.

"The offer is on the table. We fuck, have fun and then you go on to the next shifter. The next one will be your mate. He can love you and the two of you can make babies." He waved a hand. "Blah, blah, blah, and all that other stuff. You may already be...how old did you say you were?"

"I didn't. I'm thirty-four. I don't have time for—"

"You might be thirty-four, but I can tell you've never really lived."

Jolene snorted. "How can you tell something like that by the ten or fifteen minutes we've spent together?"

Storm smiled. "You can't let your guard down and relax. You have no idea what a decent fuck is all about and it's been over an hour."

Jolene rubbed her face and made a groaning noise. She sounded frustrated. "I still don't even know your name." She shook her head.

"Storm."

"Well, Storm..." She lifted her eyes in thought for a second. "I must say, I prefer Golden Boy."

He choked out a laugh. "Where did you hear that?"

"It's what I've been calling you inside my head."

"I'm inside your head?" He looked down at her lips. Of course, he was inside her head.

"Don't smile like that. It's not like that. It's not an endearment, just a reflection of your ego."

"Whatever you say, Sweet Lips."

"What the hell is that?"

"It's what I've been calling you inside my head and I'm not talking about the ones on your face, although—"

She whacked him on the side of his arm. Not hard, thankfully for her.

"What?" He feigned innocence, unable to help his grin. This female was something else.

"You're a pig." Her lips twitched. Jolene was holding back a laugh, a smile at the very least. He was getting to her.

"So, what do you say?" He raised his brows. "We enjoy ourselves for a couple of weeks and then…" He shrugged. "You still get what you want. We both do."

"No." She shook her head. "Just leave me here. Pick someone else. I—"

"No can do, Sweet Lips."

She yelled when he picked her up again. Yelled even louder when he began to run in the direction of his lair. No water dragon would try to take her, but a male from one of the other tribes just might. A large group of males would be hard to beat in his human form. One thing was for sure, he was keeping this female for their allotted three-week period regardless of what anyone wanted. Storm had no doubt that he would very quickly change her mind about wanting another male, maybe ever again…That last part could be a problem, for her at least. As long as he kept reminding her it was a temporary situation, she wouldn't fall for him. Jolene was smart, mature and extremely serious. She just needed to unwind a bit. Make that a whole hell of a lot. He was just the male to help her do it.

CHAPTER 5

Storm carried her the entire way there. He refused to talk to her. On and on he ran until she fell asleep in his arms. He'd woken her up and had placed her on her feet. Then he had shifted.

Shifted.

All she could say was 'wow.' His great wings flapped, almost noiselessly. His scales gleamed in the moonlight. A beautiful iridescent green that took her breath away. Storm was gorgeous in his man form and devastating in his dragon form. His chest was a bright golden color speckled with the same green scales. It was as if his scales in that section had been infused with the precious metal. Dazzling and dangerous all rolled into one. His teeth were sharp, his tail barbed. His whole being huge and powerful. The air seemed charged with it. The hairs on her body were raised, goosebumps had settled on her arms.

She was completely unafraid as they lifted up and up and up, leaving the ground far beneath them. His claws held her firmly yet gently. If he dropped her now, she would be dead. And yet, she found this exhilarating. Everything about it was amazing, it was wonderful, it was...wrong.

It was wrong!

The thought settled inside her mind. Why wasn't Storm listening to her? He didn't get it. This wasn't about sex or having a good time. No, that wasn't true, it wasn't *only* about sex and having a good time. It was about so much more. Sex and fun were so far from the most important things in her life. Especially sex. Why didn't he believe her when she said she didn't care much about it? He was an asshole, that's why. This was all about him. Storm was a selfish asshole. It was very evident that he was used to getting everything he wanted. Used to having everyone cater to and obey his every whim.

Not this time.

If he thought she was just going to roll over and accept this, he was very wrong. She only had three precious weeks. Taking this vacation was already costing her. Someone like him wouldn't understand that.

Jolene forgot the dragon shifter for a moment as the lair appeared. There were, what seemed like hundreds of wide windows built into the side of the cliff. Most of them were dark, but several were illuminated from the inside. One-way glass made it impossible to see inside. Except for what looked like public areas, which were visible and lit up like the fourth of July.

This dragon castle was smaller than the one she had slept in the night before. The fire dragon's lair. It was no less opulent. Golden chandeliers draped with large crystals and other stones. They looked like rubies, emeralds and other gems. It couldn't be though, could it? The floors were brightly polished and looked to be made from rock, they were covered with Persian rugs. The furniture was fairly sparse but quite beautiful. Pieces rather than simply furniture. Each one unique. Ranging from highly ornate to very simple.

Her feet lightly touched the ground, making her realize that they had landed. Storm released her, landing several feet away. There was a cracking noise, and the scales pulled back, his body folding in on itself. The whole process happened quickly.

Just as before, when he changed into a dragon, Storm stood, his back to her. He might be an asshole, but he was a gorgeous ass. Make that…he had a gorgeous ass. Glutes of note. His hips were narrow and his thighs strong and powerful like the rest of him.

If she was stuck with him for the next while, at least she would have something good to look at. Pity, she hadn't brought any of her earbuds though, she had nothing to drown him out with. Hard on the ears but easy on the eyes. He walked over to a shelf and donned a pair of black cotton pants, just as a big guy walked out onto the terrace. "Welcome." The guy smiled. His eyes were a bright green, they contrasted beautifully with his brown hair.

"Hi." She smiled back.

A growl sounded from next to her and Storm stepped in, putting himself ahead of her by a half a foot.

"Good evening, or should I say morning, my lord. Welcome home."

Storm relaxed somewhat, his frame remained tense but the tightness in his jaw eased, and he breathed out what seemed to be a pent-up breath. Storm nodded and took her hand, she tried to pull away, but he held on tight while giving her a sideways glance.

"I am Beck." The guy nodded in her direction.

"Nice to meet—"

Storm growled again, louder this time. She even felt the rumble in the hand that was being clasped by his.

"Why are you doing that?" She tried to pull her hand away, but Storm shook his head.

"What is happening to me?" Storm asked the other man, Beck. "I didn't expect it to be this bad," he muttered more to himself.

"Do not be concerned with Storm. This is normal behavior. He considers you to be his and will fight any who try to take you from him." He smiled at Storm. "It is normal to feel this way, my lord."

"But you didn't try anything." She looked from Beck to Storm and back.

"You are feeling possessive, my lord?"

Storm nodded. "Big time, even though I know you won't try anything. It's weird!" He scowled.

Beck smiled. "You will be driven to eliminate even a perceived threat. It is normal."

"I'm not his though," she mumbled.

Storm clasped her hand even firmer, his brow knitting in a deep frown. "Yes, you are," he growled.

Beck shook his head. "Do not let anyone hear you say that. It is dangerous. It would be foolish for a lesser to try to take on a royal. With talk like that, however, they may be tempted, and there would be carnage as a result."

"Carnage? You can't be serious?" She felt her blood drain.

Storm had gone back to clenching his teeth. His muscles bulged beneath his skin. Wired, agitated, angry. He was all of those and more. Her hand was being squeezed half to death.

"I'm afraid I'm very serious. Blood, broken bones,

possibly even death to anyone who tried." Beck said it like it was completely matter of fact. "It would be better if he keeps holding your hand. Maybe you should carry her."

Storm turned his amethyst eyes on her. "No!" she quickly announced. "I'm fine. Are you fine though?" she asked Storm because he looked far from okay.

He squeezed her hand tighter and nodded once. "Beck, you need to come with us." Storm spoke in a low rasping voice, addressing the other shifter. "Keep the female safe if I need to fight."

Eeep! Was this really happening? It seemed crazy, and yet she could feel the aggravation coming off him in waves.

Beck nodded. "It would be my pleasure."

Should she be afraid? She couldn't see another shifter anywhere. Would someone else try to take her? If so, would Storm really hurt them that badly? What if Storm lost? Her first feeling was fear. She could even go so far as to say it upset her to think someone might rip her away. Like she wanted to actually stay with a guy who only wanted to use her. This prince. This asshole.

"Let's go," Storm said, his voice deep and gravelly.

Jolene swallowed thickly and nodded. The walk took all of a few minutes. They moved quickly and quietly. Jolene had to almost slow jog to keep up. They did pass a couple of guys who gawked at them…at her. Their eyes tracing her every move with definite interest. Storm growled loudly at one who took a step in their direction, but that was it. No fanfare otherwise.

"Are you hungry?" Storm asked her as they arrived at a large set of double doors, his hand rested on the doorknob as he spoke.

"Yes, I am actually." She realized at that moment that she was ravenous. The last time she had eaten a proper meal had been the previous morning. The energy bars they had given her were long gone as well and could hardly be considered real food.

"I will take care of it, sire," Beck said, walking backward in the direction they had just come from.

Storm opened the door and gestured for her to go in, finally relinquishing his tight hold on her hand.

Jolene did as he asked and almost stopped in her tracks. The room was huge and double volume. All open-plan. A modern kitchen, a dining area…and the bed.

That was some bed. Huge, like double king huge and four-poster. The linen was black, which added a certain amount of masculinity to what could have been girly, for lack of a better word.

The view was breathtaking. Or would be in the light of day. The entire one section of the living area was glass window. A vast expanse of darkness on the other side, a half-moon up above, shining down on the rippled surface of the ocean. The stars…they were simply amazing. The Milky Way and Orion's Belt had never looked so vivid. She found herself wishing she'd paid more attention when she visited the planetarium some years back. All of the constellations were on display, twinkling and blinking.

"Beautiful isn't it?" he asked, stepping up next to her.

"Yes." She nodded, taking it all in for a few moments more before saying what was really on her mind. "You're not going to be able to let me go, are you?"

Storm shook his head. "Nope, I guess it's how the hunt works. Once a male wins a female, he won't…can't give her up without a fight. It's an instinct thing. Shifters are governed a lot by our instincts. I fought for you. I won you. I got you here safely, which makes you mine. I am feeling possessive..." He frowned. "Not something I am used to. I didn't think it would happen to me at all, let alone this acutely. But, hey," he shrugged, "it is what it is."

His feelings reduced to hormones and chemicals. To base instincts. They hardly knew one another but still, it stung. "You *didn't* fight for me." She shook her head. "You fought for Christina *and* me. You didn't really care who you ended up with, so it's not the same."

"You are right. I initially didn't care who I ended up with, but that quickly changed. Within a half a minute of talking to the two of you, I knew I wanted you. So, by default, I fought for you, Jolene."

"Not really but we'll let it go. I have a feeling we'd argue for a while and we'd still end up disagreeing."

"Come on, this isn't so bad is it?" Storm turned in a circle, arms outstretched. "I'm not so bad, am I?"

She hated the warm fuzzy feeling she got when he said he'd chosen her in less than a minute of talking to both her and Christina. She'd always hoped for love at first sight, but this was better. He'd picked her based on more than just looks. Pity about there being no real interest attached. Nothing lasting at any rate.

Storm grinned when she didn't answer immediately. It was cocky and arrogant, reminding her of why this was a problem. "So, you've decided I'm not so bad after all. I'm glad you're over your...issue with me." Storm leaned down and pulled off his pants, stepping out of them.

Her mouth dropped open. The first two times she'd seen him naked, he'd had his back to her. Not this time. Her gaze was drawn *there*...how could it not be?

Storm was a big guy…really big. His balls hung down…heavy between his legs. She guessed that's where the saying came from – well hung. That wasn't all, his cock was big too. Especially considering he wasn't hard. It was both long and thick. Of course, she knew he would be huge after seeing him hard earlier, but still. Knowing something and seeing it for real was two different things.

She quickly averted her eyes, thankful when he didn't say anything about her staring. Jolene didn't know him well, but Storm would be a dick like that. That much she did know. Her cheeks felt hot. Her whole body felt hot. He was standing right there in all his naked glory. She looked outside. Safer that way.

He walked towards her, drawing her eyes back to him. *Keep them up.* On his face. Storm was so big and bristling – not that he was trying to be or anything. The guy had presence. She worked hard to keep her eyes from wandering where they shouldn't.

"I'm going to take a shower." He turned to a door. "You coming?" He continued towards what she knew must be the bathroom. It was like he expected her to just follow.

"No." She tried not to yell. *Was he crazy?*

Storm stopped and turned back. "I'm sure you want to get cleaned up as well. I'll wash your back and anything else that needs soaping up." His voice dropped a few octaves.

"I'm good. I can't shower with you." *Was that shrill voice hers?*

"Why not?" Storm looked really baffled.

"I would love a shower but not with you, thank you." This guy was crazy. Over-confident and crazy.

"We're going to eat and then I'm going to fuck you until you come. Just once this time since you didn't get much sleep." He winked. "It's only two hours till sunrise."

Winked.

She was too busy trying to pick her jaw up off the floor to speak, so she shook her head, clearing her throat. "No showering and no fucking."

"We're together for three weeks and we *are* going to fuck. We may as well start now."

"No!" The sheer damned arrogance irritated the hell out of her. That coupled with her body's reaction to his filthy words. She wasn't sure which one irritated her more. "We may be stuck together for the three weeks – against my will, I might add – but there will be no sleeping together, no fucking and no…I'll think of a third thing just now. There should always be three things. I'll think of a third in no time."

"Who said we can't fuck?" He shook his head. "And why can't we? Forget I asked that. The answer doesn't matter since we will be fucking." He took another step towards her, getting quite close now and it wasn't fair. He had just run for hours. Not just that, he'd carried her for hours too, and he still smelled amazing. Sure, there was an underlying scent of the earth and of sweat, but even that smelled really good.

"Don't," he growled.

"Don't what?"

"You were sniffing."

"No, I wasn't."

"Your nose was flaring and you were inhaling deeper than normal. You were sniffing me, and by your scent, I can tell you were liking what you were scenting."

"You smell sweaty," she mumbled. Not really a lie. Not the whole truth either, but he didn't have to know that.

"You like the smell of sweat?" The side of his mouth quirked up. "A little strange but it works in my favor. Fucking, if done properly, can be a major work-out."

"I do not like the smell of sweat, and we're not having sex, so please stop."

There was a knock at the door. *Oh, thank god!* Saved by the bell – or the knock in this case.

Storm kept his eyes on her. "Enter," he finally growled.

"I brought several different items," Beck began as he walked in carrying the largest tray she had ever seen. "I wasn't sure—" He stopped talking, glancing at them. "I see I have come at a bad time."

Storm was standing just inches away from her. When had he gotten so close? He was still naked and…Shit…was that? Yes, he was sporting a semi. "Not at all," she spluttered, taking a step back.

Beck smiled. "I will put the tray here and leave you to it. There are a couple of items that will still be good, even if eaten cold, or you could use the microwave to reheat anything that needs it." He placed the tray on a table.

"What does that have to do with anything?" she asked.

"I can scent your need, female. Storm will be eager to sate you. I'm sure the food will get cold."

He hadn't just said that! These guys were so forward about everything. It didn't help that they had enhanced senses.

Storm grinned. "I'm very eager! You can go now, Beck. I'll see you in a day or two."

Beck looked over at her. "You are one lucky—"

"Out!" Storm growled.

Beck half-bowed. "Let me know if you require any—"

"Out!" Another growl, louder this time.

As soon as the door closed behind Beck, Jolene covered her face with her hand. "That was so embarrassing. He could tell…or at least he thought I was…that I was…"

"Aroused?" Storm raised his brows and cocked his head.

Jolene rolled her eyes. "I'm not though." Why was she even trying to deny it? Maybe because she shouldn't be.

"Beck could scent your arousal because you are aroused, just as I am aroused." He glanced down at his— Oh, good lord but that thing was fully erect and jutting from his body. It was big and proud and…

No! No! No! Storm was sex on legs, but sex wasn't what she was after. It wasn't. "I don't know what your nose is telling you, but—"

"My nose is telling me that you're lubricated, your pussy is preparing to accept my cock into its tight confines."

Jolene made a soft choking noise but couldn't speak. Her tongue felt like it was tied up in knots. Tight ones and several of them.

Storm went on. "Your heart is beating faster as well." He leaned in, just inches away. "Aside from the sweet, sweet smell coming from your slick channel, there are pheromones in your blood that are also enhancing your scent." He sniffed. "Fucking delicious."

"No sleeping together," she croaked. "No sex and no…anything! I don't even want to be friends with you. If you don't move away, I'm going to slap you again." It was that or kiss him, and if she kissed him, there might not be any stopping. His words were affecting her. His nakedness was affecting her. She'd never been this turned on before and she had no idea why. It had been a good six months since she'd last had sex, but dry spells had never bothered her before. He was an asshole, she shouldn't want this.

Storm pulled himself back to his full height, looking down at her. "I'm sorry to hear we can't be friends." He shrugged. "It doesn't bug me though. Feel free to hit and claw me, makes hate-fucking all the more enjoyable."

"Arghhhhh," she growled. "You're incorrigible."

Storm chuckled as he turned and walked away. He glanced back over his shoulder. "For a second there I thought you were ready to give up. I thought I had you." He grinned, looking so damned sexy that it was annoying.

"Are you trying to say you would have been *unhappy* if I had agreed to let you sleep with me?" He was too much.

Storm shrugged. "I want to fuck you very badly, but I'm enjoying working for it. It's going to make the actual event all the more amazing, just you wait and see." His chest heaved, and his cock twitched. As in, it moved all on its own.

She shook her head, snapping her eyes back up. "It's not going to happen." Her voice sounded normal. Thank god, because she wasn't feeling normal.

"It's a foregone conclusion." He marched to a door and yanked it open. "I'll leave it open just in case you decide to join me." He tapped the wood and sent her another wink.

Asshole.

Cocky little bastard. Although, *little* was the wrong description of him by a long shot. Jolene had been right on the money. This was all a big game. If she gave in, he'd get what he wanted, and if she didn't, he'd get what he wanted anyway. A challenge. This was all a big challenge to him. All a damned game. Her life, reduced to a game. It wasn't fair. Right now she hated him. It didn't matter that there was something endearing and sweet about him, that part was overshadowed by the asshole part. There would be no sex. None. Golden Boy could forget that. If she left this room in three weeks' time and he still had the biggest, baddest hard-on for her, then she will have won, and if not…there was no other option. That was it!

CHAPTER 6

Unfortunately, the food didn't get cold, so there was no need for a microwave.

The human didn't welcome him into her body. All that natural lubrication had gone completely to waste. His three-hour hard-on had gone to waste as well.

In fact, she insisted on sleeping on the floor. And silent treatment was a real thing. He was at the receiving end right at that moment. Storm wasn't sure he liked it. He had to keep reminding himself of how good the sex would be once they started going at it. They were going to rut and soon. He'd meant it when he'd said it was a foregone conclusion. She might not like him much, but she was attracted to him. It was only a matter of time before he got to feel her body tighten around him. Before he got to hear the sweet sounds she would make when he was inside her.

Jolene had folded the blankets and was going about making herself some breakfast. Breakfast for one. She didn't so much as look at him, let alone ask him what he wanted. She'd ignored him when he offered to make her food earlier and was ignoring him even harder now.

Maybe making her sleep on the floor had been a bit

much.

No fucking way!

There was a perfectly good bed. A big enough bed. It wasn't like he was going to touch her without her consent. What did she think of him? Desperate had never been a part of his vocabulary and it never would be. Not wanting to share had been her choice in the end, and he was damned if he was going to be the one to sleep on the floor.

"The plates are in the top cabinet to your right." He pointed at the cabinet in question.

Jolene stopped looking through the kitchen, completely ignored him and went over and stirred her coffee instead. Her back to him, she took a sip.

Storm felt his lip twitch. She was stubborn. He walked over to the cabinet and opened it.

Jolene turned. "I can get my own plate." She stared daggers at him. Silver-tipped ones. Silver-tipped ones dripping in poison.

"I'm sure you can, but I don't mind helping you."

"I don't need your help." She brushed past him, grabbing a plate. Just the one.

"I like fruit and nuts in the morning." He suppressed a smile.

"Good for you." She huffed out a breath. "I'd rather not talk. We have nothing to say to one another." Then she seemed to think the better of that comment. "Except to ask you to put on a shirt or something."

Storm leaned up against the counter and folded his arms. "I'm a dragon shifter, this is about as much as we wear. Is my naked torso making you uncomfortable?" He rubbed his chest, watching her eyes as they tracked the movement. He was a big motherfucker, even for a shifter.

She seemed mesmerized for a second or two before turning her death stare back on him. "Bullshit like this might work on all the other women you seduce but it won't work on me."

"I'm glad to hear it." He meant it. "You should be thankful I'm not naked, I normally walk around my own chamber naked, so technically, I'm already meeting you halfway here."

"You're so not." She snorted and shook her head. "What was with all that roaring just now when you were in the shower?"

"I think you know exactly what that was."

"So loud though? That's just rude." She shook her head, putting the plate down on the counter.

"I was picturing you." It was true, he *was* picturing the lush female. Maybe he could have been much quieter about it, but Storm wanted Jolene to know exactly what he was doing, so he hadn't held back. "I was picturing your—"

She spun around to face him. "Don't." She pointed a finger at him. So gorgeous when she was angry.

"What?" He chuckled. "I'm a male. I have needs. I had a feeling you wouldn't be any more interested in letting me fuck you this morning." He looked out the window at the height of the sun. It was almost midday. "So, I took care of it myself." He sniffed in her direction watching her frown deepen. "I can scent you didn't do the same. You're still aroused and needy as fuck." Her scent made his gums itch, made his balls feel achy.

Her cheeks began to redden, and her jaw tensed.

"I would be more than happy to take care of that for you. I may have eased myself but we shifters have a ton of stamina. We can go many rounds before—"

"Stop it!" Her hands flew to her hips. Flared and plump, just like her ass and her tits. The t-shirt she was wearing strained. "Stop looking at my boobs like that as well. Why does everything have to be about sex with you?"

"I'm a male, you're one hell of a sexy female, we're together for the foreseeable future. You'll forgive me if I react to all that." He looked her up and down.

"You'll say whatever it takes to get in my pants, won't you?"

"No, I'll be straight up honest with you at all times and you can be just as honest with me when you tell me how amazing it is, how much you love riding my cock."

"Stop it!" she half-yelled. "Just stop already. I'd rather not talk to you but if you insist on flapping your mouth, you can talk about something other than sex. I dare you to try."

Her breathing had become elevated and her pupils were dilated. He didn't need to see or hear to know she was aroused right then. He only needed his nose. The sweet scent of her wet pussy permeated the air around them. It made him want to open his mouth and taste the air. So fucking delicious. He couldn't wait to slip inside her.

"No can do, Sweet Lips." He winked at her, watching as her face turned red all over again and the peppery tang of her anger mingled with all that sweetness. An amazing combination. One he had never experienced before.

"Do not call me that!" she yelled, eyes wide. They were dark and narrowed in on him. "And stop talking about sex. It's getting boring."

"Your body doesn't think so."

"Well, I do. My body is not involved in any type of

decision I make."

"Pity." He leaned back against the counter.

"You're an even bigger asshole than I first suspected." She hooked some hair behind her ear. "My life is not a game."

"It should be. You're an awesome, sexy female, why can't you relax a little? Enjoy yourself for once? You're so wound up."

"I don't want to enjoy myself." She made a noise born of frustration. "I didn't mean it like that."

"No, I think you did." He loved cranking her chain. Might be his new favorite thing. Just until he got inside her, then *that* would be his new favorite.

"I. Did. Not. Stop putting words in my mouth. I'm not twenty anymore, I have responsibilities and I'm not getting any younger. That's the long and short of it. You're messing with me."

"I'd like to mess around *with* you." He smiled, using the one he knew females loved. The smile that had them dropping their panties.

It didn't work on Jolene. In fact, it had the opposite effect. "You're such a dick. What I mean by messing with me is that I only have three weeks leave. Not something you thought about when you decided to take me as your own personal plaything despite my request that you leave me the hell alone."

"Three weeks leave?" He suspected she was talking about her job, but he wasn't sure.

"Yes, leave. I need to be back at work in three weeks. I'm not sure my boss would allow me to take any more time off. If I'm lucky, he'll grant me unpaid leave and if I'm unlucky I'll lose my job. All because of you." She pointed at him. "If I decide to stay for longer than the allotted three weeks, I'm definitely going to lose out on a promotion I've worked my ass off to get. I still might lose out on it even if I go straight back. It's a risk I was willing to take because I thought the guy I would end up with would at least be taking this seriously."

Shit! "Yeah, I hadn't thought of that." He rubbed the back of his head.

"No, you hadn't." She shook her head. "You're only thinking about yourself. The good news is that I have money saved, so unpaid leave isn't a problem. I might lose my job though. That promotion is toast. I'm losing out to a serious bitch who likes nothing more than to rub my face in it."

"I'm sorry!" What else could he say? He did feel like a dick.

"Let me go then." She implored him with her eyes.

"I can't. Even if I wanted to…I can't." Shit! Right then he wanted to try but even thinking about it made his muscles tighten and his gums itch. Made his scales scratch. "Not until the three weeks are up. I'll pay you out… I'll— "

"No! I don't need your help or your money. I'm very good at what I do, I'll find another position in a heartbeat. I like my job though," she said, more to herself. "If I have to go back, I'd rather go back to my life as it is. I don't want to lose to Carla." She mumbled to herself.

"Who is Carla?"

"I don't want to talk about it. Especially since you won't let me go anyway."

"I don't have a choice," he rasped.

"There is always a choice." She looked up at him,

imploring him with her eyes.

It made him want to sling her over his shoulder. Made him want to throw her on the bed and…He was an asshole. Jolene was right about that. He couldn't help his instincts though. They were riding him hard. Especially with her talking of leaving. "You are a resourceful, intelligent female. I'm sure your boss will understand. I doubt he would let you go."

"You can stop trying to butter me up. We aren't having sex." Jolene took a sip of her coffee.

"I'm not trying to butter you up. I say it like it is. I certainly don't say something with the purpose of making you feel good just so that I can fuck you. That's not how I'm wired. Come to think of it, I've never had to sweet talk a female. Never had to talk my way into a pair of panties." He looked up in thought. "I don't know how." He shrugged.

"Yeah right!" she mumbled. "What if—"

There was a knock at the door. Storm pushed out a breath. "That will be Beck. I have a meeting with my brother. Beck will stay with you."

"I don't need a babysitter."

"I'm worried you might decide to wander off. If a male is tempted to take what is mine, I would have to hurt him. That will entail violence, bleeding and possibly a couple of broken bones."

He noted the horrified look on her face.

"I had a feeling you wouldn't like that. If a male actually touched you, I would have to kill him…maybe even take his head as a trophy for my mantle." He pointed to the hearth. "You are the type of person who would blame yourself, so I'm going to leave Beck with you, so you can't be tempted."

"Oh." She cleared her throat. Mmmmm, the sweet scent of her arousal. It wafted around them. This female had no idea what she wanted. Good thing he knew. He really needed to make things up to her for the situation he put her in and once she let him, he would do his level best.

"Enter," Storm said.

Beck walked in, a smile on his face. It quickly disappeared and the male stopped in his tracks. "Good," he cleared his throat, "afternoon."

"I know," Storm said. "I'm sorry. Are you going to be able to watch the female?"

"Not that I want or need babysitting, but why can't he watch me? What's wrong?" Jolene frowned.

"You are highly aroused." Beck got this pained look.

Jolene gasped.

"It will be difficult for me to be in the same room with you even once you normalize…for lack of a better word."

"You go and shower," Storm said, looking Jolene head-on.

The female shook her head. "Don't order me around."

"Fine, do as you wish but if Beck tries anything – and he just might with you smelling so damned wet and sweet…"

She choked, clutching her throat; just as quickly she regained control of herself. "You really are a pig. Just when I think you can't shock me any more than you already have, you do."

"No, I'm serious, saying it like it is. You are no longer in Kansas, Dorothy. You're in dragon lands. Don't shower. Suit yourself. If you touch her," he turned his gaze to Beck, "I will maim you. I might even kill you."

"Is it really that bad?" Her eyes were wide.

"Yes." Beck nodded, face still pained. "Please tell me you're joking about killing me. You look like you mean it."

"I do," Storm growled. "Things will improve when Jolene finally decides that rutting is on the table."

The female gasped, shaking her head.

"Let's hope it happens soon." Beck turned to Jolene and Storm had to stop himself from snarling. As it stood, a low growl erupted from him. This whole possessive thing was getting old fast.

Beck glanced back at him, his friend grinned. "Easy, my lord." He turned to Jolene. "Do as Storm says, go and shower. I will finish making you brunch while you do so."

Jolene narrowed her eyes. "How do you know I haven't eaten?"

"The sounds your stomach is making."

She looked at Beck quizzically. "My stomach hasn't made any sounds."

"Your gut sounds would be different if your stomach had food inside it."

"Wow, you guys really do have fantastic senses." It didn't look like she liked that idea much.

"I will be back as soon as I can." Storm headed to the door. "Don't do anything stupid." Although he narrowed his eyes on Beck, he was technically addressing both of them.

CHAPTER 7

"Come on in and close the door." Torrent gestured to the chair opposite his desk.

"How is Candy?" Storm asked as he sat down.

His brother smiled, it was weary and yet filled with warmth. "She is doing as well as can be expected. The baby is due any day now. The healers have warned it could still be as long as another week, maybe more, before he comes. She is not sleeping so well and is uncomfortable, but it is to be expected." There was a tightness to Torrent's jaw and worry lines around his eyes. "I will be able to breathe a little easier when the baby is here safe and sound."

"I'm sure. I can't imagine how you must be feeling." Storm had a little more respect since winning the human. These instinctual emotions could be a bitch.

"Tide will cover for me. Are you still okay with looking after Rain?"

"Of course. I love that little munchkin."

"It would just be while Candy is in labor and maybe for an hour or two after."

"I would be thrilled to let her stay at my place for as long as need be."

"Are you sure about that? I recently received a report that stated you won a female in the hunt. Congratulations!" His brother smiled.

"Thank you." Storm nodded his head.

Then Torrent frowned. "You might be too busy to babysit." Then he chuckled. "I really can't believe that you actually went through with it and won a female. When I saw you'd entered, I didn't think you'd take part. I thought it was a hoax because I never pegged you as being anywhere near ready to mate."

Storm didn't say anything for a few seconds. "Jolene is a sweet and kind female, she won't mind looking after Rain. I'm sure she would enjoy it."

"Okay…good." Torrent sighed. "I could ask one of the dragon females otherwise, but Rain loves you so damned much. She will be so happy to spend time with her uncle."

"Of course she does, no female can resist me." He couldn't help but grin. It wouldn't be long before sweet Jolene gave in.

"Wait just a minute. You almost had me there." Torrent frowned. "I brought up mating and you changed the subject. You *are* going to mate this female, aren't you?"

Not a fuck! "If it works out." He shrugged.

Torrent looked him head-on for a moment or two. "You do intend to do your level best to get her to mate with you, right?" When Storm said nothing, he went on. "Tell me that you didn't win a female with no intention of actually mating her?"

"Here's the thing—"

"Fuck!" Torrent roared. "What were you thinking? I should have known." He quickly changed tack, looking irritated.

"That I'm bored to fucking death. That I haven't had this much fun since my first stag run. That…"

Torrent shook his head and then stopped. Seeming to be thinking something over. Next thing he knew, his brother laughed right in his face. Why was Torrent laughing? It took a few moments for the male's shoulders to stop shaking. "What? What's so funny?"

"You're playing with fire and you're liable to get burned. You know that don't you?"

"I'm having a bit of fun. I'm going to enjoy the company of a human for a couple of weeks, and I'm going to make damned sure she enjoys her time with me. Then we'll go our separate ways. Jolene is—"

His brother laughed some more. It was becoming irritating. Torrent finally sat back in his chair and wiped a hand over his face. "You might just have shot yourself in the foot. You tracked this female, you fought for her and then you brought her back to the lair, and in record time, I am told. All of these things are designed to get us here…" Torrent smacked a fist into his own lower belly. "To hit us hard. Right now, you are being driven to mark this female with your scent so that all others will know she is yours. You will be horny as hell and as possessive as hell. You probably think things will get better once you rut her, but they won't." Torrent shook his head, his lips quirked up in the start of a smile.

"Of course they will. It's been a couple of months since I was on a stag run. I haven't rutted any of the dragon females in a long time. Of course I'm horny." Storm chuckled like it was no big deal because it wasn't. It came out sounding strained though.

"Trust me on this. So, this female lets you rut her. Next

thing, you'll be driven to claim her—"

Not a chance! "Hold up!" Storm held up his hand. "You're dead wrong. Do I want to fuck her? Absolutely. Am I feeling possessive? Yeah, okay, you're right on that one. I won her and she's mine. For now," he quickly added the last. "That's where it ends though."

Torrent choked out another laugh. "It has begun then."

"I don't want a mate. I'm nowhere near ready. Besides, Jolene hates me. I'm not her type." He shook his head. "Her feelings for me don't matter really though since she is attracted to me, which means we'll have plenty of sex anyway. Quite frankly, it's a breath of fresh air," he said more to himself. "Soon, she'll move onto the next dragon, one who she actually likes, one she wants to mate and have kids with…stuff I'm not ready for. I plan on taking part in a good couple of hunts before that part happens."

Torrent leaned back in his chair and folded his arms. "Okay."

"What? No arguing?" That was too easy. What was going through Torrent's mind?

"You seem to have this covered. You won the female." Torrent shrugged, neatening a pile of papers on his desk. "You don't have to mate her." He put a large emerald and gold paperweight on top of the stack.

"I'm glad you feel that way," Storm said. "I do have it covered." He nodded.

"The Lores don't say you have to mate her or that she *has* to stay with you beyond the three weeks. A word of caution though, you do need to decide once you hit the end of the three-week period. At that point, you need to claim her, or she needs to go home or to another male. There is no in-between."

"Three weeks is almost too long." Storm snorted. Then again, he had a feeling it might take him a couple more days to win her over, so maybe three weeks would be perfect. Any more though…far too long with one female.

"Great! Have fun. I will stay in touch regarding Candy." His shoulders immediately tensed up.

"It's going to be fine." Storm reached over and patted Torrent on the side of his arm.

"I hope so." Torrent clenched his jaw.

"It will." Storm stood up. "You'll see. Let me know if you need anything. I might have won a female, but I am still here for you."

CHAPTER 8

Fuck!
Fuck!
Fuck!

Had Jolene changed her mind? He turned onto his back and hooked a hand behind his head, so that he could get a better look. *Stay calm!* The sheets rode low on his hips, so he tugged them up, scrunching them over his midsection. He didn't want to scare her off. She was as fiery as she was timid. Jolene finished with whatever she was doing in the closet and turned around.

Holy fuck!

"My bag arrived earlier," she said, sounding casual, relaxed even.

"I see that." His voice was thick. His dick was hard. His balls were tight. This despite taking care of his erection not even an hour ago.

The silk clung to her every curve, falling to about midthigh. The straps of her nighty were thin. He could make out the outline of her full breasts. Her nipples were hard despite the fire that raged in the hearth. Storm swallowed thickly as he watched her walk over to the bed. Her breasts swayed and jiggled with each step she took. He tried hard not to stare. Again, not wanting to scare her off. Jolene didn't like it when he ogled her tits.

Excitement coursed through him. He felt like a whelp about to experience his first taste of pussy. His dick throbbed. It was going to happen. He felt like fist-punching the air.

"Would you mind if I slept in the bed with you tonight?" She looked at him from under her lashes and half-smiled. Her lips were shiny, they scented of berries. The smile was seductive, made him swallow again, his Adam's apple bobbing.

"No." A deep rasp. Storm cleared his throat. "Not all. Be my guest." *Act casual. You got this.* He'd never had to talk himself through foreplay before. He was acting like a complete fucking amateur. Of course he had this. He was Storm. Prince of Water. God to females everywhere.

Jolene peeled away the covers. She placed one knee on the bed, her nighty rode up higher, showing off her lush as fuck thigh. She was flirting with him. He couldn't wait to part those babies. To hold onto them while he pounded into her. He was going to make her come so hard. He turned onto his side so that he could face her. So that he could drink her in.

Storm caught a glimpse of her underwear. Red. Holy fuck but they were a bright fiery red. Pity they weren't going to survive this. He was tearing them off. Shredding them with his teeth. Then he was going to fuck her into oblivion.

By claw, but she smelled delicious. So damned amazing. His nose twitched, as did his cock.

"Just one thing…" Her voice was a soft purr.

"Anything." Right now, she could name it and it was

hers. His dick throbbed. It couldn't wait to be inside her and he couldn't blame his cock for having outstanding taste.

"Do not touch me." Her face morphed back into the death stare from earlier. "You lay so much as a single finger on me and you are dead."

"You mean…" Storm frowned. *What? No! But surely?* His dick twitched again, but this time it was in pain. Agony!

"Oh," she blinked a couple of times, "you thought I was actually going to let you…that we…" She laughed, reminding him of his brother earlier. "Oh god, that's funny." She laughed harder. "You thought I'd let you sleep with me." She sobered up in an instant. "No! You misunderstood. I'm sorry if the sexy night clothes misled you. It's all I packed, since I planned on spending quality time with a guy who actually wanted me for more than just fun and games. I don't have anything baggy and down to my ankles. Something dowdy, which is what I would have worn for you."

He had no retort. Storm just lay there with a mouth full of teeth and a hard, throbbing cock. It was his balls' turn to scream in agony.

"My back is still stiff from sleeping on the floor. I'm sleeping right here." She rubbed the mattress between them, "until I go home in a couple of weeks. It's your turn to be stiff." She glanced at the crumpled sheet, still over his hard-on, and Storm had to suppress a groan. "That is, unless you want to sleep on the floor. She turned over, taking a good deal of blanket with her. "Stay on your side and I'll stay on mine."

Not a fuck!

His dick had never been so hard. To think he'd been so damned happy. He couldn't think of a time he'd been so ecstatic. Except for maybe that one time when he'd managed to put Tide on his back. It was some years back and Storm had only been a couple of months into his training. It had been some achievement for a newbie. Especially since Tide was four years his senior. Of course, he'd give his brother a run for his money nowadays for sure, but back then…

Shit!

She'd played him.

Outright fucking played him.

His dick was harder than nails. His erection not going anywhere. There she lay. Right there. So close he could touch her. Her sweet scent filled his nostrils. It didn't help that Jolene was needy and achy. She wanted him but wouldn't admit it. Her breathing was also slowing. She was falling asleep. Maybe this whole thing hadn't been such a good idea.

Bullshit.

All she had done was to step it up. This challenge was becoming tastier by the hour. The human didn't know what she was up against. Storm smiled as he turned over.

Game fucking on!

CHAPTER 9

Something smelled good.
Really good.

Mmmmmmm! Maybe bacon. Yes, it was definitely bacon. Crispy bacon at that. Her mouth watered for a taste. Jolene cracked her eyes open. It was already morning. Quite bright. A glance at her watch told her it was almost nine. She'd slept in. Not only that. She'd slept really well.

Then she remembered having slept next to Storm and the reason why she'd slept in and like the dead. It was because it had taken her so damned long to fall asleep. Who knew that faking sleep could be such hard work.

It hadn't helped that Storm had tossed and turned and tossed some more. That he'd groaned and grumbled. She was sure he'd said 'red panties' once and 'fucking played' another time. In fact, he'd been so restless, that he'd woken her a good couple of times after she'd finally fallen asleep.

Good! Wonderful! The asshole deserved everything he got. No, he deserved more.

"Morning," Storm said in a deep baritone that had her toes curling. She immediately berated her toes. No part of her was allowed to react to him. "Breakfast is almost ready," he added as she turned.

Dang!
Shoot!
Freaking hell!

Her eyes popped out of her skull, and she spent the next few seconds trying to find them on the bed, and then a few long seconds after that trying to put them back in her skull, along with her tongue. Which needed to go back into her mouth. At least, that's what it felt like because good lord!

It wasn't like she hadn't seen him naked. She had. Only, he was holding a spatula and there was something smeared on his chest.

"I made waffles with all the trimmings," he announced, bobbing his brows.

His hair was still lightly mussed. His eyes were so stunning in the morning light, she wanted to smack them. They wouldn't be as pretty if the surrounding skin was black and puffy. His stubble was thicker, highlighting his jaw. She wasn't looking down. *No way!*

Not at his chest...*Holy smokes.*

Not at his abs...*Oh lord god up above.*

Definitely not at his...*Lord have mercy on her soul.*

Head back in the game, Jolene. This was a game. One she was damn well winning. There were only two rules in this game. One, make Storm's life hell, and two, to not to let him touch her. No touching, no sucking, no licking and definitely no fucking. He was right in that her body had other ideas. Her body could go to hell and so could he. She planned on using her body and its false signals to drive him to distraction. To turn his life inside out, just like he had hers. He would be sorry he hadn't listened to her when she told him to leave her alone. Sorry he ever decided to take part in the hunt for fun. *Fun! Idiot!*

Golden Boy had clearly never had a woman say no before. Never had any kind of pushback. Things were about to change for him. She almost felt sorry for the poor schmuck.

Jolene let the blanket fall around her waist. She sat up in bed and lifted her arms, stretching and arching her back. When she finished, she looked his way.

His eyes were dark, his jaw tight. His cock...*Eyes up*. Point one may have gone to him, but the next three points were all hers. "Waffles sound yum. Hope you have syrup, I like mine extra sticky." She licked her lips.

He groaned.

Another point to her. She jumped out of bed, adding another ten points in one go. By the end of the day, he was going to let her go. There was no way he was going to want anything to do with her once she was done with him.

―⁂―

Her tits bounced as she jumped out of bed. They fucking bounced. Dragon shifters didn't have many weaknesses. Bouncing breasts on a lush female were one of them. The spatula nearly fell from his grip. The silk clung to her. It didn't help that he remembered the fiery red thong. By her scent, he was sure the lace would be soaked. Why were they messing around? Why weren't they just fucking like rabbits? He couldn't remember anymore. What would she do if he walked over to her and threw her back on the bed? If he pulled up her nighty, tore off the lace scrap and—

"You can stop looking at me like that because it isn't

going to happen. Not today and not tomorrow." Jolene pulled her shoulders back, thrusting out the most delectable set of tits he had ever seen on a female. She liked it sticky, well, he could oblige. He could oblige in spades. He just needed to pick his jaw up off the floor long enough to try to talk her into it.

"And if I were you, I'd cover that thing up." She pointed at his cock. "You might just hurt yourself otherwise." She smiled, looking amused, rather than aroused. *What the fuck?!*

Smoke. He smelled smoke. There was smoke. *Fuck!* "My waffles!" he yelled. Storm opened the waffle-maker, pulling out the scorched food. He muttered a curse as he tossed them in the trash. "Good thing I already made a batch or two. Take a seat." He gestured to the table.

Surprisingly, Jolene did as he said. There was a pot of coffee and a pitcher of juice. Not to mention a heap of crispy bacon, strawberries, cream and syrup. He placed the waffles he'd already made on the table, pushing them over to her.

She poured herself some coffee. "I'm impressed." She added cream. "This looks good," she said as she spooned in some sugar.

"You're talking to me today. Does this mean we're at least on speaking terms? A truce maybe?" he quickly added.

"Not on your life." She stirred her coffee. "I'm hungry and you cooked." She helped herself to a waffle. "You have a little something on your chest." She pointed.

Storm looked down and spotted a smear of waffle batter.

"Yum." Her eyes were bright. "I love waffles." Her

eyes dropped back down to his chest.

"You want to help me out with this? We could add a drizzle of syrup." He bobbed his brows.

Her pupils dilated and her heart-rate picked up. She fucking loved the idea. It was a great pity she shook her head so hard. "No. Not my taste."

Liar!

"I've never cooked for a female before."

"Is that supposed to impress me?" She forked a couple of bacon strips onto the waffle before giving him a hard stare.

"I thought you might like to know. I'm making an effort here. I've also never slept in the same bed as a female…actually closed my eyes that is. You are my first. I've never even had a female in my chamber before, for that matter." That should impress her.

"And that's supposed to make me feel special?" She rolled her eyes.

"Yes!"

She snorted, cutting a corner piece of the waffle. "Well, I'm not! Not in the least! You would have jumped right in there last night if I had let you."

"Damn straight, and you would have enjoyed the hell out of it." He could hear the frustration etched in his voice.

"Whatever," she muttered. "You're only making any type of effort because I'm the first woman to turn you down. You should be ashamed you never made any effort with any of the others."

"I made an effort." He threw a waffle on his own plate. "Where it actually counted." He grinned. "I always make sure I leave the female smiling and satisfied."

"Says you." She drizzled some syrup over everything.

"No." He shook his head. "I know for a fact because a body doesn't lie."

She shrugged, not looking convinced. "I think you're an asshole. I don't think you thought any more of these women you slept with than you do of me. You most likely treated them like they were objects to get off on. You used them, just like you want to use me."

"Used?" *What the fuck!* "It was mutually beneficial. I haven't had any complaints."

"I'll bet good money that you didn't stick around long enough to hear what they had to say about it. I doubt you asked."

Shit! That wasn't true. It wasn't. Sure, he hardly stuck around. It was always at their place and he left once the deed was done. The female was usually fast asleep. Completely finished and utterly sated. "No, they were satisfied. I didn't have to hear them say it to know it." He threw a couple of strawberries on top of the bacon he'd already piled on and drizzled some syrup. Not that he was all that hungry anymore.

Using her fork, she put a considerable section of waffle into her mouth. It fit just fine. His balls hurt. His dick fucking throbbed. Jolene chewed a couple of times and swallowed, taking her time licking off three fingers. "Mmmmm," she purred. "Delicious."

This was going to be a very long, very hard couple of weeks if he couldn't get her on the end of his dick.

What was he saying?

He would get between her thighs and she was going to fucking love it. Once she felt what he could do, she would beg him to take her again. Although he planned on having her a good couple of times, he would enjoy hearing her beg. He was going to love the hell out of it. In fact, he would refuse to touch her again unless she begged.

CHAPTER 10

Three days later...

With barely a backward glance, he announced, "I'll see you later," sounding bored.

"You're going out again?" she asked, as Storm made his way to the door.

"Yes." He nodded, still walking.

"Why? What is it this time? Practice, or guarding the perimeter, or something top secret again maybe?" There was more than just a hint of irritation in her voice.

"It's not like you care."

"You're right about that," she mumbled.

He grabbed the doorknob and began to turn it. "You need to stay put." Storm huffed out a breath, turning to face her. "You *are* going to stay put, aren't you?" He narrowed those amethyst jewels in on her. She hated that he still affected her. She hated that she loved the intensity of his stare. The way his muscles hardened when he was pissed at her. She mostly loved when he was pissed at her, which was often. She was so rocking this. At least, she was rocking this when he actually stayed home longer than five minutes.

"I said, you aren't going to try something stupid, like going out on your own?" Storm narrowed his eyes some more, his voice had turned deep.

"Why? Would you let me go out if someone, Beck maybe, went with me?"

"No! Not a chance. It's not—"

"Yeah, yeah…it's not safe."

"Tell me you aren't going to try anything. I don't like that look in your eyes." He scrutinized her, taking a step towards her.

It was like he could sense her plan. "Of course not." *Act nonchalant.*

"Jolene." He cocked his head. "You *do* plan on staying here, don't you?"

"Maybe, maybe not." She stuffed her hands into her jeans pockets.

Storm looked up at the ceiling for a few seconds – it looked like he was counting to ten – before walking over to the living room area and picking up the phone.

"What are you doing?" She folded her arms.

"What does it look like?" He glanced up at her before placing the device to his ear.

"You're calling a babysitter." She sighed. She was so done with all of this.

He grinned, his eyes sparkled.

"You're such a dick!" She fell back on the sofa.

"Here I was thinking you actually wanted me to stay home, to keep you company. If that's the case…Hold on Beck!" He spoke into the phone, taking it away from his ear, turning his eyes back to her. "Is that the case? Do you want me to stay home? Do you want to spend time with me?"

"What do you think?" She knew what time meant in his book. Sex. *No thanks!* She wasn't about to give up the milk for free. Jolene wanted more. More than Storm could give her.

"That's what I thought." He started to bring the phone back to his ear.

"What would be the point?"

Storm put the phone to his chest. "Why do you want me to stay so badly? You don't care. You don't want to spend time with me. You just want to torture me, so why do you want me to stay?"

Torture? A little harsh. It was because she couldn't make his life difficult if he was out there. "Because it's not fair that I'm stuck between these four walls while you are out there doing as you please." Okay, so that came out sounding jealous. Like maybe she didn't trust him. Like she didn't want him spending time with other women.

His eyes lit up. They got this look.

"I didn't mean it like that. I could care less what you do with your time and who you do it with." It still sounded jealous. Dammit! She so wasn't.

He smiled, this cocky half-smile that did things to her…it shouldn't. "Why don't I believe you?"

She shrugged. "Believe whatever you want."

Storm chuckled. "Come on, Jolene, let's have a little fun."

"By fun you mean sex?"

Storm looked her in the eyes for a moment or two before putting the phone back to his ear. "I'll call you back," he said, and pushed the off button. "No, by fun I mean fun."

"What did you have in mind?"

"I don't know. Truth or dare? Poker?"

She laughed. "Poker? As in—"

"It wouldn't be fun if it wasn't strip poker." Storm ran a hand through his hair. The glossy dark strands shiny between his fingers.

"I've seen you naked a ton of times." She fake-yawned. Storm walked around naked most of the time, but it wasn't getting old. Not even close really, and by the grin he was sporting he wasn't buying her bored act.

"You love watching me walk around naked. You can't take your eyes off my cock. Don't think I haven't noticed."

"See, not even two minutes and our conversation has already gone down the drain."

"So, no strip poker. No talk of sex. No trying to instigate sex. Let's just…" She could see his mind moving a mile a minute.

"You have no idea of what to suggest," she blurted moments later. "We have absolutely nothing in common." She shook her head.

"Why are you so negative?"

"I've had five boyfriends. I class any relationship that lasts longer than a year to be serious."

Storm scratched the back of his head. "Sheesh, a year is a long-ass time."

"For a guy who doesn't spend more than one night – my bad, not even that long – with the same girl, I would imagine that a year seems like forever."

Storm nodded. "For the record, I have had sex with the same female more than once."

"Oh really?"

He nodded. "There are a couple of single dragon shifter females."

"Convenient." She tried not to sound bitchy and failed.

Storm nodded. "Yes, it most definitely is." At least he was honest.

"We're drifting back to talk of sex and this isn't about sex. We were talking about my five exes – it sounds even worse saying it out loud. I was with my first boyfriend for a couple of years before he left me to meet other people. He felt tied down, like he was missing out – his words. Boyfriend one was married within a year of our breakup. I caught my second boyfriend red-handed. He married the person he was cheating with. The third one…let me not bore you. They all have a similar pattern."

Storm sat down. "You know this has nothing to do with you, right?"

"Boyfriend five and I broke up eight months ago. I broke up with him. We'd been living together for almost two years and still no ring. I gave him an ultimatum and he chose to leave. Guess what?"

"He's a prick."

"That too. No, he's engaged to be married. Met someone within weeks of our breakup and asked her to marry him soon after." She shook her head, feeling the pain well inside her. Not because of Brian or any of the others. Her eyes stung but she was so not going to cry, so she sucked it back. "I'm not getting any younger. I'm starting to think there's something seriously wrong with me." She hated these 'woe is me' feelings but she couldn't help it. Brian was the last straw. He'd told her he wasn't anywhere near ready. She'd heard that before somewhere and several times over. Storm was nothing new. He had just been nice enough to be upfront about it. She respected him for that, if nothing else.

"There's nothing wrong with you. In fact, there's everything right with you." His eyes tracked her body, lingering on her breasts before darting back up to her face. He leaned back into the sofa.

"Sure, they had no problem sampling the goods, but that's where it ended. That's why I'm done with casual." She shook her head.

Storm looked at her for a while. Eyes locked with hers, he seemed to be thinking things over. Serious for once. "I can understand how your past could make you feel this way. I am who I am though. Don't take my lack of wanting to commit personally because it has nothing to do with you. If I were to settle down, you would be my type."

Jolene choked out a short burst of laughter. It wasn't the least bit funny though. "Again, I've heard it all before. Thing is, I've always known what I wanted. I've never beaten around the bush when it came to things that mean a lot to me. My own parents divorced when I was really young. I'm an only child. Family has always been lacking in my life. Mom is married to her job and dad is on girlfriend number…" She tried to run through them all in her mind. "I can't remember. Must be eight or nine. I…" *How had this conversation even happened?* "I'm not sure why I'm telling you all of this. You're the enemy."

"That's where you're wrong. We could be friends." Sincerity shone in his eyes.

"Friends with benefits, I suppose." She rolled her eyes. Truth was, she was right about the benefits part and it stung. Ultimately, Storm didn't want to be friends or anything with actual substance. She was there as a booty call. Something to distract him from his boredom.

"I would be lying if I said I didn't want to fuck you

really badly." *Here we go!* He made a groaning noise that she felt low, somewhere in the pit of her stomach. "But we could just be friends. I'm a grown male, capable of controlling my…urges. I like you, Jolene."

She wasn't buying the whole friendship thing for a minute. She preferred it when he was straight with her. Better for both of them that way. "Yeah, we could but only if you let me go on my merry way. Better yet, point out a couple of really decent guys…ones you know are keen on a happily-ever-after. Guys who are more my type."

His eyes darkened and he stood up. One quick move. One second he was slouching on the couch and the next he was standing his full height and pissed. Jaw clenched, hands tight at his sides. Body rigid. "I'm sorry, Jolene." He shook his head, not sounding sorry in the least. *Why did she love it when he said her name? Especially when he used that rasping tone.*

"You're right." He looked down at her, those purple orbs piercing into her. "We can't be friends. I can't let you go, and I'm *not* introducing you to anyone else. You're mine until the end of this term, and I'll be damned if I don't spend every second trying to tear off your panties with my fucking teeth."

Her clit did this zinging thing she felt in the pit of her stomach. Storm had been flippant, teased her, worked hard at pissing her off. He'd been arrogant and downright seductive, but she'd never seen him serious to the point of anger. It was sexy. It shouldn't be, but it was. She didn't like how it made her feel, which was hot and flustered. "Um…" Jolene licked her lips and he tracked the movement of her tongue. "Firstly, I'm not some possession. I'm not yours." There wasn't much force to her voice, which had turned into a soft purr.

"You are on dragon territory. That makes you mine. Start getting used to it."

Mine! He was making her sound like a thing. His plaything, and yet it still made her feel warm and fuzzy and turned on. She was too intelligent to be feeling this way, but she was. "Unless you've changed your mind about settling down, this..." She pointed between them. "Sex." She snorted like it was the biggest joke because it was. "Isn't going to happen." She had to stick to her guns. "You will need to buy this cow before you can sample my milk." She pointed to her boobs.

Storm frowned. "You're lactating?"

"No." She shook her head. "It's just a stupid saying. One I've been telling myself since Brian and I broke up."

"The prick?"

Her lip twitched. "Yeah, the prick."

Storm rubbed the back of his head, still looking pissed. "You don't even want to be friends and yet you'd stay if I told you I was interested in more than just sex?"

"Yes."

"Not going to happen. I need some air." Storm ground his teeth as he walked to the door.

"Running away?" she threw at him. She'd all but admitted to being interested in him despite her finding him an arrogant asshole, and he had shot her down. Big time! No need to think about it.

Storm turned. "Yes, I'm running and as fast as I can. I can't be holed up with you any longer. I'm not an idiot. The sexy nighties, little dresses. Look at you now."

"A skirt and a top." She shrugged.

"A tight as fuck denim skirt, a red lacy bra and a white tank…you're driving me crazy. I can't stay." He ran a hand through his hair. "I need to blow off some steam."

"Going to find a hook-up with one of your convenient dragon women?" *Oh god, she hadn't just said that!* Thing was, he'd hurt her, and she wanted to hurt him back. She wasn't doing a great job of it though.

"Good idea!" He nodded once. The movement jerky, the muscles on either side of his neck were roped. "I might just do that," he growled, yanking the door open and slamming it shut behind him.

Jolene pushed herself up off the couch. "Asshole!" she shouted at the door. She should go after him. *No!* She should leave. Walk out that door. Explore the lair and meet other people. Sitting around was making her crazy. This whole thing wasn't fair.

The thought of him out there, enjoying himself, flirting, maybe even more, had her clenching her fists. She shouldn't care. He really wasn't her type. Jolene began to pace. Why wasn't she leaving? It wasn't like he would actually hurt or kill someone. It wasn't like anyone would try anything. *Would they?*

There was a knock at the door. Was he back? Had he changed his mind? Did he want to apologize? Or maybe he was back to tell her she could go. The thought should make her happy, but it didn't. It left her feeling oddly disappointed. Like he'd given up on her, even though there was nothing to give up on.

Stupid!

There was another knock. "Can I come in?" It was Beck.

The disappointment she felt left her reeling. What was

this? She couldn't start feeling something for Storm. All he wanted was a good time. She wanted more. It would end in disaster.

Another knock.

"Come in," she blurted.

Beck put his head around the jamb. He was smiling, but it quickly turned into a frown. "You okay?" He lifted his brows.

"I'm fine."

"That frown and those downturned lips tell me different." He sniffed the air.

"Don't go all shifter on me."

"I scent anger and frustration. Lots of it." Beck closed the door behind him.

"Well, that makes a change from arousal, I guess." She laughed. It was half-hearted.

"Ohhhh, I scent that too." He smiled, it was friendly, his green eyes glinted.

"Of course you do." Jolene groaned in frustration, rubbing a hand over her face and heaving an exasperated sigh.

"Did the two of you have a fight?" Beck asked, brows raised.

"I'm not talking to you about it. You're his best friend, you'll blab."

"I would not. Males don't gossip like you females." He shook his head. "Look, I know a little bit about what's going on. Storm filled me in on some of it."

"I thought you guys didn't gossip." She laughed.

"We don't. It wasn't like that."

"Yeah, whatever." She rolled her eyes.

"Okay, fine. We gossiped like a bunch of females and

you were the main topic." He grinned.

Why did that make her feel good? She was an idiot, that's why. "What did Storm say?"

"Like I said, he filled me in. I knew he planned on entering the hunt with no intention of mating the person he won. I told him it was a stupid idea, but once Storm decides on something, it's almost impossible to dissuade him."

"It *was* a stupid idea. Now look!" Irritation and frustration welled up in her all over again. "I wish he would just agree to let me go. We want different things. He wants to have fun and to have plenty of sex and I want so much more. It could end really badly." Only if she didn't stick to her plan.

"That's the thing. He can't just let you go." Beck shook his head. Sincerity shone in his eyes.

"What do you mean? Of course he can. He's just too damned selfish, too much of an asshole to do it." She knew that wasn't true, but she wasn't feeling forgiving right then.

Beck nodded. "Granted, he is somewhat selfish."

"Somewhat! Come on, he's a lot selfish." She looked at him head-on.

"He's a product of his upbringing," Beck said simply.

"An excuse if I ever heard one."

"Maybe, but it's still true." Beck seemed to want to say more. Maybe to tell her something personal about Storm. Come to think of it, she didn't know too much personal information about him. Unfortunately, Beck seemed to think better of it. "It's not that though. He can't let you go, as in, he physically can't."

She snorted out a laugh. "That's the most ridiculous

thing I've ever heard." *Shit!* She knew he had these possessive emotions running through him. Knew it would be difficult but impossible? *Come on!*

"No, it's not. Storm is a shifter and a royal."

"I know all of this. That's why I signed up, because shifters are supposed to actually want commitment. They're supposed to want a family. We were warned that they come on strong and when you guys mate, it's for life. That appeals to me. That's why I'm here. The problem is that Storm isn't interested in all that."

"That's true, but unfortunately for Storm it doesn't quite work that way. He wouldn't listen to me or his brother, Tide. He wouldn't listen to anyone when they tried to dissuade him. Now he's stuck. He hunted you, he won you and he marked you."

"He didn't mark me," she flung back, instantly feeling bad at how defensive her tone was.

"He will have kissed you, touched you. I could scent him on you when you arrived." Beck looked at her expectantly.

That kiss.

That scorching, toe-curling, panty-wetting bloody kiss. Jolene had tried to wipe it from her mind. It had mostly worked. She cleared her throat and nodded. "It was a tiny kiss. It meant nothing."

"It meant everything." Beck's expression was so serious that it was almost comical. "Storm brought you back and that made you his. He is driven instinctively to mark you properly."

"As in…" She let the sentence die because she knew exactly what Beck was saying.

"Yep! Every instinct, every cell, every part of him

needs…it. Even thinking of letting you go is abhorrent to him. He physically can't do it."

So that was why he had reacted so badly when she had asked him to let her go. "So, if I told him to introduce me to other guys. Ones who were not only sweet and kind but serious about settling, that might set him off?"

"You didn't!" Beck widened his eyes. "No wonder I scent so much anger, so much testosterone. He left because you would not have liked the alternative."

"Alternative?" She raised her brows.

"You don't need me to elaborate. Bottom line, you guys are stuck. I'm sure he has realized the error of his ways. Even if he hasn't yet…he will."

"So, it's purely hormonal, instinctual?"

"He does find you attractive, otherwise it wouldn't work, but yes." Beck nodded.

"And you're sure we're stuck together, I can't—"

"No! He would go nuts if you tried to leave or if someone tried to take you. He'll be extra horny and over-the-top possessive."

"That much I noticed," she mumbled. "Would it help if I slept with him?" She put up a hand. "Not that I'm going to. I can't!" She shook her head. It sounded like she was trying to talk herself out of it, which was stupid. Maybe she was trying to talk herself into it? *Nah!* It wasn't an option.

"Yes, it would help if you had sex with him. His scent would be on you and he'd be able to breathe a little easier."

Jolene almost felt sorry for Golden Boy. Ultimately though, he'd gotten himself into this mess. It was unfortunate he'd dragged her along for the bumpy ride. There was no way she was backing down from this. Storm needed to learn a tough lesson. To not mess with people's emotions, with their lives. Not everything revolved around his ass, even if it was a fine ass. Then she had a thought that scared the hell out of her. "He will be able to let me go in two and a half weeks, won't he?"

"Yes, he will. I understand why you don't want to rut him. He made a really stupid mistake."

Jolene sighed. "I can't do it. I don't want him to suffer, but I...there is no alternative."

Beck snorted. "Storm is a grown male. He will get through this. I just wanted you to have some understanding for his...behavior. He can be an asshole, and he can be selfish but he's ultimately a good male. He means well."

She nodded. It was true, but it didn't change anything. Storm had done this to himself. To them both. It did make more sense to her now. She couldn't find any sympathy for him though. Not much at any rate.

CHAPTER 11

Storm stretched his wings and pushed hard. Until his muscles ached, until he couldn't get enough air into his lungs. He must have done about fifty or sixty laps around their territory. The first few had been at breakneck speed. The ground below a blur. Hours and many wing-beats later, he felt marginally better.

Storm landed on the main balcony and shifted. His skin was sweaty, muscles fatigued, his mind somewhat cleared.

He'd overreacted. For once, it seemed that he and Jolene had made some progress. The female had opened up to him. It felt good that she trusted him with something about herself. Information on her past relationships. Why she felt the way she did. Part of why she was so hung up on finding a mate. It made sense. It also made him feel terrible. Her goading, on the other hand, had pushed him beyond his limits. Particularly when she had begged him to let her go…yet again. It was becoming tiresome. Especially since he couldn't do it. *No chance!* It wasn't just that, she'd also asked him to introduce her to other males. Males who would mate and impregnate her. Even now, hours later, he still ground his teeth at the thought. His hands still wanted to instinctively curl into fists so that he could beat any male with designs on his female. Even if the situation was temporary.

Right now, the thought of her with another male killed him. It turned his insides upside down and inside out. Made him see red. Made him want to flip her over and...he grit his teeth some more. She didn't want sex, so he'd had to leave quickly, otherwise...

Storm had briefly considered finding a dragon female, but the idea held no appeal. Then he'd considered flying straight to Walton Springs so that he could find a human female. That had left him cold as well. The only female he wanted right then hated him. Thought him arrogant. An asshole. Maybe she was right. At least to a degree.

Jolene wasn't entirely correct in her thinking though. She did need to relax a little. Why couldn't they be friends? Benefits? Absolutely. He still wanted to fuck her something fierce. Wanted it almost as much as he needed air. His balls had never felt this big. This tight. It didn't matter how often he emptied them. The need stayed. It clawed at him. It was just—

It felt like he'd hit a stone wall. Storm took a step back. He'd been so deep in his thoughts that he'd walked into someone. "Flood! I'm sorry, I..."

The male's eyes were dark and narrowed. His mouth a thin white line. The side-punch came out of nowhere. Flood was the biggest, meanest shifter, possibly in all four kingdoms. It was a good thing he couldn't breathe fire, or he would be damn near unstoppable.

"The fuck...!" Storm growled as he jumped back to his feet in a swift move that...sent him straight into Flood's waiting knee.

May as well have been a granite slab. His lip split, his

eye on the right side instantly began to puff up. Flood kept coming. Storm barely managed to roll out of the way as the male's foot came down where his face had been moments earlier.

Storm growled, rolling away a second time. He jumped to his feet. Flood was massive and fucked-up strong, but he wasn't as fast as Storm, who countered with a kick to the side of Flood's leg. He aimed for the knee, but his thrust hit a little high. The bastard was faster than he looked. Still not fast enough though.

Storm got a punch in, just as Flood was turning his head. Smack bam in the nose. There was a satisfying crunching noise and Flood roared.

This time, Storm wasn't quite fast enough, and a blow glanced off his jaw. Hurt like a motherfucker. Someone put themselves between them. Crazy bastard, since Storm was going to teach Flood a lesson or two and he was in the way. Storm might be the youngest prince, but he was still a royal. He still deserved respect. Flood needed to bleed.

The male between them grabbed at him as he made a lunge for Flood. His fist connected with the male's face with another satisfying crunch. The force barely moved the male. Flood took half a step back, his eyes narrowing. His mouth bloody. With another loud roar, he came at Storm.

Two males grabbed Flood, holding his arms while another grabbed him from behind. One of the three went flying just as two males grabbed him. Two more males rushed to hold Flood back. The male was a strong fucker.

Storm fought half-heartedly against his own captors. He had no wish to attack someone who couldn't defend himself, and right now Flood was too busy fighting the males who held him. Another one went flying after a vicious blow to the face. Storm felt sorry for the bastard. Flood's punches were like a hard, unyielding blast.

"Stop it!" Bay shouted. The haze of battle gone, Storm recognized him as the male who had stood between them just moments earlier.

"You're a fucker!" Flood shouted, eyes on him, muscles bulging as he strained against those who held him.

Storm fought against the males holding him as well, incensed by what Flood had just called him. He broke free with a mighty pull but couldn't bring himself to hit a helpless person. It felt stupid calling Flood helpless, and yet that's what he was. It took five straining males to hold him in check. Flood's face was red, veins popped up on his forehead. His muscles roped.

Bayou tried to grab back Storm's arm, but he growled at him in warning.

"Leave him!" The higher ranking Bay snapped at Bayou. The male could obviously see that Storm didn't plan on attacking Flood. He would have done so already if that were the case.

The battle haze had left him. Anger and irritation still swirled inside his belly though. "You had better start explaining before I have them let you go so that we can finish this." His eyes were locked with Flood's. They were uncommonly dark for a Water dragon, making Flood look all the meaner for it.

Flood smiled, his teeth coated with blood. "Not so pretty right now are you, my prince?" His gaze hardened. "I would like nothing better than to finish this." His nose was clearly broken. It was slightly skewed to the right.

"You deserve to be knocked down and beaten to a pulp."

"Knocked down?" Storm laughed. "I'll admit you managed to get one or two punches in, but you had to blindside me in order to do it. Well fucking done." Anger continued to bubble in him.

His words obviously affected Flood, who began to strain once more against his captors.

"Stop it!" Bay growled. "You will end up in the cage."

Flood narrowed his eyes but stopped. "You are a bastard asshole!" he growled.

"Tell me something I don't know." *Where had that come from?*

His response caused Flood to frown. The male's muscles relaxed somewhat. The wind knocked from his sails. "You shouldn't have taken part in the hunt," Flood said. There was still a growl to the male's voice and his eyes narrowed just a touch.

"No," Storm shook his head, "you are right! I should not have." He swallowed thickly. "It was stupid and selfish. I know that now."

He watched as Flood relaxed completely. "There are males who are serious about taking a mate. I am one of those males. I was right behind you. I would have won that human if you had not—"

Storm snarled, clearly testosterone still pumped full-force through his veins because he punched Flood square in the face. *Crunch!* Right then it didn't matter that the male had calmed down and that he was still being restrained. The punch landed and Flood's head snapped backwards. His nose began to gush, dripping down his chin and onto his chest.

Storm sucked in a deep breath. "I'm sorry." *Shit!* What

the fuck was wrong with him? That was uncalled for. This jealousy. This possessiveness was getting on his last damn nerve.

Flood smiled. "I am glad you did that."

"Why?" Storm felt himself frown.

"I apologize for attacking you…for blindsiding you, my lord. I was angry." The males on either side of Flood released him, realizing that the fight was over. "I will take whatever punishment you wish to deal out." The big male looked down at his feet.

Storm felt worse. He'd never been wracked with feelings of guilt before. He was the prince. He deserved to win Jolene. "I do not wish to punish you. Go and see a healer before your nose starts to knit." It was completely bent to one side after that last punch. His bones would be pulverized. Flood would most likely need the bones to be re-broken and reset several times over to get it straight. Punishment enough. "Don't try that again." He tried to inject venom into the words and failed. Truth was, the male was fully justified. It was his—cringe—own fault.

Flood flicked his eyes to him before bowing his head once more. "I wish you all the success with your female, my lord."

"Thank you." Storm watched as the male retreated.

"Are you okay, my lord?" Bay asked. "Shall I call for a healer?"

"No." Storm's lip throbbed and his eye was definitely swollen. It impeded his vision somewhat. "It's more of an aggravation than anything. Will be healed up in a couple of hours tops."

"Good." Bay sighed and then frowned. "You sure? Your lip is split."

Storm touched a finger to his mouth and it stung. "Yes, very sure." He nodded once, striding away. Bay was treating him like a wilting flower because he was the prince. Any other male would have been sent on his way with a slap on the back. Besides, he was eager to get back to Jolene. Storm needed to apologize and explain things to her. His behavior had been less than stellar.

Maybe she would open up more and tell him more about herself. Maybe they could be friends. If that led to something more, then great, and if not, at least the rest of their time would be bearable. He needed to try harder to make this – at the very least – tolerable for her. Storm hoped he could make it pleasurable, but tolerable would be the next best thing.

Jolene hadn't read anything more than a magazine in years. She wasn't sure why, since she had enjoyed the pastime once. She turned the page, engrossed. Apparently, the dragons liked to read. They didn't watch television, but they did have a stocked library. According to Beck, it was large with very high shelves. There was one of those moving ladders a person could use to climb, in order to fetch books on the top shelf. Beck had told her that dragons weren't allowed to shift indoors. It caused too much damage. Hence the need for the ladder. He'd said he would take her to see it while she was here…maybe.

The great library was apparently stocked with tons of books. Fiction and non-fiction with every genre available. When he'd asked her what she wanted to read, her first instinct had been to request a romance. She'd always loved a good historical bodice-ripper, but right then, that type of book was not advisable. Her plan still stood. No letting her guard down. No sex with Storm.

Nope, it was a murder mystery for her. A good old 'who done it' to keep her mind occupied. She had only started reading it yesterday and she was already halfway through it. She had a good idea who the killer might be. Then again, she was probably wrong. The twists were what made this type of book exciting.

Beck was sitting on the wingback chair. He was also reading. She wasn't sure what though, since he held a Kindle in his hand.

She focused back on the words and hadn't been reading for more than a few minutes when the door opened. Her whole body seemed to heat a few degrees and her skin actually felt like it tightened. Her muscles tingled, willing her to move.

Not looking!

It had to be him, but she was reading and still mad at him for walking out. *Head down! Concentrate!* She forced herself to keep at it, one word at a time.

"Evening, my lord—My lord?" Beck's voice turned…concerned. Yes, there was concern there. By the way it went up at the last word, she was sure it was being posed as a question as well.

Still not looking!

Storm had walked out. To let off some steam he had said. *Steam?* What did that even mean? She didn't want to know.

"I'm fine," Storm said, using his deep baritone. Goosebumps rose up on her arms. Reading, she was reading. Jolene turned the page, not sure of what she had just read. *Focus!*

"Are you sure? Your face doesn't look too hot." There was humor in Beck's voice. Why was he smiling? What was wrong with Storm's face?

Dang it!

Jolene lifted her eyes for a quick peek. *OM-double-G! What the heck?* "What happened to you?" Her words came out in a rush and she realized she was standing. "Are you okay?" She took a couple of steps towards him. She couldn't help it. His lip was split. There was blood on his chin and more splatters on his chest. His eye was puffed up, the skin a nasty red. A really good shiner if she ever saw one. There was a bruise forming on his jaw as well.

Storm nodded and smiled. He immediately winced, touching the tip of a finger to his lip. "I'm fine. Turns out you're not the only one who thinks I'm an asshole."

"Who did this?" Beck frowned.

"It doesn't matter. It's taken care of."

"You sure? I could hold your hand and tuck you in bed, my lord." Beck was grinning.

Storm flipped him the bird, his eyes glinting with humor. *What was so funny?* This wasn't a joke.

Beck chuckled. "If you don't need anything I'm..." He was already on his feet and moving towards the door.

"I'm good." Storm turned his eyes on her. "What about you?"

"I'm fine," she said.

"Okay then." Beck nodded. "Let me get out of your hair. Nice hanging with you, Jolene."

Storm growled, the good side of his mouth turning up. His hands curled into fists and his muscles bulged. The blood made him look mean.

Beck chuckled as he walked out the door, which clicked

softly behind him.

"Um…do you have a first aid kit or something?" They weren't on good terms right then, but he needed help and she was it. "Your lip looks sore." Raw and bloody. He must have taken some punch.

His lips turned up at the edges in the start of a smile, but he thought better of it. "I'll take a shower, clean up and I'll be fine in no time."

"You need an ice pack to bring down the swelling and you might need a stitch or two." She kept her eyes on his lip.

"Nah!" He shook his head. "I have advanced healing on my side. I'll be fine soon enough."

"Where did you go?" she blurted, folding her arms. "What happened?" She sounded accusatory even though she didn't mean it like that. "I—" she began, wanting to set the record straight.

"I—" Storm said at the same time. There was a knock at the door.

"Maybe Beck forgot something." She glanced to where they had been sitting and saw the Kindle lying there. "Yup, he forgot his…" She opened the door, stopping what she'd been saying when she saw who was there.

"Hello, human."

Jolene had to crane her neck, that's how tall the woman was. Her eyes were large and a very bright, brilliant blue. Her hair was dark, darker than Storm's. She had a smattering of freckles over her nose. "Hi," Jolene said, not sure what else to say.

"My name is Crystal." *Wow!* She was beautiful. High cheekbones, full lips.

"Um…good to meet you."

"You too. Is the prince...?" Her eyes moved over Jolene's shoulder. "There you are, my lord. I heard what happened. That Flood!" Her voice deepened, which was strange for a woman. Scales appeared on her cheek and her teeth seemed to sharpen for a second. Then she was walking forward, forcing Jolene to step aside and to let her in.

Sheesh! The dragon lady's dress was short. Just-below-the-ass short. It was a light shade of blue and not very flattering otherwise. It didn't need to be though. Not with legs like that. They went on for miles and miles. Shapely too, in an athletic way. Toned was the right word. Long and toned.

"By claw!" Crystal huffed the words out.

"Wait a minute." Jolene registered what the dragon woman had just said. "You were caught in a flood?" She directed the question at Storm.

Crystal laughed. "Heavens no. Flood is a person. Our strongest warrior."

"Why are you here?" Storm growled.

"To make sure you're okay and taken care of." Crystal glanced at her. For a second, there was accusation in her eyes, and then it was gone. "I was worried, my prince." Crystal turned back to Storm and bowed her head.

Bowed.

Shit a brick. Make that a house. No wonder Storm acted the way he did. She knew he was spoiled, but this was crazy. It was like he got everything he wanted, whenever he wanted it. If Crystal was anything to go by.

She pushed those thoughts aside. "Someone named Flood did this to you?" Jolene asked.

"He should be put in the cage." Crystal sounded pissed.

Her words short and hard. They were very much directed at Storm. "Sit, my lord." The dragon lady pushed at him, her eyes on the couch. "Let me take care of your wounds. Let me take care of you," she purred.

What?

What did she mean by that? Crystal was making it sound like she had more than just Band-Aids and antibacterial cream planned. Maybe Jolene should leave. She felt like she was intruding. Storm didn't react except to allow himself to be pushed. He sat down and the dragon lady planted herself down next to him.

It pissed her off. Jolene was living there for the time being. This was her temporary home. Storm was her temporary…she wasn't sure what he was, but this didn't feel right.

"I-I was just about to…" *Take care of it.* Jolene didn't get to finish her sentence though.

"You don't know our ways, human," the dragon lady said, sniffing the air. "You are useless to him right now." This time she definitely saw accusation mingled with animosity.

"I think we'll be okay, Crystal," Storm said. "Thank you for your offer of help, but—"

"Nonsense," the dragon woman said, moving in so that her and Storm's thighs were touching. "You need help and so here I am. I would never leave you in the lurch. You know that."

It was weird, Storm looked uncomfortable. "Um, yes, I know." Why would he be uncomfortable? Only one answer came to mind. He'd slept with her in the past. That was why. Maybe in the not too distant past and maybe even multiple times. Why did that bug her so much?

Maybe because right then, she was…his. He kept calling her his.

You are mine.

Mine!

Mine!

If she was his, then what was this woman doing there? Storm flew off the handle if she so much as talked about another guy. He didn't even fully trust his best friend around her and here he was…*Hell no!* Crystal was leaning over Storm, her one hand splayed on his chest while the other touched his face. The bruise on his jaw, his puffy eye. *Not a chance!* His lip. "Um…." Storm pulled himself upright. "I'm okay. I don't need…I mean, thanks but I…" He shook his head, looking even more uncomfortable. Why wasn't he pushing her away? Standing up?

"I am going to help you, my lord."

"I'm pretty sure we're okay on our own." If she was sure, then why did she sound so unsure?

Crystal snorted. "I don't think so, human."

"My name is Jolene." Good, there was a hard edge to her voice.

The woman ignored her flat. "He did a good job of it." She leaned in and kissed Storm. A soft peck to his busted lip.

What the hell!

Storm gripped her hip. Jolene wasn't sure whether it was to push her away or to pull her closer. "Thank you for your concern, Crystal. It is appreciated, I assure you."

Appreciated? Sure it was! Jolene realized that her breathing had turned labored. She was clenching her teeth. She wanted to grip Crystal's hair and yank her off Storm's lap. Then she wanted to give Storm another shiner. That way he could have matching eyes. Why wasn't he telling this dragon chick to 'F' right off?

"You heard Jolene. We are fine. It is superficial." Why was he being so nice all of a sudden? She knew that Storm wasn't really a bad guy, but neither was he the nice type. This wasn't him at all.

"Nonsense!" Crystal looked like she was leaning in for another kiss. Storm plastered himself against the back of the couch and turned his head. "Your healing time would be halved." More purring. More touching of his face.

Storm glanced forward and then turned his head back to the side. "Crystal." He used a harsher tone.

"Leave us, human," the shifter growled, whipping her head back and giving Jolene a hard look. Then she straddled Storm and Jolene was sure she caught a flash of butt cheeks. Very naked butt cheeks. Crystal was naked underneath that dress. "I'll make it better. You need to rut, my lord."

Rut. The word knocked around in her brain. *Rut!*

Storm lifted his hands. Holding them palms forward. Not touching the dragon but also not pushing her away. "No, I'm doing fine. Please listen to me." There was a panicked edge to his voice. He sounded like he needed saving.

It was the first time she had heard him be so damned polite. Why now? He usually growled commands and did as he pleased.

"Don't argue." More purring from the she-dragon.

"No, I…" Storm shook his head, at this point he was frowning heavily. Her own heart was pounding.

"This human is useless," she spat. "I will help you heal." She thrust her hips.

Thrust. Them. As in, against Storm. Against his...
Naked ass and thrusting. On Storm's lap.
Oh hell freaking no!

When Crystal whipped her head around, Jolene realized she'd said it out loud. "Get off of him and right now!" she yelled. "What the hell is wrong with you?" Jolene took a couple of steps towards them.

Crystal looked at her like she had gone mad. "I'm doing my duty. Someone has to, since that someone isn't you!" she yelled back.

"Get off him or I swear to god, I'll—"

"You'll what?" the stupid cow interrupted, staying right where she was. On top of Storm, whose hands were still in the air. "Touch me, human, and you will regret it." The she-dragon narrowed her eyes at Jolene.

The tone of her voice made Jolene want to take a step back, but she refrained, holding her ground. "You had..." She stopped talking when Storm finally reacted.

He lifted Crystal off his lap, dumping her on the couch next to him. "You won't so much as touch a hair on the human's head." His voice was deadly calm as he stood up.

"You can leave now." Jolene folded her arms, eyes on the she-dragon.

"No." Crystal shook her head, looking confused. "This female isn't going to give you what you need," she pleaded with Storm. "You know I can. We are compatible."

Proof! They had definitely slept together. Maybe even recently. Jealousy felt like poison in her veins.

"What I need is for you to leave...please." He tacked the word on at the end of the sentence, which made her blood boil. Why was he still being so damned nice?

"Get out!" Jolene yelled. She walked over to the door

and yanked it open.

"This human is not doing her duty."

The nerve! "Are you hard of hearing?" Jolene asked. "Get the hell out!"

"My senses are far superior, no, I am not hard of hearing. Quite the opposite," Crystal shrugged. "We are superior in all ways. Well, in everything barring having young. That's why you are here." It was flung at Jolene. Like she was the sum total of her ovaries and her womb.

Jolene sucked in a deep breath. There were so many things she could say back. Things that she knew would hurt the she-dragon, but she opted not to say them.

"Go!" Storm growled, finally issuing a command and doing so in a warning tone.

Crystal didn't flinch. "If you change your mind, my lord…" Another quick bow and she left.

Jolene shook with anger as she turned to face Storm. "You shouldn't have turned her away on account of me." She shook her head. "Beck has babysat me for almost an entire day. What was a few hours more? Even a whole night more. Hell, may as well make it the next few weeks even." She didn't wait for a response. "Then again, you were probably getting your rocks off earlier, so you didn't need her." The words kept coming. "You're probably all sexed out, hence the need for a shower and a nap. Come to think of it, you more than likely went after someone else's woman. Less chance of commitment that way. That's why you got beaten up, isn't it?"

CHAPTER 12

"That's not why I got beaten up." He narrowed his eyes. "Besides, it's a few scratches, I'm hardly beaten up. You should see the other male."

"You sure as heck look beaten to me."

"Well, I'm not. I don't have a single broken bone. I'm not missing an organ. I'm certainly not bleeding profusely, so I am not beaten up."

"Fine!" Her chest heaved. She had a ton more to say, but right then she was too busy grinding her teeth together and breathing like mad through her nose to get a word out. Her anger was still blazing as she recalled those hip thrusts against his groin area.

"Are you done?" Storm's eyes blazed.

"No!" she yelled. "Furthermore, you're an asshole!"

"Tell me something I don't already know!" he yelled back.

"If you know it, why don't you do something about it?" Jolene put her hands on her hips.

"I'm trying!" he snapped. "For the record, I didn't fuck anyone earlier today. Nor did I get beaten because of another female. Mated or otherwise."

"Oh, so you admit you got beaten up."

He groaned. Truth was, she felt something ease when he told her he hadn't been with anyone else. "I'm trying here."

"Trying my ass. You growl if I talk to your best friend. You growl if he even looks at me innocently. You keep telling me I'm yours, and yet you let that…that…her…" Jolene pointed at the door. "Sit all over you with her naked ass. She kissed you and you did nothing about it."

"I was trying to be nice." Storm ran a hand through his hair.

"Nice! Why the hell would you be nice? Why would you choose right then to be nice?" She made a noise of frustration. "You know what, don't even answer that. You were nice because you guys clearly have a history."

"Yes, we have a history and yes, that's why I was trying to be nice."

"Of course, you have a history," she muttered, shaking her head and managing to sound incredibly jealous. Which she was! Jolene hated the emotion. She shouldn't be jealous of Storm.

"Yes, we do have a history. We've rutted and that's it." He said it like it was supposed to make her feel better or something. "Up until recently, she was one of my favorites."

"Favorites!" Jolene pushed out a heavy breath. "Women are not chocolates. What is wrong with you?"

"I know that." He forced the words out.

"Doesn't sound like it. You were rude back then." She pointed at the couch.

"I was trying to be nice to Crystal. Trying to do the right thing for once."

"You were rude to me. I couldn't give a stuff about

Crystal." Jolene widened her eyes. "You disrespected me. You shouldn't have been nice to her and by doing so you made me look like an idiot."

"How can I disrespect you when you don't even like me? When you want nothing to do with me? You call me an asshole at every turn. You don't want to even try to be friends with me. How is it that—"

"Cut the bull! *You* don't want to be friends. You don't want anything to do with any type of relationship with me. You want to fuck me."

"I won't deny it. Yes, I want to bend you over and fuck you into next week." Storm stepped up close, his voice deepened. "I've never denied it. I've been open and honest from the start. It's you who feels the need to lie about that particular subject."

"Rubbish!" she yelled.

"You want me just as much as I want you. Why won't you admit it?" Another step brought him right into her personal space.

"Because it's nonsense." More like by admitting it, she would be opening herself right up to him.

"This whole blow up is because you're jealous. You're jealous because you are attracted to me and the thought of me with another female drives you nuts. Why are you lying?"

"Screw you!" *Dammit but it was true.*

"Screw you? Yes please, but first, admit it. Stop the talking in circles. Stop!" he growled in her face. "You want me to fuck you. You just won't admit it. Admit it already, Jolene. Fucking admit it!"

Maybe it was the way he growled her name. Probably because he was spot on. Jolene finally nodded. "Yes, okay!

Fine!" she yelled. "I am attracted to you. I would love you to fuck me but—"

"No buts. The time for buts has long since passed." Storm yanked her against him. One hand clasped her firmly around the waist, while the other gripped her hair in what felt like a tight fist at the base of her skull. It stung but it also felt good. His mouth plundered hers.

Storm wasn't in the least bit gentle. In fact, it was safe to say he was rough. His stubble rubbed her skin, his teeth clashed with hers. His erection was hard against her belly. She moaned in frustration because she wanted him so badly but also because it felt so good. She'd never been manhandled like this. Like Storm might just die if he didn't—

Oh shit! This couldn't happen. It didn't matter that it felt good. That she wanted this as much – maybe more than he did. He'd win if he had her though. She'd be giving the milk away for free. He couldn't have her milk. Jolene's eyes widened and she tried to pull away.

Storm didn't let her. He picked her up and began to walk, stopping only when her ass hit something. He lifted her onto that something and there was a ripping sound.

Then his fingers were there. Right there, his thumb quickly finding her clit through her lace panties.

Jolene moaned, her mind fogging over with need. She glanced down. Her denim skirt was ripped.

"I'm fucking you," Storm leaned in and whispered against her lips. "You're going to love it."

"We can't!" It came out sounding needy…desperate even.

His thumb kept moving. Her eyes felt hazed over. Her vision blurred. Her breathing was so heavy it was like she had run a good couple of miles.

"We can and we are. I know you're on birth control. You wouldn't be here otherwise and I can't give you anything so no backing out now. No excuses!" Storm pulled back, he lifted her ass up and pulled up her skirt so that it was bunched up around her waist. "We stick to our deal." His face was just inches away. His thumb continued to trace lazy circles around her clit.

No fair. Her legs shook with the need to come. Her eyes were wide. Her chest heaved. *Okay, maybe one time.*

She shouldn't!

"If you don't like it, we leave it at that." His gorgeous eyes were on her. Boring into her. His face had a pinched look that told her he was just as desperate.

She really shouldn't.

Jolene moaned as he pressed a little harder. She threw her head back for a moment before locking eyes with him. "Your lip. It's bleeding."

"Fuck my lip. Fuck all of it. All that matters is this." He pushed her panties aside and made sweet contact with her flesh. "O-ohhhh!" Right then, she couldn't think of a single argument. She couldn't remember why she was fighting him. "Yes, okay, yes!" she blurted.

There was another tearing noise and her ruined underwear went flying. She felt a moment of dizziness as he flipped her onto her belly. It was the dining room table. Her hands were splayed on the wood, on either side of her head. Her boobs were pressed against the hard surface. Her toes were only just on the ground. Her ass must be up in the air.

Using a knee, Storm shoved her legs open. She yelled as he thrust into her. It hurt. He was big. Huge! Storm didn't give her time to get used to his size. He thrust into her again, just as hard and forcefully. Her eyes widened and the air caught in her lungs. More pain. She yelled when he thrust again. She'd meant to shout stop, only the word didn't quite form as pleasure intermingled itself with the pain. It was strange how the two things could happen at the same time.

Storm took. Not just that, he all out demanded. He was just as much an asshole right now as ever. Only, in some weird way, he gave too. He was sweet too. The hand that held her hip gripped her softly. He grunted a few times, like it might be hurting him as well. It took seconds for her yells of pain to turn to those of ecstasy. For his grunts to turn to groans. "So good," he whispered.

Storm gripped the hair on the back of her head, holding her down so that he could have his way with her. The side of her face was pressed into the table. He fucked her hard. Harder than she'd ever been taken before. Even in this, there was no lying. There would be no candy, no roses. There would be no candles and no forevers. All things she needed. Craved but would never have with him.

She needed the orgasm that was building inside of her as well, craved it just as much as everything else. Her cries and pants were evidence of that. His hand tightened on her hair, her roots pulling, stinging, adding to the pleasure. He stroked her back, his touch soft and careful. "Fucking amazing." He grunted. "Fuck!" A hard groan. "Come for me, Jolene." By then, his words were choked. "Now. Come now!" he commanded.

With a hard yell, she plunged, her channel tightening around him. A deep groan was torn from her as she reached the pinnacle. Storm snarled, letting go of her hair so that he could grip both her hips. His movements became jerky and rough. His name was torn from her. Her eyes were squeezed shut. Her hands tried to find purchase on the smooth table. She couldn't seem to catch her breath. It felt like an age before she started to come down, before his movements slowed. Rough turned soft. Deep and plunging to slow and easy.

His breathing was ragged. His hands eased their hold. Then he was caging her with his body. His front to her back. Still inside. Still moving. Storm moaned. It was sexy. "You feel…so good." He was breathing hard. "I could do that several times a day and it wouldn't be enough."

There was no way she could deny what had just happened. His mind was reeling. His cock was in heaven. "So damned good." He couldn't stop moving. In fact, his dick was hardening right back up again. Not that he'd really lost his erection in the first place. "I knew fucking you would be good, I didn't realize it would be this good." He kept making these noises. Groaning, grunting, heavy breathing but he couldn't help it.

Jolene tensed underneath him. "Get off me," she whispered.

"What?" Storm wasn't sure he had heard right. After that, he was ready to go another round. Make that, a couple more rounds, yet, it seemed like she wanted him to stop.

"You heard me." Her voice held a sharp edge. She was still tense.

Storm pulled out immediately, he kept his hands on her hips. "Did I hurt you? Shit! I'm sorry. I was too rough, wasn't I?" He couldn't see any bruising but that didn't mean anything. He had been desperate for her. Blinded by need. He pulled away completely.

Jolene stood up and straightened out what was left of her skirt. She turned around. She looked…upset. There was a definite frown line on her forehead and – damn but…damn – she looked unhappy. It was her eyes.

"I'm sorry…fuck." He rubbed the back of his neck. "Do you need a healer? I was so desperate to be inside you, I—"

"You were rough, but you didn't hurt me." She shook her head.

He frowned. "What then?"

She pulled in a breath. "You said if I didn't like it…if I wasn't satisfied that we could leave it at that. Well, I'd like to leave it at that." She tugged at her skirt, trying to pull the tear together.

"Wait just a fucking minute." He was rough but she admitted he hadn't hurt her. "You came, and by the way you squeezed my dick, you came hard."

Jolene rolled her eyes. "Do you have to be so crude?"

"I'm honest. You came hard, Jolene. Don't try to deny it."

She shrugged and made a face. Like sex with him had been average. *What the hell? No way in hell. Just no!*

"Don't go there. That, right there, was fantastic sex. That was…next fucking level."

"For you maybe." She shook her head again. That upset look was gone from her eyes, instead, they shone with determination.

What the fuck!? "That was the best sex you have ever had and now you're running scared."

Jolene snorted. "Scared of what?"

"Of falling for me."

Another snort, louder this time. "Forget it! I don't like you, why on earth would I fall for you? That's absurd."

"You loved that. Your pussy loved the hell out of that. You screamed my name, for fuck sakes."

She shrugged. "An accident, I assure you."

"Accident my ass! That was the best sex you have—"

"I heard you the first time and no, it wasn't. I have had better sex." She looked like she meant it. Jolene might deny things, even to herself, but she wasn't one to all-out lie.

Yet, he couldn't believe it. "You've had better sex?" Not a chance. He narrowed his eyes on her. "You said you don't miss sex when you're not having it. Sorry but I find it hard to believe that any of your loser boyfriends did any kind of a good job if that's the case. You said you've had better. Look at you…your cheeks are flushed. You're shivering, for scale's sake. Your eyes still have a hazy, glassy look and you reek of endorphins." He sniffed the air for good measure.

"I had an orgasm, yes…sure…fine…it was okay." Another shrug. One-shouldered this time, like she couldn't be bothered to raise them both. "That explains the cheeks and all that. I'm shivering because I'm cold." She wrapped her arms around herself. "The fire has died down and I'm not wearing a sweater. Don't beat yourself up, I've had worse sex, but I've also definitely had better. I know that there is amazing somewhere in my future. I'm glad that," using her thumb, she pointed to the table behind her, "sex with me was amazing for you but it was lacking for me. Sorry! Thanks for the orgasm. It was nice, but I don't need a repeat."

Nice?

Fucking 'nice.'

She looked sincere. Jolene even winced as she said it. Like she didn't want to hurt his feelings.

"I'm not buying it." *Fuck that!*

"We agreed you wouldn't keep pursuing this if we did it once. We've been there, done that and I don't want to do it again. I'm sorry if your ego doesn't agree. In fact, we've had sex now, so this whole hormonal thing going on with you should stop, right?"

She still wanted to leave. Nothing had changed. He was so sure that sex with him would convince her to stay for the duration of their term. "Yeah." He nodded. "You're right. It might take a few hours for whatever chemical imbalances to right themselves and then you can be on your way."

"Good." She nodded, looking relieved.

Relieved! Why did that screw with his mind so badly? "Good." He nodded as well, trying hard to act cool.

CHAPTER 13

Her legs still shook. As did her hands. Cold? Forget cold. She was burning hot. Red freaking hot. Jolene had never come so hard in all of her life. It shamed her how hard she had come.

Screaming his name had been an accident. A total accident. One she would repeatedly make if they did that again. There would be no doing that again though. No way! She hadn't been lying though when she had said she'd had better.

She may not have come so hard in some instances, she hadn't come at all in others. In fact, she'd been left hanging more times than she cared to admit, but at least there had been feelings involved. Previous encounters hadn't just been hardcore fucking. It had never been sex for the sake of sex and the end result. At least, it hadn't ever been that way for her. And yes, while sex with Storm had rocked her world, it had done nothing to move her soul. It had done nothing to move his either. She could see it in his eyes the moment she turned around.

Why had she given in?

It was over! She'd given him exactly what he was after. Her body. It was done. They were done. Come morning, he was going to send her on her way. The sadness that welled in her was confusing. She should be happy. She shouldn't be jealous when other women flirted with him. She shouldn't be sad, hurt, even now that he was done with her. This fiasco was finally over. She could move on with her life.

"I'm going to take a shower." She needed to wash him away. To be just as done with him as he was with her. Walk away with dignity.

"Be my guest." He gestured to the bathroom. "Are you happy with steak for dinner? Or would you prefer pasta?"

"Steak would be good."

Now he was being polite to her. It sucked! No, it didn't. This was good. Great even. Tomorrow, she could actually start working on her life. On her dream. Her forever.

No more Storm.
No more irritation.
Forget Golden Boy.

His mind reeled. Adrenaline coursed. Storm paced up and down while Jolene was in the shower. He couldn't seem to calm himself down. No female had ever left his bed unsatisfied before. Or had they? Maybe they had and he just didn't know it.

Not a fuck!

You didn't scream a person's name if the sex was bad. Whether it was an accident or otherwise. Jolene had enjoyed it. Her pussy had tightened around him almost to the point of pain. The noises she had made. His name on her lips. The wet sucking noises her channel had made as he drove into her. None of that would have happened if she wasn't turned on as fuck. If she hadn't come damn freaking hard.

Storm only realized he'd left his chamber when he found himself walking down the long hallway. He knew what he had to do. Storm walked into the great hall and looked around him. All the males nodded when he looked their way. Several kept their eyes averted.

There! He needed answers and he knew exactly where to get them. He locked eyes with the person in question. "Can I have a word?" he whispered as he drew nearer.

"Yes, my lord." Her smile morphed, turning seductive.

Storm sighed. "It's not like that, Crystal." If only Jolene was this interested. That would make his day. His fucking life.

"Oh." She made a face. "What did you want to ask?"

He looked around. There were dozens of shifters all around them. "It's personal, can we go somewhere a little more private?"

"You sure you're not just trying to get me alone?" She giggled and fluttered her lashes. A move that had worked well for her in the past. Right then, it only served to irritate him.

"Very sure," he growled. "I just need to talk to you about something. It's important."

She frowned. "Okay." Then she smirked. "Your loss though." They walked in silence for a minute, leaving the great hall and making their way through the hallways.

Storm gestured to a door. It led to one of the many balconies. He opened the door and Crystal walked through first. "What's got you so rattled, my lord?" she asked as she turned to face him. "Falling for the human?"

"No," he snorted. "Of course not." It was ridiculous!

"You're welcome, by the way." She laughed.

"What are you talking about?" Females of all species were infuriating. They talked in circles, the lot of them.

"I can scent she finally gave in and did her duty. The human just needed a push in the right direction." Crystal winked at him.

"So that's why you came to my chamber earlier. To help give my female a push in the right direction?" He raised his brows. That didn't sound like Crystal at all.

"No, I came to do my duty as your subject." She touched his jaw with just the tip of her finger. One quick brush. "Almost fully healed. You do realize that you just called her your female?" She looked at him knowingly. "Yet, you're not planning on keeping her, I hear."

"You know what I mean, and no, I'm not keeping her." Jolene was leaving in the morning. It was on the tip of his tongue, but he couldn't bring himself to say it. He was still pumped full of those blasted hormones. It wouldn't take long and she'd be out of his hair. His life would be able to get back to normal. *Thank fuck!*

Crystal nodded. "Understood."

"I came to ask you something." He sucked in a deep breath, looking up at the sky before locking eyes with her. "Your opinion."

Crystal cocked her head. She looked taken aback for a few moments. Then she smiled. "My, my but you are in a strange mood today. All the 'pleases' earlier and now you want my opinion. Are you feeling okay?"

"I was trying to be nice earlier," he grumbled. "It was recently brought to my attention that I might not have treated you – any of the females I rutted – with respect and kindness. That's not true is it?" He shook his head.

Crystal shrugged. "What does it matter? We were rutting. You're a prince, you have a certain commanding way about you. You're not…kind." She laughed. "That would be silly. I mean, you're you. Storm, Prince of Water."

The youngest of four. Heir to nothing. Storm nodded. "Am I an asshole?" He already knew the answer to that question.

Crystal widened her eyes. She smiled, looking shocked. Like she couldn't quite believe he had asked her that. She pulled in a breath. It looked like she was mulling it over.

"Look," Storm folded his arms, "you can tell me. You have to be honest. I don't want you glossing things over because I'm the prince and you want to stay on my good side. If you think I'm an asshole, you can say it."

It took a few more long seconds before she finally answered. "Yes, I guess you are a bit of an asshole, but you're royalty, you're allowed to be. You're a touch arrogant and a lot spoiled. Asshole comes with the territory. I like it." She winked at him.

Crystal was both honest and she glossed her answer over like a pro. "There's more," he said.

"Ask away, my lord." Crystal bowed her head.

"This conversation needs to stay between us."

"No problem! I can keep a secret," Crystal said.

"It's not a secret *per se*," he quickly said. "Just not something I want…talked about. It's delicate." He was turning into a pussy. He sure as hell sounded like one. He didn't want word of that getting around. Storm had a reputation to uphold.

"Okay. You can count on me."

"Did you…" Storm locked his lips. "Were you…" He

ran a hand through his hair. "Did I please you, sexually?" *A fucking pussy!* "You've always maintained that we're compatible. Is it really true or were you buttering me up?"

Crystal chuckled. It was deep and throaty. "Good lord, but that human has done a number on you."

"Answer the question, Crystal, please."

"We are compatible." She answered but said nothing more.

"Was it good though? Have you had better?" He didn't like where this was going. He could see the answer to his question written in her eyes.

"Other males work harder at pleasing me, so, yes, I have had better but…"

Storm groaned. He couldn't believe what he was hearing. He'd always rated himself highly. He'd always seen himself as the best at fucking because he was usually the best at things. Fighting, flying, strategizing, picking up human females…it had all come easy to him. He assumed being amazing between the sheets was a given.

Crystal laughed softly, not unkindly. "Don't be hard on yourself. You are very good. Fantastic in fact, but…"

"Not the best." He sounded defeated.

"No." She shook her head. "You do have one thing most males don't have, you're a prin—"

"Don't tell me I'm a prince and that it makes it all better." It didn't make it better. Not even close.

She shrugged. "You are though. You're gorgeous and a royal and that makes rutting with you awesome." Her eyes glinted. "You're arrogant and don't give a damn. You have this way about you." She smiled. "You like demanding that a female has an orgasm instead of making her achieve one, and you know what? It works." She laughed. "It worked on me in the past." She took a step closer, taking his hand. "All of this talk of rutting is making me—"

"No. This is serious. What you are saying is that the only thing I have going for me is this." He touched his golden chest, feeling stricken. Like someone had just told him his cock was going to shrivel up.

"You're good, my prince, better than good but you're not…you're…well, you're all about the endgame. You think you're god's gift to females because well, look at you and because you're—"

"Yeah, yeah, I'm a royal." He wanted to roll his eyes. "Humans don't know I'm a royal though. Humans love me anyway."

"Humans are easy to please."

If only that were true!

She smirked. "All except for your human, it would seem." There was a humorous lilt to Crystal's words.

"Jolene wasn't impressed at all," he mumbled. "She doesn't think we're compatible." His voice was deep. He sounded a touch choked and it shocked him when he realized he was.

"You don't feel the same way though?"

"I thought we were highly compatible."

Crystal touched the side of his arm. The female looked like she felt sorry for him. "I'm going to give you some advice on how to fix things. On how to change her mind about you. More importantly, I'm going to give you a few tips that will blow her mind between the sheets." She bobbed her eyebrows. "You need a few pointers, that's all."

"No!" Storm shook his head. "Thanks, but don't worry about it. She's leaving in the morning. Going to another male. One more suitable."

"It's probably for the best. From what I've heard and have seen, the two of you are polar opposites."

He nodded. "Definitely, and Crystal…?"

"Yes, my lord."

"Thank you. I appreciate your help." He touched the side of her arm in the same way she had touched his. This 'being nice' business was new to him. He hoped he was doing it right.

Crystal smirked. "This human might be leaving in the morning and she might only have been in your life for less than a week, but," she cocked her head, "you've changed."

"Jolene isn't afraid to tell me like it is. Forget glossing anything over. It's helped me open my eyes to a few things. A couple of things I don't like about myself."

"Don't go changing too much."

Storm chuckled. "I won't." He narrowed his eyes on hers. "Don't go telling anyone about this conversation. It stays between us." He had turned into a pussy. It wasn't something he wanted everyone knowing.

"And if I disclose all?" She rubbed her lips together.

"Don't do it, Crystal! You don't want to know what will happen if you do, only that you won't like it."

"Now there's the prince I know and love."

He chuckled, heading back to his chamber.

CHAPTER 14

Crap! Double freaking crap. What was wrong with her? Why was she feeling so glum?

Storm put her bag down next to her. He looked completely relaxed. Totally accepting of this whole thing. Jolene had known having sex with the dragon shifter would clear her from his system, she hadn't been wrong. In fact, she had never been more right on the money about anything. Storm didn't give a shit about her anymore.

He practically ignored her this morning. No, that wasn't true. He'd been nothing but polite and nice.

Polite?

Nice?

That wasn't Storm. He had no interest in her anymore. That much was clear. It rubbed her the wrong way, even though it shouldn't. This is what she had wanted.

She'd given in and had lost. Not that this was a game. Well, it *had* been a game. Not to her, but to him…and she'd lost. She'd given him the milk for free, dammit. Now that he'd had a taste, he didn't want more. Again, her choice but it still stung.

Jolene looked around the room. She swallowed thickly. There were at least a hundred and fifty guys surrounding them. No-one made a sound. No-one spoke or fidgeted or anything. All of their eyes were on her. It was freaky.

"Oh my!" she muttered. "So many," she whispered.

Storm smiled. "Yeah, every unmated male in the kingdom is here. They are all hoping you will choose them."

There were a few shouts of agreement. A hum of chatter picked up around the hall but soon died down.

"Oh…okay." Her hands suddenly felt clammy and her mouth dry.

"This is what you wanted, isn't it?" Storm asked, eyes questioning.

As opposed to going home. "Yes," she quickly said, glancing at Storm. He was the picture of calm. Golden Boy had no qualms about giving her away. Her eyes stung a little. Damn her and her girl emotions. She'd gone and slept with him and just as much as she was out of his system, he was very firmly embedded in hers. It didn't matter that it had been hardcore fucking, for lack of a better word. That he hadn't inserted even the tiniest bit of emotion into the action. That there had been no promises attached, whether verbal or nonverbal. The nonverbal ones, now, she'd read those loud and clear.

None of that mattered. She'd felt. She was still feeling. She was a stupid idiot because she actually felt something for the guy. What had she done to herself?

It didn't matter. Her stupid wayward emotions would

be under control in no time. She'd choose someone else. Someone great. He would be awesome and she would be happy. They would fall in love and have a family and a long, happy life together. She could feel it. Not! Didn't matter. She would feel it soon. She couldn't give Storm the satisfaction of going home, head bowed. Jolene pulled her shoulders back and looked around the room. Looked at all the hopeful expressions.

There were tall guys. Even taller guys and veritable giants. There were all hair colors from black to white-blond and everything in-between. Some of them had green eyes and others blue. A few of them had dark eyes and others that amethyst color, like Storm. Not exactly like Storm. His were so vivid they were unique and—

No, no comparisons! She was closing one door – locking it – and moving on. "How do I choose?" she whispered.

Storm chuckled. It was throaty and sexy, damn him. "You could draw a number and allow it to be completely random, you could have each one step forward, one at a time to tell you something about themselves or you could ask random questions to males of your choosing. We could also tailor-make your—"

Jolene huffed out a breath. "Hold on." She shook her head, which was spinning. "This is all a little overwhelming." Asking each of them a question would take all day. "I need to be sure that everyone here is really serious."

"Of course." Something seemed to darken in Storm's eyes and his jaw tightened.

"Hello and thanks for coming..." Jolene raised her

voice.

There was a loud murmur across the room as all the men responded in kind.

"Um…" her cheeks heated. It was disconcerting having all those stares focused on her. She licked her lips. "I'm going to ask a few questions, if that's okay?"

Again, the men answered. There were shouts of agreement and plenty nods of the head.

"Great! Thank you," she said when the noise finally died down. "I need to know who is not interested in mating, please leave the room."

There were a couple of snickers and one or two mutters.

"Silence," Storm growled. There was instant obedience. "You heard the human. Anyone not interested in mating this female, leave now."

No-one moved. One or two of the guys planted their feet more firmly on the ground or folded their arms, looking deadly serious.

"O-okay," she muttered, once it was clear that no one was leaving. "Anyone not interested in having children, please leave," she said, voice raised.

A few of the men turned to look at those beside them, but nobody left.

"What else is important to you?" Storm asked. "I know one," he quickly said. "This female enjoys waffles for breakfast. Those of you who know how to prepare such a meal, should stay."

There were grumbles and all-out yells, but in the end, half the guys filed out.

"Jolene might request to sleep alone tonight, would you offer to give her the bed, or would you make her sleep on the floor? Those of you that say floor, should leave now."

Most stayed where they were, but there were a handful of guys who left.

"I have one," she said, putting her hand up.

"Go right ahead." Storm nodded once.

"If you've ever had sex with one of the dragon females, you should please leave now." There weren't many dragon females. She hated the idea that most of these guys had slept with them. The thought of Crystal rubbed her the wrong way.

"You sure?" Storm whispered, his eyes wide.

"Very sure."

"That won't leave many males and," he shook his head, "those who remain…" He chuckled, not finishing the sentence.

Most of the men filed out. As in, there were only fifteen guys left. She did a quick count. Sixteen. There were sixteen. These dragon women certainly got around.

"Really?" she snorted. "A handful of women and all those guys."

Storm shrugged. "Guess so. It's how it is. Our females are respected and cherished. They get to decide who they want to be with. Most of the males try their luck."

"It's gross!"

"It's nature."

"Says you, Golden Boy." She shook her head. "I think it's pretty gross."

Storm smiled, his eyes glinted. "We'll have to agree to

disagree once again, Sweet-Lips." He winked at her.

Something ignited inside her when he called her by that nickname. A need, a want, a longing. That particular feeling could go right to hell. Jolene turned back to the group. They were all good-looking guys. They all seemed eager. "You." She pointed to a light-haired shifter in the middle of the group. He had deep blue eyes. He looked nothing like Storm and would probably be nothing like Storm. Which meant that he would be perfect.

The guy touched his silver chest, eyes wide. He even looked around. "Me?"

"Yes, you."

"Thank you," he said, stepping forward. "It is an honor you would choose me. An honor I cherish." He sounded dumbstruck. Like he'd just won the lottery.

"I'm glad you feel that way." Jolene smiled.

"My name is Hail." He was a big guy, almost as big and built as Storm. *Stop!* She really needed to stop comparing everyone to Golden Boy. It wasn't fair or right. That door was firmly closed.

Hail strode over to her. His eyes were wide and really quite exquisite. As soon as he reached her, he dropped to one knee and took her hand. His fingers were calloused, his clasp soft. "It is a privilege to meet you." He smiled, almost shyly.

Storm shifted his weight from one foot to the other. Jolene tried hard to ignore him.

"You too, Hail. I'm Jolene."

The shifter pressed the top of her hand to his lips for a second or two before rising to his feet.

"Let it be known that the human has picked Hail. No-one is to interfere by my order," he growled the command, sounding formidable.

Goosebumps rose up on her arms.

"Thank you, my lord." Hail sounded shocked. When she looked his way, she noted Hail was frowning heavily, looking slightly confused even.

"Sure. All the best," Storm said. She turned back to him…to where he had been moments before, since Storm was already halfway to the door. Typical. She tried not to let his attitude get to her. Golden Boy couldn't even say a proper goodbye to her. She swallowed thickly, turning back to Hail. This was it.

The shifter smiled at her, picking up her bag and hoisting it onto his back. "Would you like me to carry you as well?" he asked, completely sincere.

"No, I can walk just fine, thanks."

He nodded. "Come with me, I will show you my chamber. I'm afraid that it is not as big as Storm's, but it will be quite comfortable. Once we are mated, we will be given a new home, one with several rooms to accommodate our family." He gripped her hand in his. "Is this okay?" He squeezed lightly.

Mated.

Family.

She had only just met him. Her heart raced. "Yes, it's fine." This was exactly what she wanted, she reminded herself. "Um, let's get to know each other first. We have plenty of time."

"There is no pressure, Jolene. I will happily sleep on the

floor until you are comfortable sharing my bed. There is no rush for sex either. In fact, I will not bring it up until you are ready."

"Okay. Thank you! I appreciate that."

"Tell me something about yourself," he said, glancing at her.

This was new. It was really nice. A guy who actually cared about her. Not her boobs or having a good time but her.

"I enjoy watching romantic comedies. I love chocolate brownies…anything chocolate really but brownies are my favorite."

"I don't think I've ever had one of those. Here we are." He opened a door and stepped aside. "Welcome to your new home."

Her heart stuttered and her hands became clammy in an instant. Shifters could come on strong. It was normal. It was Storm who was completely abnormal. Not this guy. Hail was great.

The place was much smaller. Not as opulent. "It's cozy."

"Cozy means small." Hail smiled shyly.

"Cozy means cozy. I'm not too fussed about things like that, so don't worry about it."

"I am glad."

"The view is still spectacular." She took it in as a group of dragons flew by. One of them had a golden chest. Storm perhaps? Jolene tried not to think about it. "I'll bake you some brownies and then you'll know how they taste." She forced her gaze off the dragon formation in the sky.

"That would be great." Hail came and stood beside her. "Let me know what you will need. I have to order a couple of things anyway since I don't have the ingredients in the house to make waffles."

"Oh…" She shook her head. "You don't have to do that."

"I want to. I want things to work between us."

Maybe this was what her friend Ruth meant about coming on too strong. Did she do this? Perhaps to a lesser degree but, come to think of it, she did.

"Let's just relax and take it one day at a time, shall we?" It sounded stilted. They were being far too polite to one another and it felt awkward.

Hail's eyes clouded. He nodded once.

Damn, now she'd gone and hurt his feelings and he really was a nice guy. "Do you read?" She pointed to a pile of books on the coffee table.

Hail nodded. "I love science fiction novels. Anything to do with space rockets and journeys to outer space." His eyes lit up. "And what about you?"

She shrugged. "I'm more of a movie fan myself."

"Of course, you said so earlier." He chuckled, looking down at the floor before locking eyes with her.

"Yep, although I used to read, way back when I was still in school. I just started again, since there are no televisions in dragon land – and I'm enjoying it." She picked up her bag.

"I'll get that for you." Hail took the bag from her. "I'll clear out a part of my closet for your things."

"That would be great." She paused. "I take it we're

stuck here until…until we officially become a couple…if you know what I mean." She couldn't even bring herself to think about having sex with Hail. Not so soon after Storm. She should probably fess up and tell Hail that there probably wasn't going to be anything between them. Jolene didn't move from one guy to the next on a whim, and this was what it felt like. Hail was a nice guy and she didn't want to hurt his feelings. *This was a mess!*

"Nope, we aren't stuck at all. We can go wherever we please."

"Oh." She frowned. "Storm didn't want me going anywhere. I was stuck in his apartment."

"It was different between the two of you."

Oh yes! Very different. Jolene had a feeling she and Hail weren't thinking the same thing. She nodded, urging him to go on.

"Storm won you and brought you back, so it stood to reason he was possessive over you. He kept you home because other males would have been in danger if they had so much as looked at you. He would have ended up fighting. Especially since he hadn't properly marked you, until recently, if you know what I mean."

She swallowed thickly. "I know exactly what you mean," she mumbled. "I take it you don't have the same jealousy problem?" She narrowed her eyes at him.

Hail shook his head. "Not yet. Soon…I hope, but not right now. Storm forbade anyone from trying to take you from me, so we can venture out even though I haven't marked you…yet. Storm would kick serious butt if anyone tried anything." He smiled broadly, like it was the best thing he had ever heard.

"Oh, I see." Why would Storm do that? He'd only do it if he was one hundred percent sure he didn't want her anymore. There was this part of her that had hoped he would try to keep her. It was stupid since she had made up her mind about leaving and he would have known that. This whole internal dialog was stupid. She needed to try to put that asshole behind her and move on. "Can we go out to dinner later if that's the case? I've been cooped up since arriving here almost a week ago."

"Yes, absolutely." Hail nodded. "I would love to share a meal and to get to know you better." He touched her arm. "I'll have them set a table especially for us. I'm sure you like candles and flowers."

"No." She shook her head. "I mean yes, but no need to go to all that trouble."

He looked crestfallen.

Poor guy was just trying to be nice. Jolene smiled. "I love candles and flowers, but I would feel bad if you had to go to so much effort."

"No effort at all," Hail blurted. "It would make me happy."

"Okay then. Sounds good." He was so sweet and so kind. What was wrong with her? Why wasn't she feeling it? Why?

"Let's go sort out that closet." He winked at her.

"Great." She smiled, following him.

CHAPTER 15

What were they doing now?

Maybe they were laughing?

Storm scrubbed a hand over his face, feeling the stubble catch. He sighed. Or, maybe they were talking about babies and happily-ever-afters? That was more likely the case.

Then again, maybe they were kissing or holding hands or...*No fucking way!* Hail was too much of a wet blanket to have done any of those things. The male had better not have done any of them. He had better not have...

Storm pulled in a deep breath, pushing it out through his nose. He needed to stop, and he needed to do it immediately. Jolene did not want him. She'd told him straight out and he needed to respect that. Respect her wishes, and ultimately, he needed to respect her. The best way he could do that was by leaving her the hell alone.

If she wanted to talk happy families with Hail, then so be it. If she wanted to joke and laugh with the male – he grit his teeth – then so be it. They could hold hands and gaze at one another longingly for all he cared.

Moving the hell on!

Where was Beck? The male had invited him to dinner, and yet he was nowhere in sight.

"Hi, Storm, how are you?" Mist giggled behind her hand when he turned to look at her.

"Fine, you?" He sounded bored. Couldn't be helped. He sure as fuck didn't feel like being nice.

"Good…" She licked her lips, trying to be all coy. Why was it that every female tried with him except for Jolene? It made no sense. "I…um…"

"Have you seen Beck?" he quickly interjected, cutting her off.

Her eyes clouded. "No, sorry, I haven't." She gave a quick shake of the head.

Then he spotted them. Talking, laughing, a lit candle, a corner table away from everyone, the whole fucking nine yards. They were doing everything but touching. By the looks of things that was next on the cards.

Good thing he didn't give a shit.

Jolene picked up her mug and swirled the contents. She was enthralled with whatever Hail was saying. It couldn't be that interesting. No fucking way! Storm listened in. The male was going on and on about his training and day-to-day routines. *Yawn!*

Jolene smiled. "Doesn't it get boring, flying around your territory day in and day out?"

Fucking boring! Storm agreed. Just like their whole conversation.

Hail shook his head. "Not at all." Then he went on to explain why. *Blah fucking blah blah.* Jolene nodded every so often. Why wasn't she falling asleep? Instead, Jolene laughed.

His jaw clenched. His fists wanted to follow suit, but he wouldn't let them. There was only one way to get over someone and that was to get inside someone else.

The quicker the better.

"Mist." He could still hear her hovering. Didn't have to even look to where she was standing.

"Yes, my lord?"

"Come here." He had to force his eyes off the two love-fucking-birds and onto the she-dragon.

"Want to grab a bite?" He put an arm around her.

Her eyes brightened right up. "I thought you were meeting Beck."

"He can eat with us if he finally gets his ass over here."

She nodded, smiling up at him.

"Unless of course you had other plans?"

She shook her head, her blonde hair went flying. "No, and even if I did," she bit down on her lower lip, "I would cancel in a hot minute."

"Good!" *How fucking disappointing!* Pussy was pussy though, and Mist just happened to be there, so she would do. He felt like a jerk thinking it. Like a total asshole. Crystal was right, the human had gotten inside his head. Storm had been a lot happier when he was a selfish asshole. This whole 'being nice' business wasn't for him. "I'm going to have the lasagna. Won't you be a honey and go and pick some up for me while I wait here for Beck?"

Mist nodded. "Of course. I would love to," she gushed.

Storm sat down. He watched as Mist joined the queue of people waiting to be served. Two servers walked in carrying plates covered with platinum covers. They headed for the lovebirds.

Jolene's mouth fell open and she covered it with her hand. Her beautiful brown eyes widened. Storm couldn't believe he'd found her plain when he'd first seen her. Her skin was soft, her hair long and shiny. Her smile…not that she had smiled for him very often, but when she did—

"Why are you still eyeing that human like you're about to go over there and kick Hail's ass?" Beck plopped himself down on a chair next to Storm. He folded his arms on the table and grinned broadly.

"Not at all," Storm said. "I'm bored and they just happen to be the most interesting thing in the room."

Just then, one of the servers turned on a blow torch and proceeded to set Jolene's food on fire. She gasped and then laughed, her eyes filled with wonder.

Hail looked pleased with himself. The flame soon went out.

"See." Storm leaned back in his chair. He crooked a finger in their direction. "What did I tell you? How fucking exciting was that?"

Beck whistled low. "He's trying really hard."

"Yeah, and I can't believe a female like Jolene would fall for that bullshit."

"It's not bullshit." Beck shrugged. "Hail likes her and is trying to win her."

"I don't know…I think it's stupid." He knew he sounded like he was grumbling, like he gave two shits. He didn't!

"You *would* think it was bullshit."

Storm frowned. "How so?" he growled.

"You don't have a romantic bone in your whole body."

"That's not true." He shook his head. "I have one." Storm quirked a brow and palmed his dick.

Beck chuckled.

Right on cue, Mist returned, placing a plate of food in front of him. He pulled the she-dragon onto his lap. Mist giggled. "I'll drop my own food," she chided, grinning at him from under her lashes as she held onto her plate. Mist was tall and athletic. Wiry and toned compared to the human. Her eyes were amethyst like his. Her skin was well tanned. She was nothing like the human. She also failed to heat his blood like Jolene had.

Blast!

He needed to stop this line of thinking. Mist had suited him just fine on more than one occasion. The female was good with her mouth.

Storm looked at what was on her plate and had to stop himself from rolling his eyes. She'd picked the lasagna as well. *How original!* "Feed me," he instructed. Only fitting; she could feed him and then he could feed her later. Storm chuckled.

"What's so funny?" Beck asked.

"I was just thinking how happy I am that I'm not Hail."

Beck shook his head, looking at Storm between narrowed eyes. "For someone who's not interested in those two, you seem awfully fixated."

"I'm more interested in Mist here." He hooked an arm around her waist. "And on dinner." He accepted a mouthful of food from the she-dragon. Storm chewed and swallowed, accepting another bite.

Storm had to admit, they did seem like every bit the happy couple. Hail was holding her hand. Whatever nonsense they were discussing looked serious. Probably how many babies they were going to have or some shit.

"Want to go swimming after dinner?" Beck asked. "We could fly out at midnight."

"No," Storm growled. "Mist and I have better things to do." He took the plate out of the she-dragon's hands, plunked it on the table and picked her up as he stood himself. Then he hoisted her over his shoulder. Mist squealed as he strode from the hall.

What was he doing there?

It was Golden Boy. His chest glinting in the unnatural light. He looked bored, leaning back in his chair, arms folded. Alone at the table. *Interesting!*

No, it wasn't. She shouldn't be looking at him. He had seen her, she'd side-watched Storm stare at her and Hail. Didn't seem too interested anymore. Why hadn't he left when he saw them on a date? Didn't he feel awkward? She did. If she could leave she would but that would be rude. Hail had gone to so much trouble.

One thing was very clear, she couldn't just move on. It wasn't going to happen. Somewhere and somehow, she'd developed feelings for Storm. Sleeping with him had only made things worse. Stringing Hail along was not the right thing to do. It wasn't fair to the guy.

"Hail, there's something I—"

Two men arrived at the table and both she and Hail

looked up. The guys placed dishes covered with ornate silver – couldn't be real silver, though since non-humans were allergic to the stuff – covers on the table in front of each of them.

They then proceeded to remove the lids with a flourish. This was something Jolene had only seen in the movies. She covered her mouth with her hand, smiling broadly. Hail was such a sweet guy. She found herself wishing for the hundredth time that she actually felt something for him. He was really good-looking. His hair was a touch overgrown with a very light curl, if he'd been wearing a shirt it would have brushed the collar. His eyes were a beautiful deep blue color that reminded her of the ocean. They seemed to shine. His lips were full and always smiling. He didn't frown, or growl, or say dirty things. He was sweet and kind and polite…and Jolene wasn't in the least bit attracted to him, which really sucked.

Each of the servers switched on a blow torch. She started, clutching a hand to her chest. Jolene laughed at herself. It was all so dramatic. She noticed that Hail was watching her. He'd gone to so much trouble. It made her feel really bad.

The servers poured something over their steaks. Next thing, her food was being set alight. It was a steak with what looked like a pepper sauce over it. Orange flames rose up. Jolene sat back in her chair, feeling the heat. Almost as soon as the fire started, it died down. "That was amazing. I've never seen anything like that before."

"Enjoy your meal," one of the men said.

Hail thanked them and they left.

"I'm glad you enjoyed the show. It's called flambé." Hail was smiling broadly. "You should try your food." He gestured to her plate.

Jolene nodded. She cut into the meat, which was tender, and put the food in her mouth. Jolene nodded. "Delicious," she said once she'd swallowed. It really was good.

A loud squeal made her look to the other side of the room. There was a she-dragon on Storm's lap. She was tall and skinny and really gorgeous. Jealousy ate at her. She quickly looked away, smiling at Hail.

He put his knife and fork down, looking at her intently. "Are you okay?" he asked.

She needed to come clean.

Jolene nodded. "Yes, I guess…I…well." She pushed out a heavy breath. "I like you very much. You're a really nice guy."

"Oh shit…that bad huh?" He smiled at her. It was a little sad and a lot disappointed. "I noticed how you keep trying not to look at the prince."

"I'm sorry I…" She licked her lips. "I don't know how it happened, but I think I might have feelings for him. This is going to sound crazy, but I don't like him very much. I'm…um…it's hard to explain. You're such an amazing guy but I can't jump out of one guy's bed and into the next one. I'm not wired like that. I wish I could. I wish I could turn my stupid feelings off, but I can't."

There was more giggling from Storm's table. She couldn't help but look over for a few seconds, then she wished she hadn't. The gorgeous dragon lady was feeding him. His hands were all over her. Not all over, around her waist but still.

"You're hurt?" Hail asked.

"No…yes…maybe…I shouldn't be." She shook her head. "I have no right to be. He's been nothing but honest with me, and still…I was stupid that's all."

"You weren't stupid."

"Trust me, I was stupid. I should never have…Never mind."

"Rutted? You should never have rutted the male, is that what you were going to say?" He raised his brows.

"Yes," she blurted. "It was a stupid thing to do."

"You have feelings for him, even if you don't like those feelings, and you're attracted to him. It's normal to have sex in a situation like that." Hail paused for a moment or two, looking at her pointedly. "You did nothing wrong. It definitely wasn't stupid."

"Storm doesn't feel the same way about me, that makes me, sleeping with him, a stupid thing to have done. Again, it's complicated." She sighed. "I planned to come here, meet a sweet, kind guy like yourself and then to fall completely and totally in love. I want a house full of kids and lots of laughter and happiness. Instead, I'm attracted to an asshole prince who's quite happy to move on without a backward glance."

"Have you asked him how he feels? Maybe he has also changed his mind." Hail cut a piece of his steak. "You should eat that, otherwise, he will have ruined your dinner as well." He pointed his fork at her steak.

She laughed. "You're right." Jolene picked up her knife

and fork. "I don't need to ask him about how he feels. Trust me, he's made his position very clear."

"Maybe you shoul—"

There was another squeal. Louder this time. *Great!* Again, Jolene should not have looked. Storm had the blonde she-dragon over his shoulder. She had been over that shoulder not even a week ago. Storm headed out of the hall, moving quickly and confidently. No need to guess where the two of them were headed.

"Have fun!" Beck shouted after them.

Her heart hurt in that moment. It gave a painful squeeze. Why, she couldn't say. Why she even had feelings for a guy like that in the first place was beyond her. Jolene was an intelligent woman. She owned her apartment. Her car was fully paid for. She had a really great position in her company. The younger staff looked up to her. She was in line for that promotion. Why was she stupid when it came to Storm?

Her lip quivered so she stuck a big slice of steak into her mouth.

"I'm really sorry," Hail said in a soft tone.

Jolene looked up into his eyes, which were filled with concern. That, and a good dose of pity as well.

"Thank you," she said around her food. Then chewed quickly and swallowed, using her napkin to wipe her mouth. "I'm not sorry though." *Yes, she was! No! She was not!* "This is for the best." She shrugged. It was. There would be no going back. No temptation to throw herself at Storm's feet and to beg him to give her a chance. A real chance, not just a fling. It seemed like a fling was all he was capable of.

Hail pushed his chair back and stood up.

"Where are you going?"

"I'll get us a couple of take-out containers. Let's get out of here. We can read or play a board game or something. I can see you're uncomfortable."

"No." Jolene shook her head. "You've made so much effort. The food is delicious. I'm going to try to forget all about 'you know who.' Sit," she looked at his chair, "let's enjoy our evening."

"You sure?"

She nodded. "Very."

He sat back down. "You know that you will be expected to stay with me for three weeks?"

She nodded. "I know."

"I know you have feelings for… 'he who shall not be spoken about,' but I would appreciate it if you would still give me a chance."

"I like you, Hail. I really like you, but not in that way." She felt so bad. "I wish I did but I can't help the way I feel. I doubt that's going to change."

Hail looked down at the table, when he looked back, his eyes had clouded. "Thanks for being honest with me. At least I haven't developed feelings for you yet. That would have been bad." He smiled.

"You can take part in the next hunt, I'm sure there's—"

Hail shook his head, making her stop what she was saying. "I'm not very athletic."

"You're not?" She widened her eyes. He wasn't as built

as Storm, but he was still seriously packing some decent muscles.

"Nope, I'm not that good a fighter and I'm not all that fast on my feet. Realistically, I don't stand much of a chance against the other males. Quite frankly, it was a shock when you picked me."

"Don't say that. Don't put yourself down. You are a serious catch!"

"Not to a dragon female." He shook his head. "They like the strongest, higher-ranking males."

She made a snorting noise. "Forget the she-dragons. I've only met one or two and I don't like them. They're more spoiled than… 'you know who' – and that's saying something."

Hail laughed, he put a finger in front of his mouth. "Don't let anyone hear you saying that." He chuckled some more. "It's true though."

"Let me tell you, you would be a serious catch to a human woman."

"You think so?" He looked at her skeptically.

"I know so." She waved a hand. "I'm clearly an idiot, so don't judge anything based on me. Human women would lap you up."

"Okay." He shrugged. "Maybe I will go on the next stag run."

"That's the whole 'go into town twice a year to shag' thing?"

Hail nodded. "I've never been to one. I didn't think females would be interested in me. I thought it would be the same as here. The same as the way she-dragons treat males like me."

"They would be all over you."

Hail smiled and she felt somewhat better. There was still a tightness in her chest she hated though. And this little rerun of Storm throwing that blonde over his shoulder playing over and over in her head. Her mind also kept trying to conjure up images of what the two of them would be doing right at that moment, but she wouldn't let it. Jolene squared her shoulders and smiled back at Hail. *It was for the best!*

CHAPTER 16

"Thank fuck!" the voice snarled.

Jolene sat up in bed, her heart racing. A figure stood over her. "Hail," she stammered. "Has something happened?" She tried to see his facial expression, but it was too dark. Why was he standing over her like that? She couldn't see him clearly, but she could feel anger rolling off of him. *Why?*

"U-um…" Hail stammered. Her eyes tracked his voice. The figure looming over her had not been the one who had spoken. Her blood ran cold when she realized that Hail was at the foot of her bed. If that was Hail, then who was this?

"I'm taking the female," the foreboding figure snarled.

"Storm?" Her voice was laced with confusion. "Is that you?"

"As you wish, m-my lord," Hail stammered.

"What are you doing here?" She pulled the blankets off, sliding her legs off the bed.

"We're leaving." Storm's voice was deep. Scary deep. He was using that commanding tone. The one that had gooseflesh rising up on her arms, her legs, her whole body. It could also be the cold causing the physical response. *Yeah, right!*

Jolene shook her head. "No." She sounded as confused as she felt.

"Yes, we are." He took a step towards her.

"No, we're not." She shook her head, fiddling with the light switch and turning on her side lamp. Jolene gasped when she saw he was naked. He looked angry. Muscles bulged and his frown deepened by the second. "What's wrong with you, barging in here like this?"

"Let's go." He gripped her by the elbow, hoisting her to her feet.

"Let *me* go." It was her turn to snarl; she tried to pull free, but he held on firmly.

"It doesn't seem like the female wants—" Hail began, sounding petrified.

Storm snarled at him. A terrifying noise that reminded her of a show she'd seen about lions of the man-eating variety.

Hail stood his ground. By his silhouette, she could see his shoulders were bowed, his head tilted down. "But, my lord—"

"But nothing," Storm growled as he picked her up, reminding her of how he had hoisted that she-dragon over his shoulder just hours earlier. Anger bubbled through her veins.

"Put me down!" she yelled. "Have you been drinking or taking drugs or something?"

Storm ignored her and began to walk to…not the front

door, but to the balcony.

Hail stepped into their path. "I'm going to have to ask you…" he looked at his feet, "beg you…to let her go. Please, my lord."

"Move or bleed." Gone was all trace of growling and snarling. His voice was calm. In many ways, it was even more terrifying. Storm tightened his arms around her. The muscles on his neck roped and his jaw clenched. His eyes were a dark purple, swirling and angry.

"It's fine, Hail." She could tell that Storm was taking her whether she liked it or not. Fighting it was futile. She only wished she knew what he wanted.

Hail's blue eyes flashed to hers. She read uncertainty there. "Are you sure?"

Jolene forced a smile. "Yes." She didn't want to see a nice guy like Hail get hurt. When Storm said he would make Hail bleed, she knew he meant it. That he would do it.

Especially since the dragon prince seemed to vibrate with anger. Literally. He even ground his teeth. What was he so angry about?

She sighed with relief when Hail stepped to the side, his eyes still on the ground at his feet. Storm strode out onto the balcony.

He put her down as he changed, his limbs lengthened. Scales sprouted up from beneath his skin. His jaw elongated. His arms stretched out into impossibly wide, yet soft looking wings. Within seconds, a formidable dragon stood before her. Eyes tempestuous and zoned in on her.

Jolene shivered when he picked her up in his claws. It had nothing to do with the chilly wind that hit her skin.

Her stomach gave a lurch as they took to the sky. Her nightgown whipped around her legs, as did her hair, which stung her cheeks. Within seconds they were freefalling. Jolene bit back a scream. Storm's great wings beat slower as they neared the ground. Slower and slower still until her feet touched the soft sand. They could not have been in the air for more than a minute. She could smell salt in the air. Could hear how the waves beat against the rocks.

Jolene hugged herself. "Why did you bring me here?" she asked, watching as Storm folded in on himself. It was only his eyes that stayed the same. He turned those on her. With just a half moon to light the night sky, it was difficult to make out his expression. He stood tall. His muscles still bulged.

"He didn't touch you." Storm sighed, his voice still had a guttural edge.

She swallowed. "Is that a question?"

"No, it's a statement of fact. I can't scent him on you." Storm paced away, before walking back to her. He seemed relieved and yet agitated.

"Why would you even care?" She didn't wait for a reply. "Why did you bring me here? What are you doing?"

"I couldn't stand the thought of him touching you," Storm growled out the words. "I would have killed him if he had."

"You have no right to even say something like that." She pointed at him.

"You are still mine." He advanced on her.

Jolene took a step back. "Don't come near me."

He didn't listen. Storm gripped her nightgown in clenched fists and began to tug it up. "Stop!" She pushed at his chest. "Isn't one woman in one night enough? You disgust me," she spat.

Storm let her clothing go and raked a hand through his hair. He pushed out a humorless laugh. "I didn't touch Mist or anyone else. I couldn't." He sounded angry. "All I could think about was you."

"What?"

"Of how happy the two of you looked at dinner." It sounded like he was gritting his teeth.

Wait a minute. Jolene frowned. "You're jealous?" She couldn't believe how happy that made her feel. Jolene had lain awake for hours picturing Storm with the she-dragon. Picturing all the things they would be doing. She'd been wracked with feelings of jealousy herself, only to find out that it hadn't happened. He'd been jealous this whole time too. Maybe he'd lain awake picturing her and Hail doing things together. She shook her head, could hardly believe it possible. "You left with her though. I saw you."

"I didn't touch her. I told you! I wanted to but only to try to forget about you. I couldn't." He shook his head. "I'm seriously fucking jealous. I saw you holding his hand. It made me half lose my mind. I'm keeping you. Hail can go to hell!" he snarled, grabbing at her nightgown again and yanking. It shredded like paper between his fingers. Falling in tatters at her feet.

The cold air abraded her skin. Her nipples tightened. "You can't just—" She wanted to hug herself but didn't, forcing her arms to stay at her sides.

"I can," he insisted.

"Whatever happened to asking?" His whole alpha vibe shouldn't turn her on, but it did.

"I don't ask, I take." She could see that his chest was heaving, he looked down at her body, and she had to work all over again not to cover herself. This was the first time he was seeing her naked from head to toe. "Fucking beautiful." She didn't have to see into his eyes to know that he meant it.

Her heart raced. They shouldn't do this. They should sit down like rational adults and discuss things properly.

She yelped when Storm plopped himself down in the sand in front of her. Like he'd read her mind. Maybe about the sitting part but not about the talking part. His hands gripped her thighs lightly. "Ride me." His voice was gruff. So sexy.

He pulled her onto his lap so that she straddled him. She put her hands on his shoulders. His finger immediately found her clit.

Screw talking.

Her head fell back and she moaned.

"I want you so badly." He kissed the pulse at the base of her throat as his finger breached her. He somehow managed to rub on her clit and finger her at the same time. His hot mouth found one of her nipples. He suckled her, hard before nipping at her flesh. She yelped feeling the sting. Then mewled as he licked the same spot better.

Then two, maybe more fingers were crooked inside her. She panted and moaned, her fingers digging into his shoulders.

"Ride me," he commanded again, placing both hands on her hips so he could lift her. She fumbled for his cock. Desperate to have him inside her. "Yes," she moaned as she circled his thick girth. "Oh yes!" she moaned louder as his tip breached her.

Forget going slow.
Forget her setting the pace.
Forget her doing much of anything.

Storm yanked her down, thrusting up simultaneously with his hips. She cried out, thankful he had prepared her. Not enough though. Her flesh stretched to accommodate him. Her ass hit his thighs. She bit down on her lip as pain blossomed.

Storm grunted loudly. "Fuck yes," he snarled, lifting her and thrusting into her again.

She yelled again as his cock hit deep inside. Hitting nerves that sent her spiraling out of control from the start. She yelled even more loudly on the next thrust. Her boobs bounced. She tried to take over the movement, but he wouldn't let her. He growled, low and deep, a warning, his fingers digging into her hips. It turned her on. His thrusts became more urgent. Her body seemed to suck him in, it made wet noises. Her breasts jerked hard. She grit her teeth, trying to hold on. Her orgasm close. They had only been going at it for less than a minute. She couldn't come so quickly, so easily. Could she?

"Now," Storm groaned. "Come for me," he snarled.

It was like he owned her body because it obeyed; an orgasm ripped through her. Jolene groaned. He kept thrusting. Then his finger was rubbing on her clit. It was too much. Sensory overload. "Again," he demanded.

"No," she bit out.

"Yes." His finger moved quickly but softly. His dick thrust deep and hard. "Now," another growled command that sent her tumbling over the edge all over again.

Jolene shouted his name. This orgasm was harder and faster. It tore through her, taking no prisoners. She finally slumped against his chest, forehead damp, breathing heavily.

Storm rubbed her back. He kissed the top of her head. It was almost tender. She didn't know what to make of this.

―――

Storm felt better inside Jolene. He wanted her again. Maybe this time on her back with her legs hooked over his shoulders. Then again, he had enjoyed watching her ass bounce when he fucked her from behind. "I told you it was a mistake to leave me."

"You didn't put up much of a fight." She sounded like she was smiling. He pulled back a little so that he could look at her and her full lips were indeed curved in a smile.

"I didn't want to hold you back."

She nestled back into his chest. "And taking me from my bed in the middle of the night isn't holding me back?"

Storm chuckled. "You didn't hold back. My ears are still ringing."

"Hey." She whacked the side of his arm.

"I rescued you." Storm grinned.

"What did you rescue me from exactly?" Jolene

sounded skeptical.

"Hail is boring as fuck."

She tensed up, a frown creased her brow. "Don't say that, I happen to like him."

Storm felt everything go cold. His muscles turned hard as steel as those same feelings of jealousy returned and with a vengeance. He snarled as he tossed her onto her back. The sand would be soft against her skin. "You can't possibly...like Hail." *Not a fuck!* "Tell me you don't actually feel something for the male."

"I do like him but not in that way. I think he's a good guy."

Something eased in him. "I'm surprised your ears didn't bleed earlier. The way he went on and on about tactical movements and perimeter patrols." Storm rolled his eyes.

She gasped. "You listened in on our conversation. That's rude!"

Storm chuckled. "Just to some of it. It was too boring to get into." He smiled. "You think everything is rude."

"Everything about you." She smiled.

"And you love it." He moved inside her, pushing a little deeper.

Jolene gasped. "Wait, we should talk." Her voice was strained. Her heart-rate picked up.

"Talking is boring." He leaned in and captured her lips, surprised at how much he liked the feel of them. Storm had never been much of a kisser.

She tasted good. Felt good. Jolene moaned and he ate up the sound, loving the feel of her tongue entwined with his. Her pussy was so snug and wet. So tight it almost hurt to take her. Storm made small circular thrusting motions. He broke the kiss and pulled up onto his elbows, admiring her for a moment or two from his position above her. Jolene's lips were parted. Her eyes were hazy with desire. Her cheeks were flushed. Her hair a mess. He rose to his knees and lifted her legs, holding them together. Then he hugged them against his body. With her legs closed, her pussy tightened and Storm groaned. She felt so damned good.

There was no lasting with this female. Not a chance. He pulled out for a second, pushing his thumb inside her. Within moments it was wet with her juices. He pushed his cock back inside her, hugging her legs tighter, thrusting hard and deep, loving her moans and pants. Then he moved his thumb to her other hole and pressed.

"Oh god!" she yelped. Shock and surprise very evident by the sound of her voice.

Storm smiled. This was going to be new for her. He could tell. He kept fucking her, keeping his movements hard but easy. Not too fast. He pushed a little harder with his thumb. Breaching her ass but only just. She yelped. Another push and his thumb went to his knuckle. "Oh god! Oh god!" She panted out the words. It was almost impossible but her pussy tightened even more. Storm groaned.

He felt his balls pull up. It was as if his skin shrunk around his muscles and bone. Like somebody turned up the heat because sweat formed on his brow.

She was making the most amazing noises. Music to his ears. One more push of the finger and he was all the way in. "Ooooooh," she moaned and then groaned his name, it sounded like a warning. One he was going to ignore. Storm grit his teeth and fingered her ass. In, out, in, out. Jolene went off like a rocket, shouting something garbled that sounded very much like '*asshole*.' It was hard to tell since she was screaming her release.

Asshole.

Storm would have laughed right then since his finger was buried very deep inside hers. Problem was, his balls were exploding with an orgasm that sucked the air out of his lungs. He grunted and his body jerked. Sweat dripped, his knees dug into the sand. His body shook with the intensity. It rushed through him. Fast and yet slow. Like a flood and warm molasses all at once. He hugged her legs, continuing to move for a while. Jolene was panting and mewling. It sounded like she'd enjoyed it just as much.

He smiled as he pulled out his thumb. He opened her legs, letting her feet plant into the sand on either side of him. He grunted when he pulled out. Storm placed his head on her chest. And what a magnificent chest it was. Like built-in pillows that felt good and looked good as well. She was trying hard to catch her breath, which was good because so was he.

After a few minutes, she swallowed and licked her lips. He could hear her do it. "I can't believe you did that." She sounded incredulous.

"Did what?" He grinned, knowing exactly what she was referring to.

"You know…what you did." She choked out a laugh. "I don't like anal." She sounded sheepish.

Storm choked out a laugh. "*You* might not like anal, but your body likes the fuck out of it."

Jolene shook beneath him as she laughed softly. "Okay," she moaned the word. "It was really good. It just seems a little dirty and I don't know…"

"Dirty and rude are not always bad things." He lifted his head from between her breasts so that he could look at her. "Dirty isn't always bad. It can be pleasurable too."

"I guess." Her cheeks went from pink and glowing to all-out red. Then she sighed. "We probably shouldn't have done that without talking first."

"Not everything should be planned and discussed. Sometimes things just need to happen."

"Not things like this."

"Why not? You have to admit it. That was the best sex you've ever had, right?" Why was he asking her this again? Why was it so important to him?

Her eyes clouded and she looked distinctly uncomfortable.

Damn.

Fuck!

By claw, she wasn't about to say what he suspected she was. Jolene shook her head. "It was good. Really good. Shockingly good, can't we leave it at that?"

No! Now that he had asked, he needed to know. Even though he knew what she was going to say, he still had to hear the words. He kept his eyes on hers.

Jolene shook her head, she tried to sit up. Storm could cage her in. He could hold her down if he wanted to, but he didn't. He moved so that she could sit up. Hair mussed and covered with sand, she was still beautiful. Exquisite even. "It was good. Great even but, if you really must know, it wasn't the best I've ever had. I'm sorry if that bruises your ego. Is that what this was all about?" She looked down, chewing on her lip. She looked upset. Then her big brown eyes flashed to him. "Was this all about you proving to me that you are the best lover? Because you're not. Sorry! You can stop trying because you'll probably never get it right." Then she pushed out a heavy breath, looking crestfallen. "You might be jealous but you have no intention of doing anything about it, so we may as well drop this." Is that why she was upset, because for a second there she thought he might have changed his mind about settling down? Thing was, Jolene didn't want him in that way, so that couldn't be it.

"I'm not sure what you mean." Storm looked at her head on. "I did do something about it."

She raised her brows. "Sex is…well, it's sex, it's not 'something.'"

"It was good wasn't it?" He didn't understand her. Not even a little bit. Was this why she intrigued him so much?

She laughed and shook her head and looked sad. "I think you should take me back to Hail."

"Fuck that!" he snarled. The venom in his voice shocked even him.

Her eyes widened and her mouth dropped open. "I don't get you," she finally said. "You don't want me, but you don't want anyone else to have me either."

Storm shrugged. "I guess. I'm not sure I understand it myself." He looked out at the vast ocean, at the rolling waves, before looking back at her. "Why can't you just relax and let go for a while? Stop with all the planning, all the preparing and just let go. Breathe. Live. Be." *Shit!* He was beginning to sound like a pussy, but he didn't care. He wanted this for her.

"I'm too anal for that," she blurted. Then she chewed on her bottom lip, her eyes glinting.

"I can help with that." He winked.

She laughed but quickly turned sober. "Why can't you be a little more serious? Take things a little more seriously?"

"I get bored easily." There was no need to think on an answer. "I hate being bored. Life is too short, even for a non-human. With you being human, life is very fucking short. Have you thought about that?"

"I think about it often. That's why I want to settle down so badly. I also happen to like planning. I enjoy being prepared. I know what I want and I like going for it, whether it's job-related or relationship-related." She sighed, her eyes lifting in thought. "I realize I can come on a bit strong. That I'm too serious at times."

"Okay, I realize I can be a loose cannon at times and that I don't always consider others." He gripped her hands in his. "I don't want you to go just yet. I can't make any promises beyond the next two weeks. I just can't. All I know is that I want you to stay." He blew a breath out through his nose. "I've never begged a female before for anything but I'm begging you now to consider it."

"It can't all be about sex though." She shook her head.

"We can have sex though, right?" he blurted feeling

panicked. "Often, that is?"

She laughed. "Yes, we can have sex, but we need to do other things as well."

"What kinds of things? Are you going to make me set up a candle-lit dinner?" He made a gagging noise. "Please don't make me do that."

"No, it doesn't have to be romantic dinners. It doesn't have to be romantic anything. Just anything other than sex. If I stay, we need to have fun outside the bedroom as well. Outside your apartment would be nice."

"I'm sure I can think of a couple of things." He nodded, his mind working. Something fun. Something that would get her right out of her comfort zone. "You can't get pushy about a relationship and a future though. You can't get on to me about being an asshole and about being a commitment-phobe."

"I never called you a commitment-phobe." Then she laughed but it had a hurt edge to it. "Even if you are, don't worry, I'll cure you of that problem. You'll marry the next girl you meet for sure."

Storm recoiled at the idea. "Like hell. This should be about having fun and…" He pushed out a breath. "Maybe extending ourselves beyond our comfort zones just a little, but again, no serious future talk allowed."

"Of course not." She sounded affronted. "I know anything serious is not your style, Golden Boy."

"You would be welcome to try to change me." He raised his brows and smirked at her.

"No thanks." She shook her head. "Not interested."

"You can try to change me, and I will make it my

mission to be the best lay you have ever had. That, and to show you the best time you have ever had."

"So, my only option is to stay with you?" There was a joking edge to her voice and something else that he couldn't quite pin down.

His good old mate jealousy made a quick comeback. "Or, you could go home right now because I'm not allowing another shifter anywhere near you."

"I know I'm not supposed to call you out on it, but that was a seriously asshole thing to say." She tried to make light of what she was saying but it didn't work.

He touched his chest. "I am who I am. Do we have a deal? Two weeks, come on Jolene, let's have some fun together and then you can go on with your boring as fuck life."

"Hey, that's a rude thing to say."

Storm shrugged. "Maybe after this, you'll change your outlook a bit."

"Maybe you'll change yours." She raised her brows in a challenge – and Jolene knew how to challenge him like no other.

Change. It *was* something he was afraid of. Love and settling down were not on the cards for him…not yet anyhow, but change wasn't necessarily a bad thing for either of them.

"You never know, maybe you'll have turned me into a boring pussy by the end of all this."

"Maybe you'll turn me into a reckless wanton."

"A guy can hope." He held out his hand.

Jolene laughed, she looked down at his outstretched

hand for a few beats before taking it and shaking it. "I'm probably going to regret this."

"Not a chance." He lifted her hand to his mouth and kissed her palm. Then he nibbled on the tip of one of her fingers. Jolene giggled. When he sucked on the digit, she bit down on her lip. "Now that's how you kiss a female's hand."

"You were jealous of Hail kissing my hand?" She made a face, a smile tugged on the corners of her lips.

"I'm still considering cutting his lips off."

She gasped. "You can't be serious."

"I won't hurt him." He gripped her by the hips and flipped her onto her knees. "Not if you make it up to me." Her heart-shaped ass was covered in sand. Gorgeous. He gave it a light slap, watching the sand sprinkle onto the ground. Jolene yelped. She giggled straight after and he scented arousal.

Then she swallowed thickly. "What did you have in mind?"

"Your question should be," he found her clit and started on it, "what *don't* I have in mind? Because I can tell you..." he lined his cock up with her opening, "I have so much in store for us." He thrust inside her. Loving her surprised gasp. Loving the feel of her tight around him. "And most of it is dirty and as rude as fuck." He grunted. "You're going to love it."

Jolene moaned something that sounded like, "Doubt it!'

The game was still on. Only the stakes were higher. More fun that way.

CHAPTER 17

Something other than fucking.

Something other than... He scrubbed a hand over his face, trying to will his brain to come up with something.

"Why are you looking so glum?" Beck's eyes narrowed, and his nostrils flared. "What the hell! I thought you spent the night with Mist but all I'm getting is human. Lots of human." He pretended to cough and waved a hand as if to dissipate the scent.

Storm snorted. "Spent the night? I've never spent the night with that she-dragon before and I'm not about to start." He *had* spent the night with Jolene though. It was the first time he'd spent the night with someone he was fucking. Weird but kind of nice too. Okay, it was very fucking nice. Especially considering he'd woken up to her sweet scent. Her soft body. He'd made quick work of that.

Good morning?

Not a chance.

It was a great morning. Sex as the sun rose. Sex in the shower. Sex on the dining room table during breakfast. The things that were possible with maple syrup and breasts boggled his mind. He'd used half a jug. His sweet tooth still hadn't been satisfied. Not even close.

"Why do you have a goofy smile on your face?" Beck cocked his head, eyes wide.

"I may or may not have fetched what was mine from that…" He cleared his throat. Jolene liked the male – as a friend and nothing more – so, he couldn't say shitty things about him. "From Hail."

Beck smiled, he nodded his head slowly. "I see. I take it you guys made up."

"Several times over."

"Spare me the details." Beck held his hand up.

"I wasn't about to give you any, dickhead." Not a chance. It had nothing to do with Beck or any of them.

"Why are you here then?"

"Jolene kicked me out."

Beck threw out a laugh. "I thought you said you guys had made up."

"Yeah, we did. We came to an agreement. Plenty of sex but we have to do other stuff as well."

"What other stuff?"

"Fucked if I know." Storm shook his head.

Beck laughed some more. "You're not going soft on me, are you?"

"Not a chance. We also agreed there would be no romantic shit. If I ever turn into Hail or my pussy brothers, you can punch me in the face."

"I have your full permission?" Beck's brows quirked.

"Absolutely." Storm got this weird shivery feeling at the thought. "Punch me hard if it ever happens. I'd deserve it."

Beck chuckled. "You got it, bro. So, you have no idea what to do with a female other than fuck her?" He looked amused.

"None. I've never done anything more than that with a female. I like Jolene." He shrugged. "I think I would enjoy doing *other* stuff with her. It's just, she's not a male and she's not my girlfriend." He made a face. "It's not like that, I mean."

"So, you need something fun where she doesn't accidentally die."

"Exactly!" Storm blurted. "You see my dilemma. She also needs to enjoy herself and not get any ideas, although, I don't think she would. Jolene is not only beautiful but intelligent too."

Beck looked at him funny. "Any more of such talk and I'm going to have to punch you."

Storm laughed. "Nah, it's ultimately about the sex, which is fucking amazing." Although it still irked him that he wasn't Jolene's best. He needed to speak to Crystal about those pointers she had promised to give him.

"How so?" Beck's eyes lit up. "What's different with this human?"

'Everything' was the first word that came to mind, and this was the second time Beck had asked him to spill about Jolene. They normally spoke openly about who they bedded. Talking about his sexual relationship with Jolene didn't sit right though. He respected her and knew she wouldn't like it, so he refrained. "You're supposed to help me with a good idea."

"Take her out on that new toy of yours."

"That would be dangerous."

"Bull! You've practiced. You're getting really proficient. You haven't crashed in over a week."

Storm nodded. "Yeah, I guess I am but why not just shift and take her for a flight in the most conventional way. It would be safer." Not as much fun though. Was he becoming Hail? *Not a fuck!*

"I think she'd prefer being able to have an actual conversation with you. That's what this whole 'do other stuff' thing is all about, isn't it?"

"It's about having fun." Storm thought it over. "I think she would like a spin in the chopper. No, I think she'd love it."

"Problem solved," Beck said.

───

Shiiiiiit! She clutched her shoulder harness tighter, trying not to hyperventilate as the helicopter lifted.

Storm glanced at her. He chuckled.

"Eyes on the controls," she said as the blood drained out of her face. "How long did you say you've been flying this thing?"

"A few weeks." Storm pressed his lips together to hold back another laugh. His eyes glinted with mischief. Thankfully they were focused on the controls.

"Oh, dear god, please don't take me now."

He laughed. "You are funny."

"You said you taught yourself how to fly. *Yourself?* Is that even a thing? Can someone teach themselves how to fly a helicopter?"

He shrugged. "I can fly, so I know a thing about weight and lift and aerodynamics. I also relied heavily on Google."

"Google? Please be joking." She was going to die. More blood drained. Her mouth felt dry as a bone in the desert.

"No, I'm not." He flicked a switch on the busy control panel. "I haven't crashed a chopper in almost two weeks."

"What?" she yelled. Forget trying not to hyperventilate. It was too late for that. She struggled to breathe. "You're not joking, are you? Good god, what were you thinking taking me up here?"

"I have this. I know what I'm doing, okay?"

"Not okay." She shook her head. "You've crashed helicopters? *Crashed* them." Panic was beginning to set in.

"Maybe bringing up my early incidences wasn't the best idea."

"Ya think?" *Calm down! Calm down!*

"I can fly, as in, I have wings. You realize that, don't you? If anything goes wrong – and it won't – I will fly us to safety. You don't have to worry. This was supposed to be fun. Look at the scenery."

"How many?" She couldn't help herself.

"How many what?" It did help calm her somewhat that he was so relaxed. That and his ability to fly. It would come in handy.

"How many helicopters did you crash?"

"This isn't a good line of conversation right now. We should look outside and admire the beauty. The weather is perfect. Not too hot. Not too cold. No storms or thermals predicted." He glanced at her. His eyes so vivid, so unique and utterly gorgeous. So filled with humor.

She smiled. "You promise you know what you're doing?"

"I would never risk your safety." He turned back to what he was doing. "Never, I swear. We're perfectly safe. If anything changes, I'll fly us to safety. No harm, no foul."

"Why would you even want to fly a machine when you can fly yourself?" She smiled, her hands relaxing…just a little. She kept them firmly on the harness though.

Storm gave her his signature half-smile. "It's fun learning new things. I can shift and fly. That's easy. I can whip most dragons' asses." He shrugged. "I wanted to experience something new."

"Never happy with what you have."

He shrugged. "I'm happy. I want more though. I want 'different.'"

Jolene pushed aside the pang that rose up in her and looked out the window. It was beautiful. So incredibly beautiful. Mountains, fields and streams as far as the eye could see. No, that wasn't entirely true. Far in the distance, there was the ocean. Wilderness. Unspoiled. Untouched.

"What the fuck!" Storm snarled. His voice crackled over the headset.

"What? What is it?" Just as she had just started to relax. "Is there something wrong with the helicopter?"

"No, I can see something in the distance that looks very much like another chopper." He sounded deep in thought.

"Oh!" She clutched at her chest before realizing she'd let her harness go with that hand. She grabbed it again. "I thought it was something bad. Don't scare me like that."

"Yep, it's definitely another bird." Storm was frowning. "I'm going to get us out of here. Hold on." He pushed the stick slightly to the right and the chopper started to bank.

"It's just that—" Before he could continue, a voice came in over the radio and into their headsets.

"Foreign craft. Come in foreign craft. Over."

"Fuck!" Storm muttered. "They must have radar. There's no way they could have spotted us with the naked eye."

"Is everything okay?" Jolene frowned. She got the distinct impression everything was not fine.

"Yes." Storm nodded. "Just fine." He glanced her way, a smile plastered on his face.

Why didn't she believe him? "Who was that talking? Is there a problem?"

Instead of answering her, Storm pushed a switch, holding it down while he spoke. "This is the foreign craft. Over."

Nothing.

More nothing.

"Should I be worried?" she asked.

"I've got this," Storm reassured her.

"This is Alpha nine, one, zero, two. Who am I speaking to? Over."

"Shit!" Storm snapped before sucking in a deep breath. He pressed the button. "Whiskey, four, six, one, four. Over."

The radio crackled immediately. "Whiskey, four, six, one, four did you know this was restricted airspace? You are currently flying in restricted airspace. Over."

"Yes, I knew that," he said out loud but to himself. "Don't say a word, Jolene."

She nodded. "Okay." She quickly added when she realized he wasn't looking at her.

"Negative, I didn't know," he sounded panicked. Not like Storm at all. "I'm taking my girlfriend for a spin. I must have drifted off course."

She was quite sure they were in a dangerous situation. Everything about this screamed 'wrong'! Yet, when he called her his girlfriend, something warmed in her. It wasn't true of course and yet…

"What should I do? Over." Storm released the button.

There was a long piece of radio silence. "What's going

on?" Jolene asked, starting to feel scared. She could make out the other helicopter now. It looked like it was gaining on them.

"They're right, this is restricted airspace. I know that because it was we, the dragon shifters, who implemented the restriction in the first place. It's a long story as to how we got it right. No craft, civilian or otherwise is permitted to enter our airspace. They are the ones trespassing. Not me!"

"Come in Whiskey, four, six, one, four. Over." The radio crackled in her ears.

"Go ahead. Over," Storm said.

"I can't pick up your registration in the database. Over."

"Fuck!" Storm snarled. "They can't pick my reg. up because this helicopter isn't registered. I made that up on the spot. They're in an old military chopper. That bad boy is bigger and quicker than ours, and by the looks of things, they're coming in hot."

"Hot. What does that mean?"

"I think they're armed. We've had some trouble with unidentified choppers flying over our territories over the last year or so. Thus far we've avoided them and remained hidden." He looked her way, his violet eyes solemn. "I think the time for hiding just came to an end."

"You think these guys mean us harm?" Panic welled in her. She sucked in a deep breath, quelling the emotion. It wasn't going to help them get out of this.

"I think so." Storm pressed the button. "Are you sure? That doesn't sound right. Over."

"Yes. Whiskey four, six, one, four is not in the database. Over."

"Did you say Whiskey four, six, one, four? Over," Storm asked. "They're definitely armed. Normally I would call this in and handle it myself, but I need to keep you safe. I think these are hunters. We're sure word of our existence leaked after the first human Bride Hunt. We've changed things since then. We're stricter about background checks and paperwork."

"You're telling me." The endless interviews. All the documentation giving them permission to check all aspects of her life. The agreements and contracts. She'd almost backed out a couple of times.

"Affirmative, that's Whiskey four, six, one, four. Over."

"Sorry, I'm not sure how it happened but it should be Whiskey four, seven, one, four. I repeat Whiskey four, seven, one, four. Over." Storm turned a dial and pressed the button again. "Whiskey four, seven, one, four to base, come in base. Over," he said, releasing the button and glancing at her. "I'm letting home know there's a problem and then we're getting out of here. You need to hold on tight and close your eyes if you have to."

She nodded, her eyes felt huge in her head and her mouth felt really dry.

Storm pushed a breath out through his nose. "I'm going to get you out of this in one piece. I promise."

She nodded again.

"This is base. Go ahead Whiskey four, seven, one, four. Over."

"I've just been informed by an Alpha nine, one, zero, two, that I'm flying in restricted airspace. Over," Storm said releasing the button.

"Clever, you're letting home know we have company,

right?" she asked.

"Exactly. I'm sure the other chopper has all the equipment to listen in to whatever channel I select. I'm buying us time. I don't want to tip them off that we're onto them just yet. They're gaining on us but they're not flying top speed yet. Not even close."

"Whiskey four, seven, one, four, come in. Over."

"Shit," she said. "That's the bad guys."

Storm nodded once. "This is Whiskey four, seven, one, four. Over."

"This is base. What are your coordinates? Over." It was the dragons.

Storm turned the dial. "I don't know. We should have been flying over the Fire Mountains heading East, but we're lost. I plan to follow the shoreline in that direction. Over." He turned to her. "Our species call this part of the dragon lands the Fire Mountains. It's just within the Fire Dragons' territory." He shrugged. "The range is vast. It might take them a few minutes to find us."

"So, when you told them where we should be flying, you were actually telling them where we are now?"

He nodded.

"Quick thinking." She smiled.

The radio crackled. "That registration isn't in the database either. Who are you really? Over."

"Playtime is over," Storm said. "Hold on." They banked sharply, dropping altitude and Jolene grit her teeth. What she really wanted to do was scream but that would be counterproductive.

"Whiskey four, seven, one, four you had better tell us who you are, or we will be forced to shoot you down. You are in restricted airspace. Over." The person talking had raised his voice.

"You first. Over," Storm said, releasing the button. "You sure as fuck aren't Alpha nine, one, zero, two. Over and out."

Silence.

More silence.

"I thought so," Storm muttered. "They're gaining on us."

Jolene squeezed her eyes shut as the chopper banked again. They were moving at what felt like an alarming speed. Every time the chopper dipped or banked, her stomach gave a lurch. She held onto her harness for dear life.

"Good thing I know these mountains better than the back of my hand," Storm said, as the helicopter banked the other way. "I sure as hell know them better than those human hunters."

There was a loud noise followed by a loud bang. Jolene squealed as they banked sharply again.

"Fuckers are shooting at us," Storm growled.

"Oh god!" she shrieked, opening her eyes and then wishing she hadn't. They were flying in a narrow gully that twisted and turned, left and right and left again. Storm was flying like a pro. Any wrong move, though, and they'd hit sheer cliff on either side.

She glanced back and then wished she hadn't. The much larger helicopter had gained on them. "They're shooting!" she yelled when she caught sight of orange flames coming out of what looked like large machine guns on either side of the chopper.

"Bastards!" They veered sharply to the right, following the gully. The spray of bullets just missed them, tearing huge chunks of rock face from the cliff.

"That was too close." Storm shook his head. "When we get out of this, I'm ditching this chopper and buying something faster."

"*If* we get out of this."

"We will, Sweet Lips," Storm growled. "Hopefully the cavalry will get to us first, but if not, I have a plan." Storm sounded confident. He looked confident. "Hold on!" he yelled, pulling to the right again.

This time he was too late. There was a pinging, tearing noise as bullets ripped through the side of the chopper, which shook, almost colliding with sheer rock.

Jolene screamed.

"You injured?" Storm barked, trying to look her way and steer.

"No!" she called back.

He huffed out a breath. "Forget waiting. It's time for plan B." Storm steered them into the middle of an S-bend. When he reached the center, he pulled up, hovering.

"Um…what are you doing?" She could hear the panic in her voice.

"I have lightning fast reflexes. Make sure your straps are tight and face ahead, chin on your chest," Storm said, voice calm.

Her heart galloped in her chest as she did as he said.

"Come on cocksuckers. Come on," he coaxed. Two seconds later, the engine whined as he yanked the helicopter up. Jolene's stomach dropped as they flew up.

Something caught them on their undercarriage – Jolene screamed as the chopper spun out of control. Storm cursed through clenched teeth, fighting for control. There was a bright orange ball of flames and excessive heat that rolled out just as quickly as it had rolled in.

"Got them!" Storm yelled, the chopper steadying.

Jolene looked out the window at the gully below. There were pieces of chopper strewn everywhere, some of them still on fire. She looked at Storm, who was grinning.

"I thought we were goners." She must have been holding her breath because she was panting.

"Such little faith. I'm disappointed." He winked at her.

Jolene laughed, feeling hyped. It must have been the adrenaline coursing through her system. Her hands shook. "How long did you say you've been flying? It can't be weeks."

"You'd better believe it baby." He rose up above the mountain range. "It did take four crashed choppers to get here though."

"Four?" she chuckled, shaking her head. "I'm glad you didn't tell me that before we took off. I would never have gone with you."

"Finally." Storm waved as four dragons appeared around them. He pointed down, to where smoke billowed and then gave the thumbs up. "We're fine!" he yelled. One of the dragons gave a nod of his great head. It dropped out of the sky, almost freefalling to the crash site. The other three followed suit. "Time to get you back on solid ground."

"That would be nice." Jolene licked her lips.

Storm flew them quickly. Fields, streams and gullies passed beneath them. Neither of them spoke. It couldn't have been more than ten or fifteen minutes, and he was setting the chopper down on the same grassy bank from earlier.

Her heart still raced. Her whole body vibrated.

Storm flicked a few switches and the helicopter was powering down. He pulled off the headset, placing it on the dash. She did the same.

"We nearly died," she blurted.

"Hardly—" he began, but Jolene didn't let him finish. Careful to avoid joysticks and various equipment, she pulled up her skirt and straddled Storm, covering his lips with her own and clasping his jaw with her hands.

He grew hard against her core in seconds. Their tongues dueled, their lips smacked. Her breathing turned into hard panting. Storm pulled back, he grinned. "I think I might try and kill us more often." His eyes dropped to her mouth.

"Don't you dare," she said as she pulled his cotton pants down, watching as his cock sprang free.

There was a tearing noise and a pulling sensation as Storm ripped off her panties. He tried to undo his harness. "Leave it." She looked him in the eyes.

"You giving the orders now?"

"Yes," she growled the word.

"Okay then." He half-smiled, looking sexy. "You want the harness to stay, it stays."

Jolene gripped his wide girth and sank herself onto his hard length in one thrust. No need for foreplay. She was soaking wet. Storm closed his eyes and groaned.

Using hard, quick strokes, she repeatedly impaled herself on his cock. Storm grunted. She watched his Adam's apple work. His eyes turn stormy. His jaw tightened. Within minutes, she was yelling his name.

Storm groaned hers. His grip on her hips tightened. His eyes widened. "Fuck," he finally whispered, letting his head fall against her chest, his arms circled her. "You need to know that almost dying and letting you fuck me have become my new favorite things." He was breathing heavily.

Jolene was still breathing hard herself. She giggled. "That's the last time."

"That you fuck me?" It was comical how panicked he sounded.

"No, crazy guy, that we almost die. I didn't enjoy that at all."

"Liar. You haven't had so much fun…ever."

"Fun!" she snorted, sounding shocked. "Dying is not my idea of fun."

"Almost dying is not the same as dying." He reached up and kissed her softly. "And I agree, we won't try that again. I would hate for something to happen to you." He hugged her close.

Even though this felt like a moment, she reminded herself that it was just afterglow after good, adrenaline-fueled sex. Nothing more!

CHAPTER 18

The next day...

Crystal bellowed, clutching her sides.

Forget laughing. Laughing was too tame. The female bent over her middle and let it rip.

"It's not that funny." Storm shook his head.

"I think it is." Crystal finally said, coming up for air, a huge smile still plastered to her face. Her eyes were wet. Her lashes glinted.

"It really isn't," Storm said. "You were the one who offered and I'm taking you up on it."

"Why has this human got you so rattled?"

Storm shrugged. "I guess I don't want her to forget me when she goes."

Crystal looked at him pointedly. "You really think she's going to forget you? You? Storm, Prince of Water?"

Just nine short days ago, he would've said the same. But now, he wasn't so sure.

"Come on," she rasped. "Not happening. How often does a human get whisked away and seduced by a dragon prince? Never…okay? It doesn't happen."

"I know she won't forget me…this." He gestured around them. "Thing is, I'm competitive."

"I know," she said when he didn't elaborate.

"I don't like that I'm not her best. I want to be her best. Moreover, I want to always be her best. I don't want another guy *ever* beating me."

"That's crazy!" Crystal looked at him like he'd gone mad. "Why do you want to be her best for all time? What you're saying is you want her to leave here and pine for you. That's what you're saying, right? Not just in the immediate future but always."

"Hearing you put it like that…it sounds like a dick move." He rubbed the back of his neck. "But," he shrugged, "that's what I want."

Crystal narrowed her eyes. "It is a dick move. One I don't understand, but hey," she shrugged, "I made a deal with you, so, I'll teach you everything I know. Did you bring a pen and paper?"

"I don't need a pen and paper, Crystal."

"Yes, you do. You really, really do."

Fuck! He was so bad, he needed a notepad and a pen to write this shit down. Why had no-one ever told him? Crystal burst out laughing. "You should see your face. She really has you in a flat spin."

Storm heaved a sigh. "Don't do that. I might have to put you in the cage. Or ban any of the males from sharing your bed."

"You wouldn't! Tell me you're not that cruel."

"Chill! I wouldn't do that. Now, spill."

"There are one or two fundamental things and then quite a number of tips." She winked. "Let's start with the most important."

Storm nodded, focusing on her every word.

"Glad you could finally make it." Torrent's face was red. He had that *I'm-going-to-fuck-you-up* look that Storm knew well. Thankfully he wouldn't be able to follow through on the threat his eyes were making.

"Apologies, sire." He bowed his head and lowered his eyes before turning to the Fire King. "Good to see you, my lord. How are your lovely mate and your sweet whelps?"

Blaze didn't quite smile but his eyes twinkled in amusement.

"First, you are late and then you waste our time with small-talk," his brother growled.

Blaze finally cracked a smile. "My mate is well, and my young are…busy…" He widened his eyes before smiling again. "But I wouldn't have it any other way."

Storm nodded in Flood's direction and the male nodded back. He still managed to keep that serious disposition he wore so well.

"Apologies for being late," he spoke to Blaze.

"It was only by three minutes," the Fire King shrugged. The four kings were so competitive. He knew Blaze would take an opposite stance to Torrent, if he played them right, and he clearly had.

"What was so important?" Torrent couldn't let it go.

"My female was quite traumatized after yesterday's

event, she didn't sleep at all last night." All true but it had nothing to do with their traumatic event. "Jolene didn't want me to leave her." Again, true, but for different reasons than he was hinting at.

Torrent rolled his eyes. His brother knew bullshit when he heard it.

"That's terrible." Blaze's eyes turned solemn. "You will need to send her our apologies. We have redoubled patrols in the area. I am discussing doing the same in all four kingdoms."

"The time has come to fight back," Storm said.

"That would give us away," Torrent snapped.

"Yes." Blaze nodded his head. "I am inclined to side with the Water King on this one. It would indeed alert them to our presence if their aircraft began disappearing."

"I think it's clear that they know we are here. It's been months and they're still coming into our airspace."

"Still," Torrent shook his head, "they suspect but they're not sure. One crashed helicopter is something that can happen. Multiple disappearances would only serve to bolster their belief that they are onto something. They would only send in more."

"Yes, and it would also send a clear signal that we are not to be messed with," Storm said. "They can't keep snooping around our territory."

"We are not far enough along in our silver resistance therapy," Torrent rasped.

"Please, can you relay to Storm what you told us before he got here?" Blaze asked Flood.

The male cleared his throat. His arms were folded over

his front. "The artillery was all silver-infused."

"So, they know what they are looking for," Storm growled. "I knew it!"

"They suspect," Torrent countered.

"They know. Why keep coming back month after month? Those bastards know we are here. They're armed to the teeth with silver weaponry. They're just itching for a target," Storm added.

"And we aren't going to give them one!" Torrent yelled. "Your flying machine is grounded until further—"

"What?"

"Don't you 'what' me!" Torrent pointed a finger at his face.

"I do think there is some merit in what your brother is saying," Blaze addressed Torrent. "I think they definitely know we are here. They know we are non-human. In fact, I think they know exactly what we are."

"It would be good to know why they are looking. Why they won't give up," Storm said.

"Who cares?" Torrent shrugged. "Does it matter?"

"No! The only thing that matters is that they mean us harm. We need to convene a meeting. All four of us." Again, the Fire King addressed Torrent. "We can't keep hiding. At some point we will need to retaliate. The lives of our families are at stake."

Torrent sighed. "Maybe you are right."

"It's only a matter of time before they see something. Before they find one of the lairs…and then what?" Storm hated being the negative one. The kings were playing it too safe.

"Then we crush them like the bugs they are." Torrent squeezed his hand into a fist.

"Yes." Storm nodded his head, hoping it never came to pass. The damage could be devastating.

CHAPTER 19

Storm angled the knife, slicing the carrot.

"You seem preoccupied with something. Are you okay?" Jolene asked, stopping what she was doing so that she could turn to face him.

"I'm just feeling bad we couldn't go swimming in the ocean like I promised."

"That's okay." Jolene shook her head. "I don't mind. This is fun too."

"We're cooking stir-fry for lunch as our fun thing to do for the day," Storm muttered. "It's boring as fuck."

"It's not!" She put her hands on her hips. "Are you telling me being cooped up with me is boring?" Then she widened her eyes. "Sex aside of course." She pointed the knife at him. The one she'd been using to cut chicken with moments earlier. "That better not be what you are saying."

"Not at all. I live for chopping vegetables…especially when I get to do it with you." He chuckled.

"Now you're teasing."

"I'm enjoying myself just fine. I was just looking forward to taking you out, that's all." After what had happened the day before, they were tightening security around the lairs. That chopper had been far too close to home. It was forbidden right then for humans to leave the safety of the lair. There had been several reports of unknown helicopters scouting the area. They were probably looking for their friends. Hopefully, they found the wreckage soon so that things could go back to normal.

"Yeah, it was scary. Who were they and what did they want?" She took a sip of her white wine.

Storm shrugged. "I don't know."

"You said that it's happened before. That these people started coming into restricted airspace after the first Bride Hunt?"

"Yep." He nodded. "We went about things differently back then."

"You said there were fewer background checks."

"Less! There were no background checks and no contractual agreements. The success rates weren't as high either. Sometimes a female is not a good fit. We sometimes picked females who were just plain nasty. Females like that ended up going back home."

"They knew about you. About this place."

"I'm not sure how they managed to pinpoint where we were, we made them wear blindfolds, but yeah." He nodded. Storm took a big sip of his beer.

"Well," her eyes turned up in thought, "I think if someone knew you existed, it wouldn't be that hard to learn where you might be located. I mean, these are vast areas of wilderness. There's the ocean and the mountains. I think the main giveaway is the restricted airspace, together with the rest of the facts."

If someone was to put all those together. "I think you might be right. The very thing that's protecting us is also a dead giveaway."

"They have no idea, though, where within all these thousands of square miles you are located? Not exactly."

"Thankfully not." Storm shook his head. "That's why they keep flying over. It's like they're working a systematic grid. If they keep trying hard enough, they might just find something."

"You have systems in place, right? Patrols that would alert you if they came too near?"

"Yes, but still. The thing is, even an old military chopper like the one from yesterday could do untold damage to a lair. A silver-infused missile, aimed just right – or wrong, depending on how you looked at it – could take out whole sections at once. What if the royal chamber was hit? We're all at risk."

"I'm sure it won't come to that." Jolene's eyes were filled with concern.

"We were almost hunted to extinction centuries ago. That was when dragon slayers still carried silver knives and spears. Now they have missiles and bullets. All silver-infused. All waiting to find their mark. We wouldn't stand a chance. Our species could be decimated."

"Killing for the sake of killing." She shook her head. "Surely not?" Jolene looked upset. Her eyes blazed. "Then again…I guess it happens all the time."

Storm had a good idea of what they would be after. He didn't voice his suspicions. "You're right, it does happen all the time. Bloodlust runs strong in all of our veins, except many humans have no honor."

"The government would never allow it. They would put a stop to it." She sounded skeptical.

"You can't stop what you don't even know is happening. According to the world, we don't even exist. Easy pickings."

"No." She shook her head. "Don't say that."

"That's why we need to take them the fuck out. We won't go easily but, hey…" He lowered his voice to a rumble as he walked over to her, putting his hands on either side of the counter. This way he could close her in. "All this talk of war and death. It's putting a serious damper on our afternoon."

Jolene looked up at him through her lashes. "We have a lunch that needs cooking."

He leaned in so that they were just half an inch apart, speaking directly into her ear. "And you have a pussy that needs eating."

She gasped, her face turned pink. Jolene giggled when he picked her up.

Storm worried about whether or not she could sense his nervousness. He wondered if she would know. His heart beat wildly as he lay her out on the bed. "Let me help you out of these." He peeled off her leggings, placing kisses along her legs as he did. "Your pussy is about to become well acquainted with my lips," he murmured, only because it was something 'cocky him' would say. He didn't want to let on he wasn't feeling very cocky at that moment.

Jolene smiled, and giggled and smiled some more.

Good, she didn't notice his tension. Storm could relax a little. She was into it...thank claw!

When Storm knelt down on the bed beside her, she pulled her lip between her teeth and bit down lightly. Her gorgeous brown eyes on his. "Let me help you out of this as well," he said, tugging on her blouse.

She raised her brows. "The perfect gentleman all of a sudden. Normally you just rip my clothes off."

"There's a time and a place for everything. This is about being patient and taking things slow."

"I like that." Her voice had turned husky.

Storm undid the buttons on her top and peeled it off. Her bra was a thing of fucking beauty. It was turquoise and lace. "You have the most amazing tits I've ever seen on a female," he rasped, tugging on the cups so that her boobs spilled over. Her nipples were pink and succulent looking.

She giggled. "I'm not sure that's a compliment."

"I've seen plenty of breasts, so trust me, it's a compliment." He leaned in and swirled his tongue around one of her puckered beauties.

When he pulled up, her smile had widened. "You're not supposed to talk about previous conquests."

"Why not?"

"It spoils the mood."

"Let's do a quick check." He pulled her lace panties to the side, feasting his eyes on her glistening pussy. "That's what I thought."

"That's not..." She moaned when he leaned in and licked her slit. This couldn't be all that different from fucking. Find her sweet spots – good thing he already knew where those were – and push them. Not too hard. Stroke them was probably a better way to describe it. "Let's teach this gorgeous pussy of yours how to French kiss."

She laughed. "You're so rude." Her little nub lay nestled between her folds. He found it and licked it. She whimpered, her breathing turning ragged.

Good. This was working. Crystal had given him two tips when it came to going down on a female. Just two. He closed his mouth over her clit and sucked on it. The sucking thing was tip one. A female's clit was the same as the tip of a male's cock and should be treated in a similar fashion. He needed to give Jolene head.

"Oh god!" Jolene groaned.

Bingo! It seemed the she-dragon might know her stuff. He licked a couple of times and suckled on that baby again. "Oh, good lord!" Jolene gasped, grabbing his hair so tight it pulled at the roots.

Storm smiled against her pussy. This was working. He pulled her legs over his shoulders and shredded the panel of her underwear for better access. "Feels good," Jolene mumbled, he could hear she was smiling. She was panting too. Panting plenty.

Everything in him told him to suckle her while fingering her hard. He wanted her to come hard but then he remembered Crystal's second tip. He needed to prolong her pleasure. He wasn't allowed to be too impatient.

He circled her clit with his tongue, listening to how her

moans turned slightly frustrated. Then he inserted a finger into her tight channel. Just the one. Slow and easy. Her moans reignited. She even rocked into his hand. One quick suckle had her crying out, but he quickly eased off. Not too hurried.

Minutes later and she was begging. "Storm, please...oh god...Storm!" she moaned when he suckled on her. She groaned loudly when he let her clit go. "Please... god... please."

Aside from loving how she tasted, he loved driving her crazy. It was time, though, to step it up a level, so he added a second finger, plunging them both into her dripping pussy. Her moans turned to keens. "Please, Storm, oh, please." Her hands tightened on his head some more. At this rate, he was going to be bald by the end of this.

Jolene was close. So very close. At this point, he could be cruel and ease off a whole lot, or he could let her come. Call him impatient because he couldn't wait anymore. Storm grinned before crooking his fingers and thrusting just that little bit deeper. He closed his mouth over her clit, loving how she screamed his name. Her thighs closed around his head. Her hands pulled on his hair.

He slowed as she came down. Working his hand slower. Using his tongue instead of his mouth.

When he looked up at her, her head was flung back. Her eyes closed. Her chest heaving. "That was...that was..."

"Good?" he asked.

"No." She shook her head, still lying flat on the mattress. Her legs were still slung over his shoulders.

"Not good?" *Damn, did he screw it up?* Did he get it wrong and not even know about it?

"It was the best," she mumbled.

"As in the best you ever had?" he asked, sounding skeptical. It couldn't be.

"I know stupid things like that are important to you." She looked up for a second, letting her head fall back. "So, I'm telling you. Yes, it was the best!"

"What?" Storm frowned and he frowned hard. "How can I be the best at something I've never done before?"

She lifted her head, looking at him through still hazy eyes. "What? That was the first time you've ever gone down on a woman?"

Storm swallowed thickly. *Shit!* He hadn't meant to tell her that. "Yes," he nodded, feeling like an idiot, "that was the first time." He shrugged.

Jolene smiled. It was sweet and shy and yet really sultry all at once. "That explains things." She let her head fall back onto the mattress.

"What does that mean?"

"You wouldn't understand," she said.

"No really," he climbed on top of her, caging her in with his body. "Tell me."

"Nah, I don't think I will."

"Then I might need to punish you." He lined up with her opening and pushed inside her. *So tight. So damn good!*

Jolene's mouth dropped open. Her eyes hazed over. "I think I might like your form of punishment."

"Me too." He thrust again and again until both of them were spent.

CHAPTER 20

Three days later...

The door opened. Jolene shrieked, clutching her dress to her front. Thankfully she wore underwear and thankfully the huge guy who walked through the door didn't seem to care about her state of dress. Or in this instance, undress.

Her mouth fell open as he strode to her, eyes on hers. "Where is he?" The big guy growled at her. He was formidable, commanding and just plain scary. His muscles roped. His eyes bulged from their sockets. His hands were clenched into tight fists at his side. His chest was gold and gleaming. There were flecks of green in the gold, signifying that he was a water dragon.

Wait a minute...

Gold with the green! That meant...that had to mean...yes, he was a member of Storm's family. Now that she thought about it, there was a resemblance. This guy looked older, harder. Also, his hair was blond, but they had similar facial features. Their eyes too. "Who are you?"

she finally blurted. "I mean, you must be family to Storm but...I'm sorry, we've never met. I would shake hands, but I'm trying to prevent us from becoming a little too well acquainted, if you know what I mean?" *Stop blabbing, Jolene!* She pressed her lips together.

He pushed out a heavy breath, his shoulders easing forward a little. "I'm sorry. I'm Torrent, Storm's brother."

Oh shit! "The king...you're the king?"

She did a really bad curtsey since she had no idea how to do one and since she was practically naked.

His lip twitched. "Yes, that would be me. Do you know where he is?" The anxiety from before was back. There were worry lines on his brow and tension radiated from him.

"Storm said he needed to put in some work hours. He felt bad for his teammates because of the extra shifts caused by all of the extra patrols," she went on. Blabbing again. Jolene cleared her throat. "He'll be back in about an hour and a half."

The king muttered a curse, looking both angry and frustrated.

"Is everything okay?"

"No...yes. It's just that I needed him here. I should have told him not to go anywhere." He shook his head, looking out the window.

"Is there anything I can do?"

"Have him come to my chamber as soon as he gets back. On second thought, I'll have someone meet his team."

"Okay."

"I need to go." Torrent turned and began to walk towards the exit. He stopped almost mid-step and looked back at her. "It was good meeting you. Again, sorry for just barging in."

"I'm sure you have a good reason."

The king smiled, it was tense. He swallowed thickly. "My female's birthing pains have begun. It is our second child. It's going more quickly this time." He scrubbed a hand over his face, looking worried. "Storm was supposed to look after our daughter."

"Oh! He would never have gone if he had known."

"I know, I will have one of the she-dragon's watch Rain. It's just that she loves her uncle and was looking forward to spending time with him. She seems...apprehensive about having a sibling."

"She doesn't realize it yet but having a brother or a sister will be amazing. It isn't fun being an only child. Playing on your own isn't the same. Ask me, I know."

"It was good meeting you, Jolene."

"Oh, you know my name." She smiled, feeling like an idiot. "I'm sorry, I didn't introduce myself."

"Storm has spoken of you. I feel I know you already."

"Oh." She frowned. "Has he?" She wanted to ask what he had said about her, but that would be stupid given the circumstances. She could also see that he was still facing the door and pretty much on his way out. Still looking tense. Couldn't blame him with his wife in labor. "I'm sorry," she flapped a hand, "you get back to your mate."

His expression changed to one of relief. "Thank you."

"Sorry, one more thing..."

He turned back to her, looking flustered.

"Maybe you can send the she-dragon here with Rain. I would be happy to help out until Storm gets here."

His expression morphed to relief. "Are you sure? She's only four and can be quite a handful."

"I'm sure." She nodded.

"I will send Crystal right over."

Shoot! Why Crystal? "Perfect." She plastered a smile on her face. Not wanting to worry Torrent with stupid things like Storm's ex-partner and her jealousy over a man who wasn't even hers. Not really. "You go and concentrate on your wife and on meeting your baby."

Torrent's eyes glinted and he smiled. "Thank you." He still looked tense. She couldn't blame him.

It didn't take long for the knock to sound. Jolene opened the door. Crystal smiled; she held the most adorable little girl's hand. She got down on her haunches. "You must be Rain?"

The little girl buried her face into Crystal's dress, she had a doll clutched to her chest. "Don't mind little Rain. She's a bit shy."

Jolene stood up, she moved to the side. "Come on in." She worked hard at, at least trying to smile at Crystal. She really needed to get over herself. "Can I get you guys something to drink?" she asked.

Rain kept her face buried in Crystal's thigh.

Crystal looked down. "Do you want something, Rain?"

The little girl shook her head and mumbled. "Na-ah."

"You're being rude, Rain," Crystal said. "You should look at someone when you talk to them."

"Don't worry about it." Jolene shook her head. "It's a big day, she might be feeling a bit overwhelmed."

"The day isn't big!" Rain yelled, putting on a growly voice. "Mummy's tummy is big." She finally lifted her head from Crystal's side. Her face was scrunched up in anger. Even her little fists were clenched tight. "But not for much longer." She narrowed her eyes. "She's having my baby brother today."

"How lucky are you?" Crystal said in a sing-song voice.

Rain didn't look like she was feeling lucky. "Don't say that." She put her tiny hands on her hips. "I don't want a brother!" she exclaimed, eyes firmly on Crystal. It looked like the little girl was waiting for her to argue with her.

Crystal smiled. "Why don't you go and play with your dolly while Jolene and I fix you a sandwich?"

Some of the fire left Rain's eyes. She looked at the she-dragon for a few moments longer before nodding. "I like peanut butter and jelly. The bread must be cut like mommy does it."

"Of course, sweetheart," Crystal said. They watched as Rain sat down on the rug and began talking to her doll.

The she-dragon gestured to the kitchen with her eyes. Jolene nodded. "I don't know if we have peanut butter," she whispered.

Crystal widened her eyes. "We'd better pray you do. I'm sorry, she's not normally like this."

"It's completely understandable." Jolene herself had longed for a sibling her whole childhood – what she wouldn't have given to have had a brother or a sister – she could see it from Rain's perspective though. "Her whole life is about to change."

"Yes, it certainly is." Crystal turned to Jolene, locking eyes with her. She looked down at the ground before looking back at Jolene. "I need to apologize for the last time I saw you. I was worried about the prince. I…I shouldn't have done what I did. It wasn't right." She sighed. "I guess I was feeling jealous."

"Jealous?" This was the last thing she expected to hear. "Of me? You?" Jolene had to laugh. "You're gorgeous. Tall, toned…" She shook her head, opening a cabinet, she began rummaging inside. "If you want, you can look in the pantry, it's through that door." She pointed.

"Don't be silly." The she-dragon snorted, walking to the door in question. "None of that matters. You have child-bearing hips. Dragon females can only long to have breasts like yours. No wonder Storm is so besotted with you."

Jolene stopped what she was doing. "Child-bearing hips?" She choked out a laugh. Crystal had said it like it was a good thing. "He's not besotted with me." She shook her head.

"He is doing everything in his power to please you. From being polite – or trying to be, at any rate," Crystal smiled, "to asking for advice on how to please you in other ways." The she-dragon winked.

Oh no, hell no!

"I can see from your face that you're upset. Please don't be. He wants you happy. I probably shouldn't have said anything."

"I think it's more about making himself happy," she

mumbled, rolling her eyes as she took another look in the cabinet for the peanut butter. "That and appeasing his humungous ego." Storm couldn't take it that he wasn't the best at something.

Crystal chuckled. "He does have a big ego. Don't be too hard on him though. I definitely shouldn't have said anything." She shook her head. "The only reason I did is because I think it's sweet. I truly believe he is trying to please you and is ultimately doing it for the right reasons."

"Which are?" Jolene was frowning. It couldn't be what the she-dragon was hinting at.

"He has feelings for you. That's why. I saw it that day when I came here. That's why I was so jealous. It's why I acted the way I did. Like an idiot." Crystal stepped back into the pantry. "Got it." She re-emerged holding a large jar of peanut butter, grinning broadly.

Jolene wasn't about to argue with the she-dragon. It wasn't like that at all though. In a week's time, she was leaving and she was okay with that. She reminded herself daily – make that, several times a day – that their fling was just that, a fling.

She wasn't sure what the she-dragon saw, only that it wasn't what she thought it was. Storm didn't feel that way about her, and wanting to please her sexually, was just that, it was his ego talking and not his heart. In fact, she wasn't going to even bring it up with him. She should, but what would be the point? Again, it wasn't like they were in a real relationship or anything. She grabbed the jelly out of the fridge.

Crystal had already put two slices of bread on a plate.

"Do you want some juice, honey?"

Rain looked up from what she was doing. Her eyes were huge. She looked so sad, poor kid. Rain nodded once. "Yes peez."

"I'll get it," Jolene said, since Crystal was busy smearing peanut butter on the bread. They finished making lunch for the little girl. Crystal seemed to know what she was doing. She first checked with Rain before cutting the bread. Turned out her mom cut it into squares. Not triangles, or rectangles but squares.

Rain ate a few bites of one piece before moving to another. She drank some of the juice before announcing she was full.

"You sure?" Crystal asked. "You hardly touched your food."

"My mom makes it better," Rain said, shrugging a shoulder.

"Of course, she does, sweety. Do you want to watch a movie on my iPad?"

Rain smiled. It was a sad smile. She nodded. "The one about the shark."

"Okay, honey. You sit on the sofa and we can choose something together."

Rain nodded. She slid off the chair and headed for the sofa, her doll still clutched to her chest.

"Why didn't I think of watching a movie online?" Jolene muttered to herself. Storm had an iPad as well as a desktop computer.

Crystal set up the movie while she cleaned up.

"How is she?" Jolene asked.

Crystal shrugged. "She's happy now. I found that shark movie she wanted." The she-dragon smiled. "I wonder how the queen is getting on. I must say, that's one good thing about being infertile, I don't have to worry about giving birth." Although Crystal smiled, she could see a pinched look on her face and her eyes had clouded. Then she smiled and it was gone.

Jolene couldn't imagine what it must be like. To long for a child, a family and not be able to have one. It kind of put things into perspective. She'd been mad at Storm for choosing her with no intention of taking it further, but at least she could move on.

Storm was right. She did take things too seriously. She did push too hard. When she did meet someone one day — hopefully in the not too distant future — she was going to do things differently. It would be about getting to know one another and about fun. Like she and Storm were doing now, only…it would be more serious.

"I can't imagine how it must be for you," Jolene said.

Crystal shrugged. "It is what it is. I've resigned myself to it. I'll never be a mom and that's okay."

"It must be hard on you…all of you she-dragons, watching your men mate human women."

"Yes," she nodded, "it is. I can only hope to mate one day. Most of our males want young and…" She shrugged.

"So, they hold out for a human."

"Exactly and that does hurt. I'm not good enough." She sighed. "Oh well. There is a new human doctor. She is working with Tide's mate, Meghan. Doctor Sheila has offered to test us. She wants to try to get to the bottom of our fertility problems."

"Oh, that's great!"

"Yes, but at the same time I am worried it will just get my hopes up. I don't think it is really possible for us to ever have young."

"I think you should try though. You will regret it otherwise."

"Maybe you are right." Crystal smiled. "Doctor Sheila also wants to test why it is that only male children result from human and non-human pairings. It doesn't matter what the species is whether vampire or shifter, so far, only male children have been born. It's also a problem with the rare dragon shifter females who are fertile."

"That's interesting. Are you saying—"

The front door opened and Storm raced in, his chest heaving. The pants he was wearing were twisted slightly to the right, like he'd hurriedly pulled them on.

"I'm sorry I'm late," he growled. "I'm not sure why no-one sent for me." He walked towards them, a frown creasing his brow.

"Calm down, my lord. Jolene and I have things under control. Is there news of the queen?"

He nodded. "Although the birthing process is progressing quickly, all is well. I should not have left the lair. I promised Torrent I would look after Rain." He looked around the chamber. "Where is my niece?"

"What?" Jolene said.

Crystal frowned as her eyes landed on the now empty sofa. The iPad was lying on the chair, the movie still playing unwatched.

Storm glanced at the door behind him. It was still open.

"Maybe she left to try to find her parents," Jolene said, feeling panic mount.

Storm muttered a curse. He walked back out, sniffing the air. "Her scent trail isn't fresh. This doesn't make sense. Rain," he called out, closing the door.

Jolene walked over to him and whispered. "She's upset about all of this. She says she doesn't want a brother."

Storm nodded, eyes filled with worry. "Rain, hun...it's your favorite uncle." He tried to make his voice upbeat. "I'm sorry I'm late, angel." He swallowed thickly. "Where are you?"

Nothing.

Suddenly Storm visibly relaxed, he touched his ear and then pointed at the bed. Crystal nodded in what looked like agreement. The little girl was obviously under it. Hiding. The dragons had been able to hear her with their superior senses. Jolene felt for Rain. This had to be quite frightening for a child.

"I have strawberry ice-cream. I can make you a three-scoop cone." Storm said, speaking up so Rain would hear him.

"My mommy never lets me have three scoops," a little voice sounded from below the bed.

"Your mommy's not here, sweetheart," Storm said. "I am, and I say you can have three scoops if you want."

There was a moment or two of silence, before Rain slid out from under the bed. Storm crouched down beside her. "Why were you hiding under there?"

She shrugged, big blue eyes filling with tears.

"What's wrong, angel?" Storm wrapped his arms around her. "I'm sorry I wasn't here and I'm sorry I didn't visit you this week."

"Have you been busy?" she asked as Storm released her.

"Yeah." He glanced at Jolene. "But I should still have gone to your house and seen you."

"Is that lady pregnant too?" Her eyes welled. "Are you going to have a baby of your own and forget about me, like daddy?"

"Daddy hasn't forgotten about you."

"All he can talk about is my baby brother. He keeps telling me how happy I'm going to be and how I can help mom, but I don't want to." Her lip wobbled. "Daddy won't want me anymore."

"That's not true, Rain," Storm spoke softly. "Your daddy loves you with all his heart and I love you with all my heart. No-one can ever replace you or forget you. You are one in a million and a princess. The only girl princess in the whole Water territory." Storm smiled at her, cupping her chubby cheek softly in his hand for a moment.

"That is true." She was thoughtful for a moment. "A boy can't be a princess, can he?"

"Nope. No chance of that."

"What if she has a girl?" Rain pointed at Jolene.

Storm smiled. "That's my friend, Jolene."

"I'm not pregnant," Jolene said, her voice catching. All this talk of babies was making her feel emotional. Watching Storm with his niece wasn't helping things either. He was so gentle, so sweet. So good with the little girl. He would make a wonderful father someday. Pity, she wouldn't be around to see it.

"Oh!" Rain said. "Okay." That seemed to appease her.

"What do you say to three scoops, princess?" Storm held his arms open.

Rain giggled. "Yay!!" she yelled, jumping into Storm's arms.

"That's what I thought." Storm tickled Rain who shrieked and yelled. He picked her up and held her in his arms, walking towards the kitchen. He stopped as he passed them. "Would you like some ice-cream?" he asked her. "I have sorbet," he added, looking at Crystal. Dragons didn't eat milk products.

"Sounds great," the she-dragon said.

"What about you?" He kissed her quickly on the lips.

"Yuk! You are just like daddy and mommy," Rain squealed. "You sure you don't have a baby in your tummy?"

Jolene made a face. "Out the mouths of babes. Maybe I should skip the ice-cream. I'm quite sure, honey," she said to Rain.

"Nonsense." Storm frowned. "You're perfect." He kissed her again.

"What did I tell you?" Crystal piped up.

"What did she tell you?" Storm frowned.

"Nothing," both she and Crystal said at once. Jolene felt her cheeks heat. "Okay, but only one scoop," she quickly changed the subject.

"Two," Storm said.

"Three!" Rain yelled.

Crystal laughed. "What the hell. I'll have three!"

Jolene rolled her eyes, laughing as well. "Three it is then." She watched as Storm put Rain on the countertop. The little girl kicked her legs happily. She only had eyes for her uncle and Jolene couldn't blame her.

She had this feeling inside. This pang. It was regret. It was longing. Jolene was falling for Storm. There were no two ways about it. When Rain had asked if she was pregnant, she found that she wished she was. She wished even harder that Storm was hers. That Crystal was right when she said that Storm was besotted with her, but it wasn't like that. At least, it wasn't like that for him.

CHAPTER 21

Their last night…

Her eyes lit up as she walked outside and a smile slowly curved her full lips. She clasped a hand to her mouth, her eyes wide with shock. "I thought you said you weren't doing any romantic bullshit."

"I'm not." He shook his head.

"What's this then?" She looked around the patio. "Fairy lights, flowers, candles, wine and soft music." She laughed, the sound music to his ears. "I hate to break it to you, Golden Boy but this is plenty romantic."

Storm shrugged. "I wanted our last night together to be special. You're special, Jolene." He walked over to her and clasped her hands. "I'm sorry I ruined things for you."

"No, you didn't, you—"

"Wait, hear me out." He squeezed her hands. "I kind of did." He sucked in a big breath. "No 'kind of' about it. I ruined things for you. I was a selfish asshole, but I'm happy to say that I think I've changed for the better since meeting you, so something good came of this."

"Maybe a little selfish in the beginning but you're ultimately a good guy. You were right, by the way, I was too pushy and too anal. I was far too serious about things, and that was most likely a very big part of why men couldn't commit to me in the past. I scared them away."

"They weren't good enough for you." Storm felt angry that those faceless males had turned their backs on this gorgeous, funny, sexy female. It was their loss. "If I was ready to settle down, I'd snap you up in a heartbeat." He meant it too. Every word. Her eyes clouded for a moment, but she blinked a few times and it was gone.

"Shall we eat?" He let her hands go, pulling out her chair and pushing it in as she sat.

"Venison carpaccio." He put a plate down in front of her. "With a plum jus. I put some parmesan on yours."

"Thank you."

"No problem." He sat down.

"How is your nephew doing?" she asked, picking up her knife and fork.

"Great. He's already put on some weight." Storm had to smile just thinking of the squirming little baby. "Fjord looks exactly like Torrent. I'm sorry you never got a chance to meet the little one."

"No," she put her knife down, "don't worry about it. There wasn't enough time in the end. How is Rain? Has she warmed to the baby?" She put a small forkful into her mouth.

Storm chuckled. "Like you won't believe. She's driving her mom crazy because she wants to do everything. She wants to bathe him and change him."

"I'm so glad." Jolene smiled. It was warm and beautiful. Her chocolate eyes were bright and so damned beautiful.

"If I ask permission, would you stay?"

Her eyes lightened up and she seemed to hold her breath.

"I mean for another week. I know you said you don't have any more leave, but do you think your boss would let you stay?" He pulled in a breath. "You could meet little Fjord. I know Candy, my brother's mate would really like to meet you and Rain has asked about you as well." He put down his cutlery. "What do you say?" His heart beat wildly. He didn't think Torrent would agree but his brother could go to hell. It was only a week. Only seven days.

Jolene sort of smiled. She looked down at her food for a moment before locking eyes with him. "I don't think that's a good idea."

"Why not? You've had fun, haven't you? We can finally go swimming." The humans had found the aircraft remains and hadn't been seen since. They seemed – at least for the time being – to have backed off.

"I need to get back to my job, to my life. I enjoyed myself. I enjoyed spending time with you, but…" she bit down on her lip, "I can't stay. You know that. I told you about my pending promotion."

"What about it?" Storm leaned forward, listening to her every word.

"I'm up for a promotion. Carla Jackson and I each manage the sales and marketing department. That's what our company does. I'm not going to bore you with the particulars."

"Not at all. You can tell me more." He meant it. He wanted to know so much more about this female.

Jolene smiled. "You'd die of boredom."

"I would not."

"What I do isn't important," she laughed, "I'll get into that some other time." She must have realized what she had said because her eyes clouded. There wouldn't be another time. There was a heavy pause. She pushed out a breath. "Anyway, Carla and I are both up for an Exec position. We're pretty evenly matched. Carla is cutthroat…bottom line, she's a bitch. I would have to leave if she got the job. I couldn't tell my boss that of course."

"Why not?" he blurted. Jolene was far too nice.

She shrugged. "I just couldn't. You don't do things like that." Jolene took a sip of her wine.

"Of course you can. You should tell him like it is. Stand up for yourself. This Carla female sounds like she would do the same." She sounded like she walked all over Jolene, which made him want to do something about it but there was nothing he could do. It frustrated him.

"She'll do a whole lot more," Jolene mumbled. "She's an ass-licker of note."

Storm felt horrified. "She likes to lick ass?" Who was this female?

Jolene burst out laughing. "Not literally." She chuckled some more. "It means she likes to suck up. She sucks up to my boss all the time. It might win her the promotion. It doesn't help that I left to come here at a crucial time."

Storm felt like a dick all over again. "I'm so fucking sorry. What can I do to make it up to you?"

Jolene shook her head. "You don't have to keep apologizing. I've had a good time. It was...dare I say, fun." She smiled brightly.

"Stay then," he urged.

"I can't." She shook her head. "Please understand."

"I do." He nodded. "I had to try one last time. I suppose it would be delaying the inevitable and I want you to still have every shot at that promotion." He swallowed thickly. "I really meant it when I said I would grab you and never let go if I was ready to take that next step."

She shook her head, smiling. There was this look in her eyes though. "What makes you think I'd be interested?"

"Your body, Sweet Lips...your body tells me all the time how interested you are."

She snorted, her smile widening. "Good thing my body's not in charge then, Golden Boy."

Storm choked out a laugh. "Eat up." He picked up his fork and pointed at her food. "Before it gets cold."

Jolene rolled her eyes. "Carpaccio doesn't get cold." She laughed.

Storm had planned on going with the last piece of advice Crystal had dished out but, how could he? It wouldn't be right. As much as he wanted to be the best. As much as he wanted no male to ever match up, he couldn't do it. He couldn't do it to himself and he definitely couldn't do it to Jolene.

Worship her body, the she-dragon had said. Worship every part of her. Take your time. Make it about her. It's not a race, or about how many times you can make her come. Once is enough if you put your all into it. If you put everything into it.

Only, that sounded too much like making love. Who was he kidding? That *was* making love and as much as he longed to make love to the sweet human in front of him, he couldn't. It wouldn't be fair because he couldn't keep her.

"What are you thinking about?" Jolene asked, putting another forkful of food into her mouth.

"How I can't wait to get done with dinner and about how much I'm looking forward to dessert."

"Oh, and what's for dessert?"

"You are." He let his eyes dip to her cleavage before moving back to her gaze. "I was just wondering if you were particularly attached to that dress and if this table can take a bit of a hammering." He gave it a little shake, pretending to check it.

Jolene giggled. "You've gone to so much trouble. We should enjoy it."

"Screw the food. I'm going to miss you." He meant it. He really and truly meant it. Maybe it was a good thing she was going.

Her pupils dilated.

"To hell with it," he growled, standing and swiping the plates, cutlery, candles and all the other crap from the table.

Jolene stood up as well, chest heaving. Eyes wide. He could scent arousal. He gripped her hips and turned her, so that her front was on the table, her ass in the air. *Oh, that ass.* Rounded and plump. "Fucking perfect," he growled as he pulled her dress up. "No underwear?" He could hear the shock in his voice. "That's fucking rude, a lot naughty...and I love it." He slapped her ass just enough that it would sting just a little. Jolene squealed and then giggled. The scent of her arousal grew stronger.

She groaned when he found her clit and rubbed softly while pulling at his pants and freeing his cock.

He was desperate to be inside her. Like his life depended on it. He snarled as he pushed inside her. Snarled again as he began to thrust. He pulled the zipper down on her dress, continuing to work her pussy. Loving the mewls and whimpers she was making.

Her channel was slick and tight, pulling him in. Clenching him hard. His balls slapped against her ass, which bounced with every hard thrust.

He peeled her dress down, her tits spilling out. Storm reached around and cupped her breast, her nipple hard against his palm. His balls were already pulling tight.

With one hand, he held her down. With the other, he found her clit and pinched it softly between two fingers. Jolene sobbed as her pussy spasmed around him. He roared her name as he came. His body jerked with the severity of his orgasm. He finally slumped over her, his dick still buried deep inside her. They were both breathing deeply. "Are you ready for the next course?" he asked.

Jolene shook with laughter beneath him. "How many courses are we talking?"

"A whole lot." He grinned, kissing her back. "First the chicken." He pulled out, making a grunting noise. "And then I'd like to finger your ass again," he whispered in her ear, then pulled himself up, so that she could move.

Jolene pushed out a throaty laugh. "You are so crass," she said, standing. She began fixing her dress. Tucking all her gorgeous curves away.

"But you love it." He grinned, bobbing his brows at her.

She nodded. "It's grown on me." Her eyes clouded but she looked away. If she was so sad about leaving, why didn't she stay? Storm knew he wouldn't be able to change her mind. The only thing he could do was make the most of the time they had left.

"Here, let me do up your zipper."

She turned around, holding up her hair. If only he wasn't such a damned pussy. If only things had been different.

CHAPTER 22

Storm carried her bag. It was lighter than when she'd first arrived. Many of her t-shirts, skirts, shorts, you name it, had been ripped to pieces. She was wearing her last pair of underwear. There was a lump in her throat. Her feet felt heavy and her heart heavier.

This was it.

The end.

She could do this. There was no way she was begging Storm to let her stay…for real. No way she was expressing her feelings for him. No way she was running after him. She'd done enough chasing in her life. It was her turn to be chased. There was someone out there who was going to love her and want her enough to pursue her. Someone who was going to appreciate her. Deep down she'd hoped that someone would be Storm. She swallowed down the lump.

He seemed completely relaxed. Head held high. Greeting the odd person. He slid his arm around her. It was moments like this that it felt like they were together. Really together. Sometimes when he looked in her eyes or touched the small of her back. When he kissed her. Especially when he kissed her. Whether hot and heavy or deep and tender. Those were the moments she felt the possibilities between them. When she felt herself wishing for more. It was stupid. She knew it was stupid, but she hadn't been able to help it.

She spotted Beck and Flood. There were another two guys with them she didn't recognize. Jolene waved and all the guys, barring Flood, waved back. Flood gave a deep nod of the head instead.

Storm tightened his arm around her and stopped walking. They'd technically said goodbye already. "This is it," she said, trying hard to hold it together.

"Yes, this is it." Storm swallowed hard. "You're sure I can't convince you to stay for another week?"

She shook her head. "No. Thank you. I had a really good time though."

"Me too." She wasn't sure what she expected but having Storm fold his arms around her and hug her close was not it. A cocky smirk? Sure. An even cockier remark? Definitely. But this? No. He was breathing fast. His arms tightened even more. She hugged him right back, squeezing her eyes closed. Trying hard not to cry.

All too soon he was pulling away. "You need to take care of yourself."

"Yeah, you too." She nodded.

"I would tell you that everything you ever dreamed of is coming your way. A mate and babies…but I'm a selfish bastard. I don't like thinking of you with another male." His jaw had tightened. His eyes seemed darker.

She grit her teeth together to keep from talking. She didn't have to be with anyone else. She could stay here with him. They could be very happy together. *Shit!* She was going to cry. Jolene sniffed and forced out a laugh. Amazed at how flippant it sounded. "I wouldn't worry too much about that. You'll mate the next girl you're with. You'll take part in another hunt, fully expecting to have a bit of fun," she put on a voice, "and you'll end up with her. Story of my life, remember?" She raised her brows.

"I wouldn't be too sure." He cupped her cheeks and looked her in the eyes. "I'm going to miss you, Sweet Lips."

That lump in her throat grew impossibly big. "You're going to miss my sweet lips alright." It was her turn to make the silly remarks. It couldn't be helped. It was that or cry.

"The sweetest." His eyes were trained on her mouth. There were still no flippant remarks forthcoming. Instead, he leaned in and kissed her. It was sweet, soft and tender. It spoke of things that it really shouldn't. Made her false promises. He ran a thumb along her bottom lip as he pulled back. "Go get that promotion and everything else you've been dreaming about."

You. I've been dreaming of you.

"It's all there waiting and you're worth it."

Shit! She sniffed and nodded. Then he was letting her go and taking her hand, so that he could lead her to the group of waiting dragon men.

He handed the bag to Beck. "You take good care of her." His voice was a deep rasp.

"I will…" Beck narrowed his eyes. "Are you sure you don't want to take Jolene back yourself?"

"We spoke about this and yes, I'm sure. You're okay going with Beck and the rest of the males?" Storm looked down at her as he spoke.

I want to stay.

You want me to.

Why won't you admit it?

"Yes, I'm fine with that." She nodded.

"You sure…" Beck began.

"Very sure," Storm snapped. "Get my female home safe. Follow your orders."

"Yes, my lord." Beck handed her bag to Flood.

"Does everyone know what's expected of them?"

They all responded that they did. One of the guys took a step forward. "I am Bay and this is Harbor."

"Good to meet you both."

"If you are ready, Jolene," Beck said, his eyes filled with what looked like pity. "We can head out."

"I'm ready." She nodded, squaring her shoulders. She didn't need pity.

Storm brushed his lips against hers one last time. This was it. She turned away, tears stinging her eyes, not sure how much longer she could hold them back. Maybe the pity was fine since she was about to have a pity party.

The four men spread out and changed into their dragon forms. Flood took to the air, he clutched her bag in one of his claws. Beck leaped into the sky, hovering above her so that he could pick her up. He made one screeching roar before lifting. Then they were on their way. It didn't take long for the tears to fall. Hot and heavy. Her heart felt like it was being ripped from her chest. Jolene forced her eyes on the horizon ahead. No looking back.

CHAPTER 23

"I had hoped you wouldn't be here," his brother said, from somewhere behind him. Torrent sighed before continuing. "I must say, I had really hoped to hear you'd decided to keep that female."

Storm had watched until the flying formation was long gone. He couldn't bring himself to leave. Everything in him screamed to follow. To bring her back. Jolene was his. She was.

No, that was just hormones speaking. Stupid instincts brought about because of the hunt. The sex had been good. Watching her go, not so much. He'd get over it though.

"You can still go after her, you know?" Torrent said, stepping in next to him. It was precisely what he didn't need to hear. An echo of his own thoughts.

"Why are you being so hard-assed about this? You have feelings for that female. Admit it."

"I'm in lust with her. That's all," Storm growled, his hands tightening on the rails. "I don't want to mate her so there's no point in bringing her back. You made that clear from the start."

"You don't see her as yours?"

Yes! Fuck! What was he thinking? "No," he growled, a little too harshly.

Torrent chuckled, making him want to punch the male.

"Don't," Storm warned.

"I'm sorry." His brother shook his head, sounding genuinely apologetic. "It's not just lust. I wish I could make you see that. I'm afraid that by the time you do, it will be too late."

"I'm not going to change my mind." Torrent didn't know what he was talking about.

"You will and by then, someone will have snapped her up. Mark my words."

Storm ground his teeth together at the thought of another male touching his…her…Jolene. "By then I will have moved on as well. These blasted hormones will be out of my system."

"Granted. This whole thing started out as a hormonal issue. An instinctual problem, if you can call it that, but it has evolved since then into something far more. I understand why you might be apprehensive about getting into a relationship. In hindsight, some of my own issues, Lake to a lesser degree and Tide's too, stemmed from what happened with mom and dad."

"No," Storm said. "That's not it at all. I told you, I'm young. Years younger than you and Tide were when you mated. Lake doesn't count, he's always been sweet on Sky. Thing is, I don't want to be tied down to one female for the rest of my life. I'm not ready to be a father."

"No-one said anything about becoming a father." Torrent got this sappy look. "Although it is wonderful. I'm talking about building a life with a female you love. Someone you love spending time with. I promise you it's not the hardship you think it is. I think deep down inside you know that. You're just afraid of the other side to love."

Torrent was right; being 'tied down' to Jolene didn't sound like a hardship. Even having a couple of kids with her didn't sound all that bad. *What was he thinking?* He shook his head. "I have plenty of time for all that."

"Okay."

"That was too easy." Storm narrowed his eyes. "Why aren't you arguing some more?"

"You have clearly made up your mind and." he shrugged, "it is not my place."

"I *have* made up my mind."

Torrent's whole frame tensed. His eyes narrowed, seeming to track something on the horizon. Storm turned to see what it was. *Was that? No! Surely not!* "That isn't...is that...?" He scrunched his eyes up, trying to get a better look.

"It's Bay," Torrent said under his breath. "At least, it looks like Bay. Hard to tell from this distance."

"What the hell is he doing?" Storm growled, feeling his scales rub. "Why isn't he with the others?" He felt his muscles bulge, preparing to transform.

"He's moving fast. Too fast." Torrent shook his head.

"Something must have happened." Adrenaline coursed through him. "Fuck! Jolene. Something must have happened to…" His voice was thickening. Storm realized that he was shifting. He couldn't seem to help it.

"Wait!" his brother shouted, banding strong arms around him. "You need to hear what Bay has to say. You can't rush off half-cocked."

Storm sucked in deep breaths, trying hard to keep himself under control. He could feel scales rising on his arm. He couldn't quite shift back fully to his human form. Not completely. Not with this much adrenaline coursing through him. Jolene. If anything had happened to her he would never forgive himself. He was too big of a pussy to take her back himself. He didn't think he could say goodbye if he took her all the way back. Bottom line, he just couldn't bring himself to do it because he was yet again an asshole and now she was possibly in danger. He kept dragging air into his lungs, trying hard to calm himself down.

They watched Bay approach. Torrent was right. He was moving at an alarming rate. The male did a partial crash-landing, rolling once in a ball of wings and claws, before finding his feet. "What happened?" Storm snarled, walking to where Bay was, still in mid-shift.

"Where is Jolene?" His voice was a deep rasp. More scales shoved their way through his skin and his teeth felt sharper. His vision became more acute. His muscles hurt with the need to fully change.

Bay was covered in a sheen of sweat. He was breathing in ragged pants. "Humans," he managed to push out.

"What about them?" Storm growled, taking another step towards Bay. "What the fuck happened? My human?"

he snarled. "What of Jolene?"

Torrent grabbed his arm and pulled him back. "Give Bay space. He needs half a minute to catch his breath. Nod if the female is okay."

Bay crouched over, putting his hands on his thighs. His mouth was open as he gulped in air. He nodded once. "She was okay."

"Was?" Everything in him tightened. He wanted to lunge at Bay and demand immediate answers.

"I was at the rear." Bay gulped more air, his face no longer as red as it had been. "I thought I saw something." He shrugged. "Helicopters, two of them." He sucked in a few more breaths and Storm wanted to scream. He had to bite back a snarl. His brother's hand tightened on his arm.

"We all dropped."

"Dropped?" Storm yelled. "What the fuck does that mean?"

"There was a rocky outcrop, I used that for cover." More breathing. "While the others were closer to a treed section, so they headed for that. The choppers must have seen something because they began to circle. One even landed. Three humans made their way to the wooded area on foot." He swallowed, licking his lips. "While the focus was on them I bolted for home."

"So, you don't know what happened? Were they armed?" His voice was becoming more corded. His muscles had started to rope, his limbs to lengthen. He could feel the stumps of his wings pushing through on his back.

"Wait, Storm!" His brother spoke in a gruff voice.

"You can't fly in there. You could start a shit-storm. You could get her killed!"

"Like hell!" he snarled. "I need to save her. Kill them." A snarl, his words thick.

"We need a plan." Torrent yelled. "We also need to try to stay hidden."

More scales pushed up. Claws began to emerge. "Fuck staying—" he didn't get to finish what he was saying. His brother's fist came out of nowhere.

Flood shoved her behind him, motioning for her to crouch down, which she did. A twig snapped under her sneaker, making her flinch. How did these shifters move so noiselessly? She could even hear herself breathing. Nothing else seemed to make a sound. There was no wind. Even the birds had stopped chirping.

The boulder was hard and cold against her back. She wouldn't be able to hold this position for long since her thighs were already feeling strained. She was too nervous to sit on her ass in case she had to move quickly. Sweat trickled between her breasts.

Beck crouched down beside Flood. He whispered something and Flood nodded, turning to her. "Bay made it to the other side of the ridge, we're sure he would have gone for help."

"Good." She swallowed, her throat feeling dry. "It's more of those hunters, isn't it?"

Flood nodded, his face looking pinched. His forehead marred with deep worry lines. "I'm afraid so. Two choppers."

She could hear the engines and the *whoosh whoosh* of the blades.

Flood pointed upwards. "They're circling. They may have spotted something even though we were far away." His frown deepened. "I was so sure we were too far for the human eye to have seen much of anything."

"Maybe they were using binoculars," she said.

"Good point," Flood whispered. "If that's the case, they may have seen us in our dragon forms. They may know we are hiding in here."

"Then again." She shook her head. "We dropped like rocks." Her stomach still felt queasy. "Even with binoculars, it would have been difficult to see much of anything."

"I hope you're right," Beck whispered.

Harbor was a little to the left, his eyes trained at the canopy above.

"We can't be sure of anything. We should rather expect and prepare for the worst," Flood growled.

"I think you are right. They must have seen something, or they would have moved on by now," Jolene said.

Beck narrowed his eyes. "Maybe not or they would have landed, or shot at us, or—"

Jolene felt like the ground dropped out from below her. Her stomach gave a clench and her heart picked up its pace. Adrenaline surged. What if they opened fire? There was nowhere to hide from cold hard bullets.

"You're scaring the female," Flood snarled silently. It was both vicious and quiet, which was weird. "Do not worry, human." He spoke softly and carefully, like he wasn't used to talking in this way. "I will protect you," he added. "I promised the prince I would lay down my life and I will, in a heartbeat."

"We all did," Beck said. "We will do it too. Of that you can be certain."

"So, do not worry…" Harbor looked up, sucking in a breath.

She nodded once. "Thank you." She frowned, the way the men were acting told her that something was up. "What is it?"

Then she knew. One of the choppers was descending. There was that telltale powering down, and yet the noise was getting louder as the chopper dropped lower and lower.

Flood crouched over her, pushing her more firmly against the rock.

Beck cursed. "Let me go and check it out."

Flood nodded once.

Within minutes, Beck was back. He crouched back down. "Three males left the helicopter. They're armed, on foot and headed this way."

"We could ambush them," Harbor said.

Beck frowned. "We could take them, but…"

"No," Flood growled low. "At this stage, it looks as if they are trying to feel things out. I don't think they're sure of anything. We need to hide."

The outcrop of trees was maybe a square mile. Not too much more. There couldn't be too many places to hide in here. Not from armed men at any rate. In the meanwhile, the second chopper continued to circle, so there was no direct escape.

"Up," Flood whispered.

"Up?" she squeaked. "What does that mean?"

"These trees are tall. Their boughs are wide. We need to hide in the canopy. That way we can drop down and kill them if need be."

"Yes," Beck nodded. "Let's do it."

"Human, climb on my back and do not let go. We have a minute tops to get into position." He spoke quickly and quietly, looking from Harbor to Beck. "No noise and no falling," he said the last while locking eyes with her.

She swallowed thickly. "O-okay."

The other two shifters stood up. Flood stayed where he was. Using his thumb, he pointed to his back and she clambered onboard. Jolene gripped his shoulders and secured her ankles around his middle.

Her mouth fell open as she watched Beck scramble up a tree, barely breaking a sweat. Flood gripped a tree trunk and pulled them up. She had to dig her fingers into his shoulders to keep from slipping off.

Moving quickly, he heaved them onto a branch above. Flood grunted softly as he pulled them onto the branch, his hand reaching for the next limb. His biceps bulged. He pulled them up, swinging to a thicker bough.

No falling and no noise. Jolene bit back a yell as her hand slipped, almost losing its grip. She folded her arms around him, holding on like a baby monkey. Only, she suspected a baby monkey would be much better at this sort of thing. Hopefully, she wasn't choking him. Her muscles ached from holding on by the time he pulled them onto a wide branch, when in reality, Flood had only been climbing for twenty seconds max. The branch sloped downwards but was relatively level at the truck.

He motioned for her to lie on the branch. "Do not fall," he mouthed. Then he held his finger over his lips and climbed higher. Making it look easy.

She lay down like he said, careful not to let any limbs dangle over the edge. At first, her heart beat frantically and her senses reached out for anything. Any noise. Any flicker of movement below. Not that she could see much through the branches. She measured her breathing, fearful that they would hear her. Stupid, of course since she was too high up.

Seconds ticked by, turning into minutes. The noise of the chopper flying overhead didn't let up. The engine whine grew softer and softer before becoming louder again. *Whoosh whoosh* went the rotor blades. No-one moved. No-one made a sound.

Then there was the sound of a twig snapping and leaves crushing. If she hadn't been straining though she might have missed it. Someone was below them. Jolene wanted to hold her breath, but she was afraid of passing out and falling. Instead, she took small breaths. There was a crunch of gravel further off. Then silence, except for the circling chopper. Had the guy moved off or was he right under them and she didn't know it? Were they still circling the outcrop of trees? She strained to hear something other than the engine noise and the whoosh of the rotors.

More minutes ticked by.

More still.

What was that? She stopped breathing. Even stilled her inner voice as her hearing strained. *Yes!* It was the second helicopter. It was lifting. Then it was moving off. They both were.

Several more minutes ticked by. There was movement from above. Flood came into view. He was climbing back down.

"They're gone," Beck called up from below.

"Thank god!" She pushed out a breath. It didn't take more than a second or two for Flood to reach her. She climbed onto his back.

"No falling." He winked at her.

She choked out a laugh, her body still buzzing with adrenaline. "Don't drop me."

Flood chuckled, his body shook. It didn't last for more than three seconds and he was back to being Mister Serious. Jolene squeezed her eyes shut, holding on tight.

She was thrilled to put her feet on solid ground.

All three dragons cocked their heads, all listening for something at the same time. Beck smiled and Harbor relaxed.

"What is it?"

"Several dragons are incoming," Flood said. "Let's make our way there." The guys surrounded her, two in front and one behind.

Within minutes they were exiting the forest. There were fifteen dragons. Only two of them shifted after landing. One, she noticed, had a golden chest. She was both disappointed and relieved to see it wasn't Storm. More disappointed, she realized when her lip quivered. She bit down on it, sucking in a deep breath.

"We made sure they were well out of our territory," the dragon said as soon as he was in hearing distance of them. "I have another fifteen of our best warriors trailing to ensure they don't double back." Then he turned blue eyes on her. "I am Tide. I'm Storm's brother." He held out his hand and Jolene shook it. "I'm sorry this happened," he said, eyes narrowing with concern.

"It's not your fault these assholes are snooping around your land."

Tide broke out in a wide grin that reminded her so much of Storm that her heart actually stuttered inside her chest.

"I can see why Storm likes you so much." He gave the side of her arm a light tap.

Why did everyone keep insisting Storm had feelings for her? If that were true, surely he would be there himself? Surely, he would have taken her home himself? "I'm sorry my little brother couldn't make it out himself." Tide said, obviously reading disappointment on her face. "He wanted to. In fact, he was ready to rush in without thought or backup. Would've got himself – all of you – killed, if he had."

"Where is he then?" she asked.

"Nursing a headache by now, I would suspect." Tide flashed a quick smile.

He must have caught her confused look because he went on.

"He was so gung-ho, my brother…Torrent…the king…I think you met him – knocked him out cold. Had to."

Beck choked out a laugh.

"Is he okay?" Jolene asked, worried.

"He's absolutely fine. Like I said, he'll be nursing one hell of a headache, but he'll be okay." Tide snickered. "He'll have one or two loose teeth and maybe a cracked jaw." He shook his head, still grinning.

"You call that fine!" she yelled. What was wrong with these shifters?

Tide made a face. "Torrent packs one hell of a punch. Don't forget, we heal quickly. Now," he smiled at her, his eyes clouding with concern, "would you like to continue home, or would you rather return to the lair? Torrent has invited you to spend one last night with us. He thought you might be too shaken to continue. Thought you might want to see Storm."

It would be wonderful to go back. To see Storm. To feel his arms around her, comforting and warm. To see that he was fine with her own eyes. "Are you sure he's okay?" she asked Tide, who nodded.

"Very." He smiled.

"Then I think it's best I go home. Please thank Torrent. Tell Storm I hope he gets better soon." In the end, she couldn't go through it again. To watch the minutes tick by, knowing it was one of the last she would ever spend with the man she loved. No, it was better this way.

"You sure?" Beck asked, frowning. "I'm sure Storm will be worried about you."

"You can reassure him."

"I will do that," Beck said.

"Shall we head out?" Flood asked.

Jolene nodded. She was doing the right thing. Why did it feel so wrong?

CHAPTER 24

Two weeks and one day later...

Jolene knocked twice, turning her head so that she could listen to his response.

"Come in," he said immediately. Then again, he was expecting her. He'd set up this meeting and his PA had announced her upon her arrival.

Rob smiled as she walked in, lines crinkled the skin around his eyes. "Take a seat." He gestured to one of the chairs at his desk. He tossed a pen onto the note-pad in front of him and ran a hand through his thick, salt and pepper—more salt than pepper – hair.

"I'm sure you know why you're here?" He leaned back in his chair, clearly loving the fact that he held her future in his hands. His smile straddled the line somewhere between humor and a smirk. He folded his arms.

Jolene sat down. "Yes." She nodded. This was either one of those talks where he would let her down gently, or he would be promoting her. Her stomach felt wound up. Carla Jackson had a meeting straight after this. It was impossible to tell just by looking at him which way this was going. They would soon know their fate though. "I need you to know something, Rob." She shouldn't do this. The old Jolene told her not to. The old Jolene begged her even. The new Jolene, on the other hand, was a little more impulsive. The old Jolene could go to hell. Fact was, Storm was right, she was great at what she did. If this blew up in her face, Jolene would find another position and easily. She owed it to herself to be straight. To go for it, and she would.

"Sure. Okay." Rob looked at her with narrowed eyes, sizing her up. "Go ahead," he prompted.

Her tongue suddenly felt thick in her mouth. Her lips dry. She could do this. Jolene sucked in a deep breath. "I hope you're about to tell me that I've been promoted. Why?" She leaned back in her own chair, folding her arms across her lap. She suddenly felt calm and very sure of herself. "For several reasons. Firstly, because I deserve it. I've made this company a lot of money over the years, especially since bringing on Dell Apples as a client. They're our biggest client, as you know." She paused. "And then, secondly, because I won't be able to work for Carla. She's good, very good – not as good as I am, but an understandable candidate and a formidable adversary. Bottom line, it won't work. I sincerely hope you choose me, but if not, I'll be handing in my resignation. I wanted you to know that before you said anything."

A slow smile spread on Rob's lips.

She forced herself to stay where she was. To stay relaxed. Not to fidget. Dammit, but she loved this job.

Had she just thrown it away? It didn't matter. It was true, she couldn't work for Carla. No damned way.

"Are you saying that if I decided on Carla, that I should change my mind? Are you threatening me, Miss Pierce?"

"Not a threat." She shook her head. "I thought it was best you knew, and yes, if you decided on Carla, I'm giving you a chance to change your mind…sir." She quickly tacked on the last, not wanting to sound too pushy.

Rob laughed. "Just so you know, I picked you, Jolene. You have the position if you want it." He shook his head, his smile wide. "I have to say, I was a little worried about choosing you. You know your stuff, you're a hard worker and a good leader, but you tend to be a little too rigid sometimes. You're not much of a risk taker and that worried me, but today," he chuckled, "you proved me wrong. It took some balls to lay it out there. Heck, there's a good chance I would've changed my mind if I had gone with Carla. You're the new Marketing Director." He stood up. "Congratulations."

Jolene thought she would be thrilled. This is what she had been working so hard for. Nothing. She forced a smile. "Great! I'm glad to hear it. Thank you."

Rob held out his hand and she shook it, feeling numb. "You're going to—"

Just then, a buzz sounded at his desk. "Just a second," Rob said, picking up his phone. He listened and frowned. "My appointment with her isn't for another ten minutes." He looked at his watch and then at Jolene. "Okay, I'll tell her." He put the phone down. "That was my PA, she says Carla is looking for you and that you need to head back to your desk."

"Why?"

"Your guess is as good as mine. Maybe Carla has organized a celebration for her new boss."

"But Carla doesn't know, does she?"

"I told her this morning," Rob said. "She asked me straight and I told her. Our meeting in ten minutes is a formality." He shrugged.

If nothing else, Carla was straight. That and an ass-licker. It wouldn't surprise her if she *was* throwing a celebration party downstairs. Jolene nodded. "I'd better go then."

"Celebratory drinks with the board at Hershies after work?" He raised his brows in question. It wasn't really a question though, she would be expected to attend.

Hey, it wasn't like she had anything better to do. It wasn't lost on her either that Carla had kids. She was a divorcee with way more responsibility. The fact that Jolene didn't would have counted in her favor. Corporate sucked. "I'll be there."

Rob was already sitting back at his desk, eyes on his computer. Pen back in hand. "Six sharp," he said as she walked out.

Had Carla organized a celebration? She wouldn't put it past the woman to immediately start sucking up now that she was her boss. Jolene halted in her tracks, she needed a minute to soak it in. Marketing Director. It felt good, but it didn't feel great. It didn't feel like she thought it would feel. Her mind wandered back to Storm, to her time with the dragons. She was still hurting. Still missing him. Jolene sucked in a deep breath, swallowing down a lump. That same damn lump that always clogged her throat whenever she allowed herself to think of him. There was no time for that right now. Jolene began walking back to her office. For now, she'd throw herself into her work. She'd be the best damned Marketing... *What?*

The guy standing in her office was big. He had his back to her, so it was hard to tell if she knew him. He had broad shoulders and was well-muscled. He reminded her of a shifter. Couldn't be though. Not here. It was that, or he was a *GQ* model. He was wearing a collared shirt and a pair of black suit pants. What was a *GQ* model doing in her office?

Carla was giggling and twisting a lock of hair around her finger. Her cheeks were a bright pink. Jolene's heart beat a whole lot faster as she rounded the corner.

"Beck," she gasped, clasping her chest. "What are you doing here?" She couldn't help but smile. It was so good to see him.

"Hello, Jolene." His eyes sparkled. "I came to fetch you."

"Fetch me?" She felt confused. Must have looked confused.

"Yes, the prince wants to see you."

"Prince!" Carla spluttered. "What prince?" She looked from Beck to her and back again.

"Did Jolene not tell you all about her—"

"Stop," Jolene interrupted. "I didn't say much of anything about my vacation. It's not anyone's business. Especially since this is my place of business."

Beck nodded. "Makes sense." He winked at Jolene.

"You met a prince while you were on holiday, didn't you?" Carla gaped at her.

"Maybe," Jolene muttered, wanting Carla off her back. "It was nothing," she quickly added.

"Couldn't have been nothing, since it looks like he wants to see you again." Carla was smiling from ear to ear. "I thought your whole 'taking a cruise' thing was silly. Looks like I was wrong."

Jolene ignored Carla. Her mind racing. What the hell was going on?

"Get your things together," Beck said. "We need to go. Our flight leaves in half an hour."

"Oh, you're too late then." Carla looked happy. In fact, she was gloating. "Boarding gates will have closed. Poor thing." She shook her head, faking concern.

"Actually, we're on a private jet, so I think we'll make it just fine." Beck hooked his thumbs into his pants pockets.

"I can't just up and leave." Jolene shook her head, feeling excitement build inside her regardless. She tried to tamp it down. She needed more answers first.

"The prince insisted that I not take no for an answer."

Carla giggled, her eyes on Beck. "Can I get your number? You take the prince," Carla glanced her way, "I'll take the bodyguard. I like buff guys." She winked at Beck, flirting with him shamelessly.

Beck chuckled. "Oh female, that's where you would be wrong. The prince is bigger than I am."

"He is?" Carla's mouth dropped open.

Beck nodded. "And more good-looking. His cock is bigger than mine is as well."

Jolene bit down on her bottom lip to keep from laughing. The look on Carla's face was comical. It shut her right up. She sat down, with a bump, on the edge of Jolene's desk. *'What the hell is this?'* she asked herself for the tenth time since seeing it was Beck.

"Let's go," he insisted. "I don't want to have to throw you over my shoulder."

Carla made a squeaking noise and started fanning herself. "If you don't go, I will."

Like hell! "I can clear my schedule for the afternoon but will need to be back by six."

"No can do." Beck smiled. "You'll be lucky to make it back by tomorrow."

"I can't just leave. Trust Golden Boy to expect me to drop everything and come running when he crooks a finger." Her heart was pounding. This was probably all a game to him. One last fling. Or something stupid like that. "You're sure you don't know what this is about?"

"I wasn't briefed beyond taking you to a certain location. At a certain time." He looked at his watch and frowned. "By any means necessary."

Carla squeaked again. "You sure you don't want my number?"

"You have one minute," Beck said. She could see he meant it.

"Pushy much?"

"I'm under order." Beck winked at her and Carla swooned, clutching at her chest.

"Do I need anything?" she asked.

Beck shook his head. "It's all arranged."

Jolene pushed out a breath. She picked up her phone and asked to speak to her boss.

"Yes," he said, sounded irritated at being interrupted.

"Hi, Rob, something has come up, I need to reschedule our six o'clock."

"What?" He sounded flustered. That and a touch angry. "You can't make the board reschedule. Drinks are tonight. You need to be there!"

"I can't make it. Have drinks without me then. Please apologize on my behalf, but it can't be helped."

"It's your night. You can't not be there."

Shit! Was she killing her career before it even began? Maybe. Was she going to go anyway? How could she not? "I'm sorry, there's nothing I can do."

He pushed out a breath. "I'll see what I can do about rescheduling and Jolene…"

"Yes?"

"Don't make a habit of this."

"I won't and thank you! I owe you one." She licked her lips. A habit? Yes, she really hoped that meeting with the prince would soon become a habit. *'Oh Storm,'* she silently prayed, *'please don't let me down. Don't let this be another game.'*

CHAPTER 25

This time there was no Christina to egg her on. To push her to walk one more mile. To go that little bit faster. Nevertheless, she trudged on, putting one foot in front of the other. Boob sweat was still very much a thing. It was happening right then.

Why the hell was she out here? Where was Storm? He was getting a piece of her mind when he finally turned up. This was just like him.

It was all game.

All a freaking game to him.

Once again, her career was in jeopardy because he couldn't think further than his own damned nose. She stopped and covered her face with her hand and groaned. She'd made her boss – the CEO of her company – reschedule with the board. She'd treated the guy who paid her bloody salary – who held her livelihood in his hands – like her own personal assistant.

Jolene groaned again. She should have refused. Should never have come.

Beck had dropped her off over an hour ago. He'd given

her a change of clothing, trainers too and had told her to head out. He'd handed her the backpack and had told her to start walking. She'd demanded to be taken back, but he had laughed, shifted and disappeared into the sky.

Jerk.

He hadn't told her anything. By the prince's orders. "He can take his orders and stick them," she mumbled.

"What's that, Sweet Lips?"

Jolene yelled and turned, almost falling over her own feet. Storm was right behind her, leaning up against a tree looking smug. He was smirking. Asshole thought this was hilarious. Her heart did beat faster though at the sight of him. His dark hair was tousled. His amethyst eyes bright and exquisite, like the rest of him. So darned handsome it took her breath away, which irritated her. Why? Because she was in love with him…and she was just a game to him.

"I said, you can take your orders and shove them where the sun don't shine, Golden Boy." She narrowed her eyes and pointed at him while she spoke. "You had better have a damned good reason for uprooting my life once again. For dragging me out here. I told the board they needed to reschedule our meeting this evening. I haven't even been officially announced as the new Marketing Director, and I'm already throwing my weight around."

Storm grinned. "You got the promotion? Of course, you got it. I'm so proud of you."

"I might not have a job when I get back after this," she grumbled. Truth was, she didn't care about the stupid job. She was scared out of her wits though. "Why am I here?" It had to be asked.

Storm shrugged. "I'm hunting you."

She rolled her eyes and groaned. "Let me guess." She locked eyes with his. "You were bored. Is that right? You needed to liven up your life and so you had Beck pick me up."

He nodded, folding his arms. "You're not far off. I was very bored. I've been bored to tears since you left. No-one to argue with. No-one to—"

"Yeah, yeah, I know where this is going. No-one to warm your bed."

He gave her a half-smile. "I was going to say fuck, but," he nodded, "I guess they're the same thing."

She snorted. "Well, you can forget coming anywhere near me."

"Still playing hard to get I see. This is almost like a repeat of the last time. I'm sorry it took me so long. Over two weeks. If it was up to me, this would have happened much sooner."

"What? What do you mean?" *Why had he said that?*

"I would've organized this whole thing sooner, only we had to wait to be sure those slayers didn't come back."

"You mean the guys in the helicopters?"

"One and the same," he said. "They haven't been back since the day they almost caught you." His jaw tensed and his eyes darkened. "I was beside myself with worry. I—"

"Your brother…" It took her a moment to recall his name. "Tide mentioned that Torrent had to knock you out."

Storm grimaced and touched his jaw. "He blindsided me with a right hook. Broke my jaw in three places and knocked out two teeth."

Her eyes widened. "Oh my god! Are you okay? You look okay, but—"

Storm chuckled. "It took me an hour to come to and another couple of hours to heal but I'm fine. Good as new." He flashed her a full set of teeth. "It was too late to come after you though. You were long gone by then and the kings put a strict lock-down on any movement in or out of the four kingdoms. That restriction was lifted this morning. The slayers seem to have backed off...at least for now. We're not sure what they're planning but that's a discussion for another day."

"Okay." She wasn't sure where he was going with this.

He pulled in a deep breath. "I wanted to recreate the hunt." He looked around them, looking pleased with himself.

"I'm sure you did." She shook her head, feeling frustrated to her core. "This isn't a game to me though, Storm. It never was. I did have fun in the end but now it's over. We don't want the same things. I need to move on with my life." She needed to try to get over him, which wasn't going to happen if they kept seeing each other.

"You told me that males always end up mating the very next female they are with after you."

"Yes." She nodded. "Why is this even relevant?" *Why rub it in?*

"You told me that I would end up serious about the next female I caught in a hunt. You said that, didn't you?" he asked when she didn't respond.

"What are you saying?" It couldn't be what it sounded

like.

He licked his lips and wrung his hands together before holding them still at his sides. Storm looked nervous all of a sudden. "Well, here we are. I just hunted and caught you, Jolene. It's my own mini-hunt." He chuckled.

She had to laugh too. Partly because she was suddenly feeling nervous too and partly because he was such an idiot. A cute, sweet idiot of a man. "We're the only two taking part so it's not technically…Wait a minute…we *are* the only two taking part, right?"

"It's just us and it's supposed to be symbolic. A romantic gesture."

"Flowers and chocolates are romantic. Boob sweat on the other hand," she mumbled, trying hard to hold back a grin and failing.

"Look," he swallowed thickly, his Adam's apple bobbing, "when I thought they had you…when…" His eyes widened for a moment. They turned a touch glassy. "It was horrendous thinking that they might get you. What they might do to you if they did. Slayers are not nice people. They're not scouring our lands for any good reason other than because they know we are here. All I know is that their intentions are evil. They wouldn't be armed to the gills with silver artillery otherwise." He pulled in another deep breath, letting it out slowly through his nose. "I'm glad Torrent knocked me out because I wasn't thinking about anything other than rescuing you, which under the circumstances would have put you in untold danger. All of us in untold danger. I hate that I had to wait two weeks." He tucked a piece of wayward hair behind her ear. "I decided not to contact you during that time because I wanted it to be a surprise. I wanted to tell you in person."

"Tell me what?" By now she was holding her breath. She bit down on her bottom lip.

"That you are my next female. You're my last female. You *are* the one I'm serious about because I'm crazy about you. I don't want anyone else. My brother was right…I did know it when you left, and I let you go anyway because I'm an asshole and an idiot and all of the other things you love calling me."

"You're not." She shook her head and sniffed. Jolene quickly wiped a hand over her eyes when she realized she was crying.

"Yeah, I am. I'm an idiot too for running scared. My dad died in a freak accident when I was six. My mom died from a broken heart less than two years later. I watched her pine for him every day and I guess it scared the shit out of me. I was looking at it all wrong though. I looked at it from the negative side. They loved each other so much. I thought that kind of love was bad, but I was wrong. I *do* want that kind of love…I have that kind of love with you. I'm not running scared anymore. I love you, Sweet Lips." He cupped her cheeks. "I'm so glad I had the good sense to throw you over my shoulder because you are the female for me. You're it! You're mine!" He leaned in and kissed her, taking her breath away.

She grabbed his ass and squeezed, rubbing herself against him. "I've missed you, Golden Boy. Missed you so much and I love you too. There were moments…lots of moments over the last two weeks where I wished it wasn't true, but it is. I'm not sure how it happened but it did."

"It happened because I'm awesome."

She choked out a laugh.

He turned serious. "Because we're awesome together. Does this mean you agree to mating me?"

"What do you think? Because," she narrowed her eyes, "if you think I'm moving in, you're sadly mistaken. I'm not giving the milk away for free."

"No moving in. I want that milk. I want it really badly."

She laughed and then realized what he was saying and stopped. "No dating?" Her heart beat faster.

"No dating!"

"No?" Faster still.

"Nope." He shook his head. "I'm making this official! You do agree to mating with me?" He looked at her, chest heaving, eyes wide.

"Of course, yes."

He hoisted her into his arms and kissed her until she struggled to breathe or think. Then he put her down and stepped away from her.

Jolene frowned "This is the part where you're supposed to throw me on the ground and make passionate love to me."

"Um…I wouldn't recommend it." He shook his head.

"Why? What's going on?"

"You didn't think I'd let you wander around alone did you?" Storm raised his brows. "Those slayers could come back." Storm whistled, and a couple of dragons took to the air around them. "I'm not risking your life, but I wanted this to be special. I wanted you to know you're it for me."

"You're so sweet and I love you."

Storm kissed her again, his lips brushing hers. "What do you say we head home?"

"Sounds good." She nodded, smiling so hard her cheeks hurt.

CHAPTER 26

Storm could hardly believe that this day was finally here and that Jolene had agreed to everything. It was the first time they had both readily agreed to the same thing at the same time. Good thing too, since this time it counted for so much.

He flapped harder, wanting to get home already. To their home. To their future together. Storm was glad he didn't have to make his way back on foot as would have been customary if his mini-hunt had actually been a real hunt.

He made straight for his own patio, again glad he didn't have to go through the main public balcony as was normally customary for a hunt. He carefully placed Jolene on her feet and then shifted as soon as his claws touched the ground.

Jolene was the most beautiful thing he had ever laid eyes on. Her hair was in a loose, wind-swept ponytail, her brown eyes wide. He cupped her face in his hands and told her so, capturing her mouth with his. "I love kissing you," he groaned as he pulled back. "You're the first female I've enjoyed it with."

She rolled her eyes. "You're not supposed to talk about previous conquests."

"Why not? You are my last and most important conquest."

"And that's supposed to make it better?" She was smiling.

"Yes." He brushed his lips against hers. "Talking about conquests." He hoisted her into his arms.

"I need to shower first," she said as she threaded her hands around his neck.

"No, you don't." He shook his head.

"We can shower together." She raised her brows.

"No!" He shook his head some more.

"I have boob sweat."

Storm choked out a laugh. "I know it's sick, but I love boob sweat."

"Ewwww."

"Let me reiterate, I love *your* boob sweat. I love anything to do with your boobs." He nuzzled his face into her chest as he walked to the door. Jolene giggled as he opened it with one hand.

"That's both really sweet and really gross." She wrinkled her nose.

He shrugged. "I like it dirty remember?" He bobbed his eyebrows. "You couldn't have forgotten already. Besides, I can't wait to lay you out on my bed." He dropped her right in the middle of said bed, watching as she bounced once. "So that I can give your pussy another lesson in French."

Her smile widened. "Now you're talking my language."

He pulled off her trainers and then her socks. *Easy! Slow! Gentle!* He had to make this special for her. Not so straightforward when he was shaking with need. When she scented of candied apples. Tart yet sweet. So delicious, it made his mouth water.

She had already unzipped her jeans and was peeling them down her thighs. He kneeled on the bed and help her get rid of them. Then she unzipped her jacket and pulled off her shirt. Her lacy black bra cupped her tits, showcasing them to perfection. Jolene thrust out her chest and giggled as she caught him gaping at her. "I did warn you about the boob sweat." She said as she unclasped the garment, letting all that lushness free.

"Fuck but you're sexy," Storm growled and he pulled her legs over his shoulders. "Even your pussy is a thing of beauty," he said as he looked down at all that loveliness between her lush thighs

"So crass, Golden Boy."

"Good thing you love it, Sweet Lips," he said as he buried his face in her folds. Stormed licked, sucked and possibly threw in a nip or two for good measure. When his hands joined the party, his sweet little human soon came crashing down, yelling his name as she did.

Finally.

Finally.

It was time. Storm pulled off his pants and crawled over Jolene, caging her with his body. Her breasts were pressed against his chest. Her heels dug into his back. His cock lined up with her wet center. He longed to drive himself into her.

Her hands draped around his neck. Her breathing was still labored from coming not half a minute ago. Her eyes were hazy, her cheeks flushed. *Gorgeous.*

Vibrating with need, Storm sank his tip inside her with a hard grunt. He leaned in to capture her mouth. To plunder it. Jolene moaned as he sank deeper inside, easing out to slowly, ever so slowly sink deeper and deeper. In and out using infinite care. He broke the kiss, moving to her neck, her ear. Jolene moaned some more.

Slow.

Easy.

Deep.

"You feel amazing," he whispered. "Are amazing." He lifted her legs, angling himself deeper. Jolene cried out.

Bingo.

It took everything in him not to fuck her. To make her come then and there. His balls pulled up just thinking of doing it. *Worship. Worship. Dammit.* This was about her. *Slow. Slow. There. Right fucking there.* Jolene dug her nails into his back and groaned. Her thighs clamped tight. She made these noises, but fuck, he was also making ridiculous noises. Grunts and groans. Pure ecstasy and pure torture rolled into one.

Poised just above her, his face an inch or two from hers. Her eyes were at half-mast, hazy with pleasure. Her lips. Rosy, parted and slightly swollen. *Fuck, those lips.* He loved them. Loved her so much. His heart swelled with the emotion. He brushed a kiss against her mouth. In and out. His balls so high and so tight, it hurt. His orgasm there.

Just there. So was hers, he could feel her legs vibrate. Her nipples were hard against his chest.

He smiled. At least, he hoped it looked like a smile, his skin felt too tight. "Are you going to come for me?" he asked, his voice a deep, panted rasp.

She sort of smiled back, her head falling back, her eyes fluttering closed. "Are you going to make me?" she moaned.

"Yes." He ran his teeth along her throat, every instinct told him to sink them into her. To mark. To take. *Not yet.* He nipped, biting without breaking the skin.

Excitement coursed through him as he nipped some more. It felt so good, so right. He thrust harder, just that tiny bit faster. He felt Jolene's body tense beneath him. Every muscle, every sinew, every fiber pulled tight. He pulled back so he didn't accidentally bite her. He wanted to watch her take her pleasure. Storm looked into her eyes. Her nails dug into him. They widened for a moment, then rolled back and her jaw turned slack. Her pussy clamped around him. It couldn't be helped. His body took over, jerking into her hard, milking her. He groaned her name as he spilled himself inside her. Jolene yelled his name and something incoherent as well. He kept going until she was completely spent, then he rolled on his back, pulling her lifeless body into his arms. If she wasn't breathing so heavily he might think she was dead.

She moaned.

"Are you okay?" he asked, feeling concerned.

No answer.

"Did I hurt you?" He swept the hair from her face. "I

thought I was being careful," he added.

Jolene smiled and lifted her head a little to look at him. She looked drunk. "I'm fine," she half-slurred. "Better than fine." She let her head drop back on his chest. Then she giggled, still sounding drunk. "That was amazing."

He caressed her hair. He couldn't help himself. He had to. "Was it the best?"

She laughed, lifting her head so she could squint at him. "Yes, okay. Yes, dammit. It was the best."

"Yes!" he yelled, fist-punching the air. "That was the first time I've ever made love to anyone ever." He chuckled. "I can't believe you thought it was the best. I think it needs work," he grumbled the last.

"Oh I've come much harder but that was the best." She kissed him on the chest.

"What?" He sat up, dragging her up too. "Are you telling me one of your loser ex-boyfriends did a better job?" Jealousy burned. It ate at him. It clawed him from the inside out. "At least I have a very long time to change your mind." The thought helped but not much.

Jolene smiled. She leaned in and cupped his jaw. "No silly. I was talking about you."

Storm frowned. "That doesn't make any sense. I made you come the hardest, but I wasn't the best?"

"Exactly." She shook her head. "Not until right now. This was the first time you put any emotion in the act. The first time it was more than just fucking. It was amazing. So special." She bit down on her bottom lip, her eyes glassy.

"It was special to me too. I wanted to make love to you before. I wanted to really badly but…I couldn't."

She put her arms around him. "It wasn't the right time."

"No." He shook his head.

"So, are we mated?" Her eyes shone. "It works with biting, right?"

"Not yet," he said. "It's not something we have to rush into. I have to bite you, as in draw blood, before it's official."

Her eyes clouded just a little. "You do still want to, don't you?"

"Oh yes. Very fucking badly." He kissed her. "I don't want to rush though. Did you like it? My teeth on you?"

She nodded. "Yes, it felt really good. Like crazy good."

"You are supposed to have a spot on your neck, an erogenous zone." He licked his lips and she tracked the movement.

"Oh really?" She raised her brows.

"When I find it, you'll beg me to bite you. I mean to really bite you."

"Will I now?" She looked at him from under her lashes.

"Yes, you most certainly will." He nodded once.

"Leaves us with a bit of a dilemma then." She cocked her head.

He loved and hated where this was going. *This female.* "What dilemma would that be, Sweet Lips?"

"Well, I have this little rule."

Fuck! "What rule is that?" He traced the underside of her breast with the tip of his finger.

"I don't beg." She shook her head.

"Not ever?"

"Never."

"Can't or won't?" he asked. He was so in love. So much so that he was going to have to make Beck punch him later. Hard!

"Both."

"I guess I'll have to change your mind about that." He squeezed her nipple softly, loving how her pupils dilated.

"Not happening." She shook her head.

"Want to bet?"

"I don't have to."

"I *will* change your mind and you *will* beg me to bite you." He leaned in and suckled on her nipple.

Jolene moaned as he released her. "Says who?" She was breathing heavily, her eyes glinting. The challenge in them apparent.

He smiled. "Your body, Sweet Lips, your body tells me so."

"Too bad my body isn't in charge, Golden Boy."

He looked up and into her gorgeous eyes. *Game on!* Jolene was going to beg him, and he was going to love the hell out of making her.

AUTHOR'S NOTE

Charlene Hartnady is a USA Today Bestselling author. She loves to write about all things paranormal including vampires, elves and shifters of all kinds. Charlene lives on an acre in the country with her husband and three sons. They have an array of pets including a couple of horses.

She is lucky enough to be able to write full time, so most days you can find her at her computer writing up a storm. Charlene believes that it is the small things that truly matter like that feeling you get when you start a new book, or when you look at a particularly beautiful sunset.

BOOKS BY THIS AUTHOR

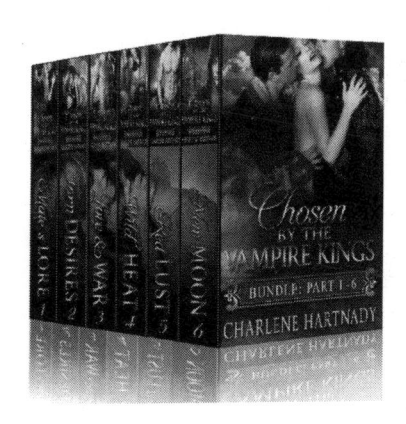

The Chosen Series:
Book 1 ~ Chosen by the Vampire Kings
Book 2 ~ Stolen by the Alpha Wolf
Book 3 ~ Unlikely Mates
Book 4 ~ Awakened by the Vampire Prince
Book 5 ~ Mated to the Vampire Kings (Short Novel)
Book 6 ~ Wolf Whisperer (Novella)
Book 7 ~ Wanted by the Elven King

The Program Series (Vampire Novels):
Book 1 ~ A Mate for York
Book 2 ~ A Mate for Gideon
Book 3 ~ A Mate for Lazarus
Book 4 ~ A Mate for Griffin
Book 5 ~ A Mate for Lance
Book 6 ~ A Mate for Kai
Book 7 ~ A Mate for Titan

Shifter Night:
Book 1 ~ Untethered
Book 2 ~ Unbound
Book 3 ~ Unchained

The Feral Series
Book 1 ~ Hunger Awakened
Book 2 ~ Power Awakened

The Bride Hunt Series (Dragon Shifter Novels)
Book 1 ~ Royal Dragon
Book 2 ~ Water Dragon
Book 3 ~ Dragon King
Book 4 ~ Lightning Dragon
Book 5 ~ Forbidden Dragon
Book 6 ~ Dragon Prince

Demon Chaser Series (No cliffhangers):
Book 1 ~ Omega
Book 2 ~ Alpha
Book 3 ~ Hybrid
Book 4 ~ Skin
Demon Chaser Boxed Set Book 1–3

Excerpt

ROYAL Dragon
THE BRIDE HUNT

CHARLENE HARTNADY

CHAPTER 1

They were damned either way. Whether the lesser kings accepted the proposal or not.

Damned.

The word rolled around in his mind. It made his gut churn and left a bad taste in his mouth. Coal looked at each of the four males, from one to the next. All of them were powerful specimens. Pure royal blood ran through their veins. Their golden chest markings were testament to that. As was his own. He felt such pride at being a royal prince, at being a fire dragon.

Granite, the earth king had dark hair and even darker eyes, like polished onyxes, much like his own. There were flecks of black within his chest marking, to show that he was an earth dragon. Of his personality, it was known far and wide that he was both strong and a hothead.

Then there was Torrent, the water king. His hair was so light it was almost white. His eyes as blue as the ocean itself. Flecks of green could be found in his golden chest markings to represent their element familiarity. The male was excessively arrogant but likeable, an odd combination.

Thunder had eyes the color of amethyst jewels. As the air king the blue flecks within his golden markings were definitely prominent. Though normally calm, the male looked agitated at the moment. This meeting needed to run smoothly. Coal only hoped that the males would accept the proposal put forward by his brother, the fire king. Blaze was the strongest of the dragons. He had eyes the color of emeralds. He, like Coal and the rest of the fire dragons, could breathe fire, which gave them a superior advantage over the others. Their golden markings were pure.

The air king held the platinum goblet with such a grip that Coal was sure it would crush at any moment. His face was red. Scales were visible through the golden tattoo on his chest, making more blue bleed through. A sure sign that he was moments away from changing.

"No," Thunder growled. The word was accompanied by a billow of smoke. It left his mouth in a lazy, curling tendril, at complete odds with the male who expelled it. The air king was fire breathing mad. Such a pity for him that a bit of useless smoke was all he could produce. Thunder had better watch his step. Blaze looked relaxed as he leaned back in his chair, but Coal knew better. His brother was not as calm as he seemed. The slight tic in his jaw was evidence of that.

The air king clenched his teeth together for a few long moments, clearly trying to get himself back under control. *Best he do that, and quickly.* Blaze would not tolerate such outbursts, even from another king. "You can forget about having one of the air females. The agreement was, your sister for one of my tribe. A fair trade."

The earth and water kings moved restlessly in their chairs, as did the princes at their sides. They were not privy to the arrangement that had been made between the fire and the air kingdoms. Had the agreement worked out, it would have put both fire and air at the top of the food chain, with their own tribe, fire, as the solid leaders over the four kingdoms. As it stood though, they were still at the head of the game despite the deal falling apart at the last minute.

Blaze twisted the ring on his finger. "I will agree to the three of you taking human mates on the condition that I get to have one of the fertile dragon females." His green eyes blazed. He dropped his hands back at his sides. There was not a single sign of tension in his body. Not true. There it was again, that tic. Only, you had to know where to look and if you blinked once too often you might miss it.

Thunder laughed. There was no humor to the sound. "You are an arrogant bastard." The male turned serious in an instant. "We are going to take humans whether you like it or not."

"Do that, and I will destroy you." Blaze's voice was

even. "That goes for all of you." He let his gaze go from one king to the next before returning to Thunder.

The other two kings didn't say a word. Although Coal wasn't sure if it was because they knew their places. Something was brewing and it was clear that these three had discussed this amongst their selves at length.

Thunder leaned forward in his chair. "You are going to single handedly destroy our species. Just because some human female broke your heart doesn't—"

"Say one more word and I'll kill you, so help me . . ." Blaze stood, tension radiated off of him. On the upside, that pesky tic was gone. He and Thunder stared at each other for what felt like a long time. Coal had to work to remain outwardly calm. To refrain from fidgeting like the others. He was the fire prince and heir to the throne, should anything happen to Blaze.

"This is how it's going to go down," Blaze said, his voice still calm and even. "I'm going to take one of your sisters. The rest of you can take humans, if it works out, we'll allow more of our males to take them as well." He sat back down.

Thunder shook his head. He ran a hand through his hair. His blue eyes were bright and filled with a multitude of emotions including anger, frustration and longing.

"Deny the males human females and it's a sure fire way to an uprising. Do you want to be overthrown by your own dragons?" Granite's deep voice reverberated around the large room.

"It wouldn't happen. One example and the coup attempt would be at an end." Blaze narrowed his eyes.

"We need to make it clear that their turn will come. Patience."

"Their patience is waning." Granite's brother, the earth prince, piped up. "Our males get two opportunities per year to be with a female. They are driven to mate and to reproduce. The testosterone in the air is nauseating. I haven't been with a female for months so I can relate." His neck muscles bulged. He was a second prince, as was the case with the water prince. It was puzzling that he was here. It was protocol for the first princes to be present at such occasions.

"I thought I could scent something odd." The earth king choked out a laugh and some of the tension in the room eased. Even Blaze managed a half smile.

"It's enough to drive even the most level headed male completely insane." Granite took a sip of wine from his goblet. "They will not wait."

"What do you propose?" Blaze cocked his head and raised his brows.

"We need to stick with tradition. All of our males need to be afforded the same opportunity despite their standing within the tribe," the earth king said.

"The hunt," Coal muttered.

Blaze nodded. He looked like he was deep in thought. Coal couldn't believe that his brother was actually considering this. Human mates. It was absurd. Humans were far lesser beings. So far below the dragon shifter species. They were small and weak. Coal had never once contemplated going on a stag run. Why, when there were two perfectly good females in their tribe and several more scattered across the kingdoms? He was lucky to have been born a prince. Human females for the lessers maybe, but for the royals, it was a travesty.

Lately, he and Scarlet had been spending more and more time together. The female had hinted about wanting to become his mate. They were discussing the possibility. The only downside was that she was infertile. The female had never gone into heat and probably never would. Granite was right when he said that they had a built-in need to reproduce. Coal wasn't immune to this drive but neither did he want a human. Scarlet would make a good mate. She would keep his bed warm, his hearth lit. He enjoyed rutting her and . . . making conversation. She was adequately attractive. No sparks flew when they were together but that wasn't important. What more did a male need?

His mind immediately moved to thoughts of emotions. His sister had often spoken of love. Of long lingering looks. Of one's heart beating faster when in the presence of another. Of lust so all consuming that it was impossible to keep one's hands to themselves. She spoke of wanting to know everything about another person. What nonsense. He didn't believe that love truly existed. He certainly didn't need it.

No. Once they got out of this meeting, he would discuss mating Scarlet with Blaze. Surely his brother wouldn't refuse him. It wasn't like he planned on taking her for himself. As the fire king, Blaze was destined for a fertile female. There was no other way.

"Yes," Granite paused for a beat. "The hunt. Tradition

and lores cannot be refuted."

Blazed laughed. He shook his head. "You speak of taking humans which is completely against our lores to begin with. Diluting the blood of our species is wrong. Diluting our royal blood is a sacrilege."

"It cannot be helped!" Thunder boomed. "Offer another alternative if you have one. We have no choice." He looked down at his lap, refusing to meet Blaze's gaze for a few beats.

"I agree." The water king leaned forward. "We need to follow this path. Our warriors deserve mates, as do the rest of us."

"Agreed," Granite added. "We are becoming desperate." He gave a humorless chuckle. Sweat dripped from his brow. There was a nervous tension in the air.

"Taking human mates is the only solution. We cannot take too many at once though, a handful of females. Males who take part in the hunt can win themselves a female. The usual rules will apply including the no fire rule." Thunder looked pointedly at Coal before turning his gaze back on Blaze. "Equal opportunity for all." The fire dragons were the only dragons capable of producing fire.

The idiot actually thought that he, prince of fire, would lower himself and take part in such a hunt? For a human? Hardly a prize. It was absurd.

"Where will we find these females?" Blaze asked. "The vampires advertised in the local newspapers, and females came flocking in droves. We, however, do not possess such luxuries. We need to remain hidden. Humans are not permitted to find out about our existence. We were all but wiped out by the humans two centuries ago and our numbers were strong back then. Humans have always feared us, and rightly so." He looked thoughtful for a moment.

"We may be much stronger but they outnumber us by at least a hundred thousand to one. In today's age, they have weapons of far greater power. We would be doomed. Back to my original question, where will we find these females?"

Granite smiled. "We'll simply take them."

"No." Blaze shook his head. "We're not animals. We're not in the business of kidnapping females."

"Granite is right," Thunder said. "We have no other option but to take some of these human females. I've had scouts on the lookout for the right ones. Young, strong, fertile and—"

"No." Blaze hit his fist against the table. "How will it look when human females suddenly start to go missing? Aside from the implications, it wouldn't be right. We are an honor bound species, we don't steal females."

"What if the females were in need of rescuing? What if they were lonely, hungry, destitute? We can save the females, offer them a better life and in the process, we can save ourselves as well."

"It's walking a fine line. Just because someone is desperate and lonely, may not mean that they want to become the mate of a dragon shifter. I don't like it."

The water king shifted in his chair. "It's not ideal," Torrent conceded. "Though dragon shifters have everything a female could want. We offer them good lives.

Females beg me to take them with me when I return from a stag run. It is the same every time without fail."

Granite shrugged. "Maybe we should forget about the hunt and bring females back with us who express an interest in becoming a shifter mate." He raised his brows.

"We've discussed this at length," Thunder growled.

Coal felt irritated at this statement. Proof that the three kings had met privately to discuss this. Why the need for all the secrecy?

The air king narrowed his eyes. "It would not work. Males would fight over females. How would we decide who is eligible to take a human mate? It would be difficult to regulate. A good number of human females would go missing and this would draw attention. What if a female was deceptive and left a mate and children behind? It could be disastrous."

"Your last two points are probably the biggest concerns." Blaze looked thoughtful for a second. "It's a worry regardless of how we proceed."

"Not if we only take females who are destitute," Thunder said. "My tribe has already earmarked numerous females. None of them have family or even many friends. They would be perfect candidates."

"Perfect candidates to abduct?" Blaze sounded exasperated. "Listen to yourself," he growled.

"To be rescued!" Thunder's booming voice filled the room.

"Let's just say that I agree to this hair-brained scheme. *I'm not agreeing,* I'm just giving the whole thing some thought." He sucked in a breath. "Females would need to be in a bad way and in need of saving. They would need to have everything explained to them and would need to be treated with respect and kindness at all times. Even if a male wins one of these females fair and square, he may not force himself on her. Any male found to be forcing a female will pay with his life. The human would need to agree to being mated and later impregnated. She would need to be a willing participant at all times."

"Females will be afraid initially. It's a given." Granite took another glug of wine.

"If a female doesn't want to be with a male, no matter how hard he tries to win her…" Blaze narrowed his eyes. "Then she will be allowed to leave, to return to her old life."

"No," the air king growled. "She would be able to reveal our existence."

"Let's hope that our males are capable of winning the hearts of these females." Blaze smiled. "To be honest though, I don't like the idea in general, whether they can make them fall for them or not. The bloodlines have to be considered. I'm not ready to commit to a yes to such a widespread mating of human females."

"It's not their hearts that we're interested in." Thunder smiled even wider.

"Females are emotional, humans are so much worse. That's why I'm infinitely glad I'm not taking a human mate. Thunder…" He looked the male head on. "Bring your sisters when you return tomorrow. I would like to meet with them. I hope that one of them will agree to becoming my mate."

Thunder's face clouded. He looked both angry and nervous. By the sheen of sweat on his brow and his suddenly pale complexion, Coal would definitely say that he was nervous. "I was very angry when I found out about your sister's pregnancy."

"As was I." Blaze didn't take his eyes off the male for a second. Their sister, Ruby had been promised to the air king. The deal was that Thunder would take Ruby and in return, Blaze could choose a fertile air princess to mate with. Unfortunately, Ruby had other plans and had become pregnant with a vampire male's child. They were mated and happy but things were clearly still heated between the fire and air kingdoms. Thunder had not been happy about the news.

The male in question leaned forward. "I may have made some rash decisions, but you can't blame me." Thunder's eyes were wide and he spoke too quickly.

Oh no.

Coal could sense that whatever Thunder was about to say was not going to be good.

Blaze nodded, urging the other king to continue.

"I gave my sisters to the earth and the water princes, it…" No wonder the second princes were in attendance. No damned wonder. Coal clenched his hands into fists.

Blaze slowly stood up. The tic was back and with a vengeance. Blaze banged his hands on the table. "You did what?" His voice was low and deep.

If what Thunder was saying was true, then there were no more available fertile dragon females left in all four kingdoms. The fire dragons were at risk. Huge risk.

Thunder sucked in a deep breath. "I did what I felt was right. There will be humans and they—"

Blaze threw his head back and roared. At once, the room was engulfed in scorching flames. Chairs crashed and furniture smashed. By the time Blaze was finished, they all had first degree burns. Thunder was missing limbs and only barely alive.

The laundry room was cramped. Clean linen lined the shelved walls. The low hum of washing machines and dryers could be heard in the background. "Room 211 is demanding a clean." Her supervisor looked at her watch. "You've got twenty minutes to get over there and to get it done."

Julie had to refrain from rolling her eyes. She pursed her lips together, holding back a choice response. "I was just there. He had a DND sign up," she finally pushed out. "That's why I called and asked to be given another room to clean." As a temp, she only got paid for the rooms she cleaned and then only after one of the managers checked them once they had been returned back into the system. If there were any errors in any of the suites, a percentage was deducted from her pay. Julie needed to clean a minimum of sixteen rooms per shift. That gave her an average of twenty-five minutes a room. She couldn't afford any errors. Literally.

Callie huffed out a breath, looking irritated. "Well, he's changed his mind." She raised her brows. "Now, do you want to keep arguing or should I give this unit to one of the ladies on the next shift?"

Callie was the best of the bunch. Most of the supervisors treated the temps like slave labor. They got the worst rooms. They had to work like dogs to earn something of an income. It wasn't fun and it certainly wasn't fair but Julie had never had it any other way. This was her life. "I'm on it." She pushed the brake on her trolley and made her way back up the hall.

"Oh and, Julie," Callie called after her.

She turned. "Yeah?"

"Pack up and clock out when you're done. I need to fetch Harry from school today so I can't hang around to wait on you."

"No problem."

"You sure?"

"No sweat." Julie gave a reassuring nod of the head.

"Okay then." Callie nodded back.

Julie continued down the hall. Callie was a single mom. She wasn't really allowed to leave until everyone had checked out but her life was one big juggling act. Rules sometimes had to be broken. Julie understood that more than most.

It was a bit of a haul to the staff elevator. Julie walked as fast as the outdated housekeeping trolley would allow. It had one squeaky wheel and if she wasn't careful the door would open and the amenity drawers would fall out. Every minute she had to work over time to get this room done would be for free. The hotel only paid for time spent on rooms cleaned within the allotted shift and then only if they were perfect. She sighed.

By the end of this month, she'd be up to date with her

rent and then she could start saving. Julie had moved plenty as a kid. They were all small towns just like Walton Springs. There had to be more. There was a whole world out there to explore. Big cities. Beautiful views. Breathtaking sunsets. So much adventure just waiting. She was done with small time. Done with small towns.

She'd never flown in an airplane, much less been to another country. Once she saved up enough though, she was leaving. Suddenly the trolley didn't feel as heavy or the lift so slow. One day . . . one day soon. She just needed to get out of this hole and ahead enough to be able to save. It was going to happen.

Julie gave a double knock on the door. Room 211. "Housekeeping," she announced. There was no answer so she tried again. Maybe the guest had gone out.

She cracked the door open. "Housekeeping." She said again before entering with her spray bottle and cloth in hand. The cumbersome trolley stayed in the hallway. It would be a simple matter of returning to it for new supplies such as bedding and amenities when needed.

"Oh god." She covered her eyes and backtracked. "I'm so sorry," she mumbled.

The guy was middle aged and not bad looking. He had an athletic build and salt and pepper hair. He was also completely naked as the day he was born. Her cheeks heated. *Floor please open up and swallow me whole.*

Why call for housekeeping if you plan on changing just then? Also, when someone announces themselves at the door, respond and ask them to wait.

"Don't be silly," the guy said. "Ignore me, do your

thing, I'll be dressed in a moment. We're both adults."

Damn. Was he a weirdo? He must be. Then again, he had a good body. Well muscled. She opened her eyes and he was searching in the closet. His ass was . . . not bad. *Not looking!* She snapped her head in the opposite direction.

This was weird. He was far too old for her but he had that whole Richard Gere thing going on. His hair had that just showered look even though it was already halfway through the afternoon. Odd! No, he couldn't be doing this on purpose. A guy like him could get a date. Surely. Definitely. She relaxed just a smidgen. He was obviously just comfortable in his own skin.

She was tempted to leave and wait outside. Every minute she stood out there would be money lost though. She needed to get up to date with her rent. If she wasn't so damned desperate. Julie suppressed a sigh, she ignored him and got to work stripping the bed. She was sure that by the time she looked again he would be dressed or even better, out the door. First she removed the cover from the duvet, then the sheet from the bed and was just removing the first pillowcase when she looked up.

What the hell!

A squeaky noise came out of her throat.

"Keep cleaning," the guy said. His face had a pinched look. His back was to the closed closet door. He wasn't dressing. He wasn't even attempting to dress. His hand worked his cock. Up and down. In slow easy strokes. Forget Richard Gere, this guy was a creep with a capital C. Gross!

"What the hell are you doing?" She sounded pissed. Which was good, because she felt pissed. Her cheeks felt hot and she could hear the sound of her heart beating. It was as if the thing was in her ears.

"Ignore me and keep cleaning. I won't touch you." His voice sounded strained. Of course it was strained. He was getting himself off. His hand was still going. Tug, tug, up and down. Her eyes tracked the movement in a kind of sick fascination.

"You're some kind of sicko," she blurted. "You like watching people clean?" What the hell! Talk about a strange fetish.

He made a groaning sound that told her she was right on the money. "There's a hundred bucks on the dresser." He pointed with his free hand. "It's yours. Just clean the room and ignore me."

She shook her head. "You are nuts. I'm out of here." No way! Forget it!

"Clean the fucking room and take the money or you'll regret it." His eyes narrowed and his hand stopped tugging.

An icy tendril of fear wound itself around her. "I'm not some kind of . . ." She grit her teeth. "I refuse to—"

"I said that I won't touch you. Clean my room and do it now. It's what you're being paid to do. There's an extra tip in it for you as well." He glanced at the dresser. "Now be a good little cleaning lady and do your fucking job."

"Fuck you," she whispered as she walked out of the room. Her back prickled and for just a second she expected him to grab her from behind or to attack her or something but he didn't. At the very least she expected an insult to be hurled at her but there wasn't. The door closed behind her.

Her heart pounded. What the hell! She'd only been working for the hotel for a couple of months and although she'd encountered some weird shit, what had just happened was top on the list. She could have done with the hundred bucks but not like that. Forget it.

The guy seemed so normal. Julie shook her head as she pushed the piece of shit trolley. The door on it opened as she arrived at the elevator and she was forced to get on her knees and pick up all the spilled amenities. That was another thing, the temps got the worst equipment. Feather dusters with only half their feathers left. Trolleys with only three wheels or like hers, doors that wouldn't close. It was a pain in the ass. She finally made it back to the laundry room just as Callie pushed her locker closed. "What happened?" Her brows were raised and concern shone in her eyes.

Her supervisor was intuitive and a smart cookie.

Julie shook her head. "The DND was still up. I knocked twice but there was no answer, so I hope you don't mind, but I left it."

Callie frowned. "That's weird"—*You don't know the half of it*—"he definitely called and asked for a room clean." Then she shrugged. "Oh well."

It was on the tip of her tongue to tell Callie what happened but she decided not to in the end. She'd sworn at the guy. It might get her fired, despite the circumstances. She'd learned a long time ago that just because you were in the right, didn't mean that you came out on top. In fact, the opposite was mostly true. She'd checked in with reception and the pervert was checking out this afternoon so none of them would have to deal with him anymore. Julie would try to put it behind her. There wasn't much that surprised her anymore. She'd seen it all.

Available in paperback, eBook or audio

Printed in Great Britain
by Amazon